Lili St. Germain is a phenomenon. The first of her seven serialised dark romance novellas, *Seven Sons*, came out in early 2014, with the following books in the series released in quick succession and selling over half a million copies worldwide. The bestselling Gypsy Brothers series focuses on a morally bankrupt biker gang and the girl who seeks her vengeance upon them. *Kingpin* is the second instalment in the Cartel series, a prequel trilogy of full-length novels that explores the beginnings of the club.

Lili quit corporate life to focus on writing and is loving every minute of it. Her other loves in life include her gorgeous husband and beautiful daughter, good coffee and Tarantino movies. She loves to read almost as much as she loves to write. Find out more about the author at lilisaintgermain.com

KINGPIN

LILI ST. GERMAIN

HarperCollins*Publishers*

HarperCollins***Publishers***
First published in Australia in 2016
by HarperCollins*Publishers* Australia Pty Limited
ABN 36 009 913 517
harpercollins.com.au

HarperCollins***Publishers***
Level 13, 201 Elizabeth Street, Sydney NSW 2000, Australia
Unit D1, 63 Apollo Drive, Rosedale, Auckland 0632, New Zealand
A 53, Sector 57, Noida, UP, India
1 London Bridge Street, London, SE1 9GF, United Kingdom
2 Bloor Street East, 20th floor, Toronto, Ontario M4W 1A8, Canada
195 Broadway, New York, NY 10007, USA

National Library of Australia Cataloguing-in-Publication data:

Saint Germain, Lili, author.
Kingpin / Lili St. Germain.
978 1 4607 5187 9 (paperback)
978 1 4607 0429 5 (ebook)
Series: Saint Germain, Lili, Gypsy brothers.
Erotic stories.
Love stories.
813.6

Cover design by HarperCollins Design Studio
Cover images by shutterstock.com
Tattoo on cover drawn by Arijana Karcic
Author photo by Kate Drennan
Typesetting in Sabon LT Std by Kirby Jones

Loving me will not be easy.
It will be war. You will
hold the gun and I will hand
you the bullets. So breathe,
and embrace the beauty of
the massacre that lies ahead.

r.m. drake

GYPSY
BROS

PROLOGUE

MARIANA

2007

I watched from where I sat, grief beating inside my chest as Dornan placed a cupcake with a single candle on the table in front of me. A tear formed in my right eye, blurring my vision and the pink frosted cupcake warped momentarily. But I would not cry. I would not break down. Because it had been too long, and I struggled to remember my life in Colombia before this. I only knew that it had been happier, freer. Mostly, I remembered being less afraid.

I blinked the tear away, making sure none of it made its way onto my cheek. Dornan saw it anyway.

'Happy birthday, baby,' he said, his voice low and husky in the quiet, still night.

My eyes filled again at the tenderness in his tone. Someone else would miss it under the rough exterior, the 'fuck you' attitude, the way he held himself.

But I heard. I saw. I *knew*.

'Aren't you going to blow out the candle?' he pressed, his rough hand caressing my cheek as he stood behind me. I nodded, swallowing thickly. I took a breath, pursed my lips and blew across the flame. It flickered at first. I hadn't leaned in close enough. I took another breath, blew a steady stream of air at the flame, and extinguished it.

'Did you make a wish?' Dornan asked me, his hand squeezing my shoulder. I turned to meet his gaze. I thought of a boy with tiny, chubby hands and bright blue eyes. Wondered what *he* wished for when he blew out his candles. Did he wish for me, like I wished for him? He would have been twelve that year. *Twelve.*

Nine years spent together with this man, and he still didn't know about the son I gave up before we met.

I nodded. I smiled. I pushed all other thoughts away.

Dornan smiled back at me, his dark brown eyes lighting up. He knelt beside me on the ground, and I turned in my seat, opening my legs so the insides of my thighs rested on either side of him. I cupped his face in my hands, pulled him closer and pressed my lips to his forehead. His skin was warm. He always ran hotter than me, like a furnace. As I gazed down into his eyes, I felt my heart jump, like it always did when I was with him.

I was twenty-eight years old.

We were in love.

And it was the saddest fucking thing in the world.

CHAPTER ONE

MARIANA

2007

NINE YEARS GONE

Five days a week, I dressed in smart business clothes. I ate breakfast and painted my face, like countless other women. I was an accountant – well, technically, I was a bookkeeper, because I had had to leave college before I could complete my degree. At the office – a tiny, cramped room in the back of a run-down strip club off La Cienega – I drank coffee and spoke to nobody and worked my ass off. Then I was driven home – the home *he* had chosen for me. Some nights, my lover escorted me to the door, opened it for me, and spent the evening worshipping my body in ways I'd never imagined possible before meeting him. He was rough, he was dominating, and he made me feel safe even with a hand wrapped around my throat, cutting off my air supply just long enough to make my head spin. I liked the way he drove me to the peak, how he dangled me over the edge and then pulled me back up just before I fell.

Dornan Ross might have been a brutal man, but to me he was shelter. Even when he hurt me, he made it feel like love. Because at least if he was hurting me, he was there. I'd become addicted to him and had stayed that way for nine years. I was either alone, or I was with very bad people like Emilio Ross, or I was with him. But mostly I was alone. So I took everything he gave me, and I took it with a smile.

If you and I passed each other on the street, you'd think I was just like all the other girls, getting through each day as best as I could.

But nothing about my life was normal. I was not just a girl who went to work and went home and cooked dinner and had sex. If you passed me on the street, you'd probably miss the biker who walked five steps behind me, the 'roommate' I'd been given who was actually my keeper for all those hours when Dornan wasn't around. You'd miss the handprints around my neck, hidden by long hair and scarves, marks left by brutal love that I looked at in the mirror and delicately touched in the safety of my bathroom, to remember what it felt like to be alive, to be on the brink of coming and passing out at the same time.

If you knocked on my door and I was alone, you'd think I wasn't there. You'd never imagine I was pressed against the other side of the door, listening to your every move, begging silently for you to go away but wanting you to stay at the same time.

You'd never guess what I really was, because that reality was too dark, too painful for any normal person to entertain.

I was a slave.

Nine years ago, I'd made a deal with the devil. Emilio Ross, Kingpin of the Il Sangue drug cartel, had been seconds away from slaughtering my entire family for a debt my father owed him. Perhaps foolishly, I'd offered myself up in return for my family's safety. As long as I stayed with the cartel and worked off my father's massive debt, they'd be safe in Colombia.

My money laundering had paid off the original debt a long time ago, at least by my count, but Emilio had since made it clear that the deal didn't have an expiration date. He owned me.

I had been prized property of the Il Sangue Cartel for nine years, and there was one thing that I knew for certain.

I was never getting out alive. Truth be told, I'm not even sure I wanted to get out. The part of me that craved my son's embrace, *she* wanted to get out. The mother inside my soul desperately craved the feeling of holding my child in my arms. Years before I'd become entangled with the cartel, I had given birth in secret. Teenage pregnancy was worse than murder in my family, and I'd been forced to give my son up hours after I pushed him into this cruel world. My father had forged my signature on adoption papers, and I never saw my son again.

Maybe when we met again, it wouldn't be in this nightmare. Maybe he'd hold me just as tightly as I wanted – needed – to hold him. Maybe, more likely, I'd never see him again. Because of the sins of my father, I'd never see my precious boy again, and that thought was harder to fathom than knowing I was a prisoner of Il Sangue. I'd happily die if it meant I could spend just one day with Luis. But I couldn't sacrifice my entire family for my selfish needs.

Besides, I didn't even know if Luis' adoptive parents would let me near him. I had no legal recompense to the child I'd carried in my womb for nine months, the child who was half me and half Esteban, my boyfriend who'd been murdered in front of me by Emilio's men.

But by far the most compelling reason to stay away from Luis was that he was probably better off without me.

I hadn't believed my father when he had told me that, as he pried my fingers loose and took my only child from me, but over the years his words had played on my mind. *He's better off without you.* It didn't matter that I was screwing the vice-president of the Gypsy Brothers, or that we were in love. None of it mattered, because if I went to my boy, my lover would probably be the one who'd plant a bullet in my back before I even got to touch Luis.

Dornan was an enigma, a combination of brutality and tenderness, wrapped up in one man. The only son of my 'owner', Il Sangue kingpin Emilio, Dornan had been the one who'd saved me from being sold into sexual slavery. Emilio had intended to reclaim the money my father owed by selling me as a whore in one of his slave auctions, but Dornan had convinced him that I was more valuable as a money launderer in the cartel business. I'd proved him right very quickly, and we'd fallen for each other even faster.

Everyone in my immediate family thought that I was dead – they thought that Emilio's men had killed me on the night they shot up my family's home – and somehow that made it simpler to disconnect from my old existence. Dornan thought it'd be easier that way – for them, because they'd be able to stop searching, and for me, because I'd be free from the soul-crushing guilt of knowing they were looking for me while I was hiding in plain sight with the Gypsy Brothers in Los Angeles. I never had a choice in the matter. The man I was falling in love with dragged me up a rocky mountain, kissed me and then made me watch as my brother and father dug up a headless corpse they'd been led to believe was me.

And I still fell in love with him. I'm smart, but maybe I'm also really, really stupid. Because I truly did love Dornan Ross, with every part of my dark soul. I needed him like I needed air to breathe. I came alive whenever he was around me. My light to his dark, a delicate balance of pleasure and pain.

We were like a match made in heaven.

Wait. That's wrong.

We were a match made in *hell*.

CHAPTER TWO

MARIANA

1999

SIX MONTHS GONE

Every cartel needs someone who can make their dirty money clean, and I was the best damn money launderer on the West Coast.

Six months after I'd arrived in Los Angeles, John Portland – president of the Gypsy Brothers Motorcycle Club and Dornan's best friend – paid me a visit. I'm not sure why he chose that particular day, or why he'd waited months to voice his suspicions about who and what I really was. Maybe he'd wanted to bide his time, watch me, make sure he wasn't raising any suspicions by visiting me at home, away from the strip club and the Gypsy Brothers clubhouse where we frequently crossed paths.

We shared the same small office at the clubhouse but John was hardly ever there. I suppose presiding over a one-percenter biker gang like the Gypsy Brothers wasn't really a job you could do from behind a desk. But he was always around, delivering big crumpled bundles of cash for me to clean and launder, picking up packages that were probably full of drugs or guns, monitoring the front business that allowed us to channel money obtained illegally through a legal avenue – peepshows and lap dances. The reality was the strip club (or 'burlesque club', as they somewhat euphemistically called it) ran at a loss, and the majority of the clientele were Gypsy Brothers, who came in for free blow jobs and beer in between their club business. The dollar bills floating around this club were usually reserved for snorting coke, not stuffing in strippers' panties.

I'd learned much about John Portland in the six months since Emilio had parked me in the back office of the VaVa Voom strip club with a pile of blood-smeared hundred dollar bills and a boxy old computer that whirred whenever it overheated. Tidbits of information that I had filed away for the future, just in case.

John had a wife who liked to shoot drugs into her arm to make her forget she was a biker's wife, a daughter who was the light in his world, and a club full of Gypsy Brothers he was responsible for leading. He was covered in tattoos, mostly over his muscled arms and up his neck, the only part not covered was his face. The club tattoo that stretched across his tanned back was the largest, and I'd seen it only once, when he'd been stabbed in the stomach by a rival gang member and he stitched his wound in front of me. Yeah, John Portland was a bad ass. His blue eyes, ringed with hazel flecks, were framed by dark blonde hair, and he alternated between clean-shaven and a full beard. With the tattoos and the bike, it didn't really take away from the tough exterior when he shaved the beard off. He still looked like he could kill you with his bare hands.

I'd learned some other things about him. He was kind. He was thoughtful. He liked to surf. When he smiled, his whole being lit up. He almost never smiled, though, instead wearing a constant hard-set expression that was halfway between a grimace and a frown. Most of all, I'd learned that he was trapped here, just like me. He might not have realised it – hell, maybe he did – but he was as much a pawn in the Il Sangue Cartel as I was ... maybe even more.

Six months in and John Portland knew nothing about me besides the fact that I carried a photograph of a small baby around with me. Christopher Murphy, a federal air marshal and Emilio's long-term link to bribing the American government, had stolen it from me and used it to try and extort sex and compliance from me in exchange for his silence. Until John arrived. He had never spoken of the photo again after he wrestled it from Murphy and silently returned it to me months later, and for that I was eternally grateful.

But John knew, and I didn't know what he would do with my secret. I'd vowed early on to give him nothing else – not one more shred of incriminating evidence that he could potentially use against me. Whenever he asked anything about me or my family I would find a way to change the subject, to deflect his questioning, to respond with something vague and non-committal. I was very, very careful with my past, with the way I interacted with people. One word answers. Blank stares. Outright ignorance. The strippers who frequented the hallways didn't call me The Ice Queen for nothing. Sometimes, if they were particularly bitter, The Ice Cunt. But I'd only heard that once, from a girl called Mindy. After Dornan threatened to knock all her teeth out and set her up as the permanent blow-job station in the corner of the club, she didn't say it again. After that, none of the girls had really spoken to me, let alone bothered me. The only person who ever spoke to me outside of the holy trinity – Dornan, Emilio and Murphy – was John.

But for all of my one-word answers, blank stares and outright ignorance, it felt like John Portland could lower my guard without me even noticing, until it was too late and I'd revealed parts of myself better left in the dark.

I don't think he knew what I really was – a prisoner – or maybe he just didn't want to admit it to himself – until he came to see me at the apartment one day. Dornan was in Mexico on Gypsy Brothers business, and I needed to be checked on, obviously. John knocked on the door. I waited for him to punch in the code and come in, but he didn't.

'Mariana!' he yelled, kicking the bottom of the door. 'I've got my hands full, can you let me in?'

I panicked.

I still wasn't trusted with the code to my own apartment. Other select people could get in, but I couldn't get out. Dornan said it was for my own protection.

And it had worked fine. Until John.

'Uh, just key in the code and come in,' I replied, rooted to my spot on the couch.

He yelled a few more times, but I couldn't move. I was paralysed with fear. I knew he suspected something wasn't right, from the first moment he'd laid his baby blue eyes on me and demanded to know who I was, and what the hell I was doing in his office. He wasn't an idiot.

Eventually, he punched in the code himself. The front door to my apartment swung open and there he was, his helmet in his hand and a question on his face. I got up and hurried to the door, as if I'd been about to open it.

'Can I get a hand here?' he asked.

Barefoot, I stepped out onto the landing with him. There was nothing there.

'I thought you said your hands were full,' I said, looking around.

Before I could stop him, John grabbed the door handle and pulled it shut.

'Oops,' he said. 'Can you open it back up for me?'

I gave him a blank look, but inside my stomach was twisting into knots. *Oh God, he knows, he knows about me. He knows I'm not normal. He knows I'm trapped in here.*

'Sure,' I replied. I stared at the keypad, tried to think of a number Dornan would use. His birthday? I punched that in and tried the door. Nothing.

I looked at John, who had one eyebrow raised. He was dressed in black from head to foot, his leather cut and jeans hugging his body as he towered over me, black steel-capped boots encasing his feet. His dark blonde hair hung in front of his eyes, adding a smudge of boyish charm juxtaposed against his ferocity.

I shrugged. 'This thing's temperamental,' I said. 'I swear it hates me.'

I tried another couple of combinations. Of course, they didn't work.

'Forget your own birthday?' He rolled his eyes, shouldering me out of the way and stabbing at the keypad with his index finger until the door gave a small metallic click.

He'd tricked me. *And how the hell did he know when my birthday was?*

Furious, I shoved the door open and tried to slam it behind me. John wedged his boot in the door before it could close. I tried to push his boot out of the way using the door, but he was much stronger than me.

'I can stay here all day,' he said. Finally, I moved back, letting him into the apartment.

He closed the door behind him and strode past me, down the hallway and into the dining room, which faced the ocean and had its own small balcony.

'It's hot today,' he said. 'Why don't you have this door open?'

I shrugged. 'I'm home alone. It feels safer with everything closed. How do you know when my birthday is?' *How did he know anything about me?*

'Bullshit,' he said. 'I bet if I try this door right now, it'll open, won't it?'

'Of course it'll open,' I responded, panic building inside me. 'It's just a door.'

He made a point of opening and closing the balcony door, then passed me again, going back to the keypad at the front door. There was one inside and one outside, and he armed the inside one with quick fingers.

He crossed the apartment again and tried the balcony door.

It wouldn't budge.

John turned to me slowly, his eyes practically bugging out of his head.

'They keep you here,' he said slowly. 'They keep you here like a fucking prisoner. Don't they?'

Fuck. What if he spoke to Dornan about this? What if he spoke to Emilio?

I pressed my teeth together in my mouth and tried not to scream.

He rushed towards me, and for a moment I had the uncanny thought that he was going to grab me by the throat and toss me against the wall. Conditioning, I suppose.

Living in the middle of a fucking drug cartel with people like Emilio Ross and Christopher Murphy always hovering on the edges of your existence could do that.

But he didn't grab my throat. He grabbed my shoulder with one hand, his touch gentle, and the other hand trailed along my chin, forcing my head up so we were eye to eye.

'Don't they?' he repeated, much quieter this time. His eyes were full of anguish, and something else I couldn't quite fathom.

'What do you want from me?' I whispered, turning my head away.

He cupped my cheek with his hand, his other palm starting to burn as it gripped my shoulder.

'You don't need to lie to me,' he said, and something in his words snapped me back to reality. I did need to lie to him – to him and to everyone else in the world if my family was going to be safe. My sacrifice, my complicity, my ownership at the hands of Emilio Ross and the Il Sangue Cartel meant that I had to lie every time I opened my fucking mouth, lest I find a gun jammed down my throat for my transgressions.

'I'm not a prisoner,' I snapped, levelling my gaze at him again as the mask slipped back over my soul. 'I'm forgetful.'

His eyes were like twin fires, his grip on my shoulder getting even tighter. 'You're hurting me,' I said, wrenching my shoulder away and stepping back.

He turned and left, and the cocky bastard didn't set the lock when he slammed the door behind him.

Was he giving me a chance to escape?

Or was he testing my loyalty?

Emilio had found countless ways to test my loyalty ever since I'd been painfully initiated into the Il Sangue Cartel, and by default, the Gypsy Brothers.

I didn't leave. I didn't take my chance to escape.

No, I re-programmed the lock myself (now that I knew the code) and sat on my couch, drinking vodka instead. You could say that I was weak, that I was suffering from Stockholm syndrome, that I was the worst kind of victim because I refused to help myself when the opportunity arose.

And I'd say *fuck that.* I'd made a deal with Emilio Ross, and at least four lives – my mother, my father, my sister and my brother – hung in the balance every single time I made a decision. Five, if you counted Luis. Oh, and then there was the small fact of my own life. That hung in the balance every single day, and everything always felt so goddamn *temporary.*

So I didn't leave. I sat, and I waited.

John came back an hour later with a box. Plain, brown cardboard packaging.

'What is this?' Did I even want to know?

He took a knife from the rack and made a slit down the side of the packaging, pulling out a cellphone. I eyed the small black phone dubiously, pulling my own cellphone from my pocket.

'For you,' he said. 'A burner phone. Nothing to identify you. Nothing to trace back to you. Nobody listening to you. But you have to keep it hidden, okay?'

'I have a phone,' I said.

John's eyes flicked to me, soft and with the hint of a smile. 'Your phone,' he said, 'is bugged. But you knew that already, right?'

I looked around the apartment nervously. Last thing I needed was for Emilio or someone else to overhear this conversation and decide I was getting too dangerous to keep around.

'How do I know you haven't bugged *this* phone?'

He smiled. 'You just saw me open the packaging. Plus, you should know by now that I don't have time to eavesdrop on your calls. I've got too much other shit to do.'

I had been standing stiff beside him; I felt the tension melt from me piece by piece as he held out the phone.

'You can trust me,' he said softly. 'I'm not like them. I'm not like Emilio.'

I nodded, looking away, salt tears burning my cheeks at the weight of his kindness.

'Mariana,' he whispered. He put his finger underneath my chin again and tilted it up, so I had no choice but to meet his cerulean gaze.

'What?' I asked.

'If you change your mind – if you decide one day you need to leave – you tell me. And I'll help you, okay? I'll make sure they can't find you. Dornan's my friend – my best friend. But he's also Emilio's son, and there are things he cannot control.'

I burst into tears, covering my face with my hands. I'd been *theirs* for six months by then, six months where the only visitor I got was Dornan, and the only person I spoke to every day was myself, in the mirror, talking myself out of doing something crazy like killing myself. And I loved Dornan. But I hated my life.

'You don't understand,' I said finally. 'He loves me. He *saved* me.'

John looked at me sadly, the smile fading from his face.

'You call *this* saved?'

***

Two weeks later, Dornan showed up with Guillermo. A Gypsy Brother. Dornan figured out I'd been operating the locks without him. It was only to get out onto the balcony, to smell the salt air rolling in from the waves below, a welcome refuge from my gilded cage. I had the code now, but I'd never try to run. I wasn't an idiot. I didn't dare try to leave, not even for a moment. And then I couldn't have, even if I'd wanted to, because somebody suddenly decided that I needed a full-time bodyguard. Dornan might have loved me, but he didn't trust me – he didn't trust anyone.

'It's for your own protection,' he said. 'I know you want to go outside.'

Because I had begged him to go outside. To shop for groceries, to feel the wet sand beneath my feet, to breathe in the fresh air on my balcony.

I got my wish.

I got to go outside, whenever I wanted, Guillermo Reyes always by my side or five steps behind.

It was easier, I decided soon afterwards, to be alone and locked up in a glass tower than to have someone watching my every move.

I realised much too late that things are almost never as bad as you think they are, and just when you think you've got everything figured out, everything will change again.

I wanted to go outside. I wanted to stop feeling so alone.

I got my wish.

I was never allowed to be alone again.

CHAPTER THREE

MARIANA

2007
NINE YEARS GONE

Sunday.

A sacred day. The one day a week when I was guaranteed time with Dornan.

I just had to jump through a few hoops first.

He'd been late to pick me up, which wasn't a surprise. Still, I didn't like it. I hovered inside the entry to the apartment – I still didn't feel right calling it *my* apartment, even though I'd spent almost a decade trapped between its walls – and paced nervously. My black patent stilettos clicked on the tiles as I walked back and forth, wanting to wait outside in the fresh air and open space, but knowing Dornan wouldn't be happy to find me out there. Because, according to him, I was something to be protected. Something to be hidden away.

I was about to fix another coffee when I heard boots thunking on the concrete stairwell, getting louder as he approached. It felt silly that even after all these years, he made my stomach buzz nervously just by showing up. I hadn't seen him in weeks, since he'd been away and then he was tied up with his wife and kids, but today was *ours*. At least, this afternoon was ours. Once we'd served our purposes to other people, we could serve each other.

There was a snort from the man sitting at the kitchen counter. 'Your master is here, bitch.'

I narrowed my eyes at Guillermo, my excitement fading.

He laughed, slapping his leg with a hand covered in gang tattoos. Guillermo was now a constant in my life. He was my unofficial bodyguard, babysitter and someone who watched over me when Dornan wasn't around. He lived in my apartment, ate my food, drank my good coffee and annoyed the living shit out of me every minute of the day. Don't get me wrong – he wasn't a bad person, or at least no worse than any other small-time gangster-slash-biker.

However, he was in my apartment. It was technically Dornan's, owned by some dummy corporation on paper, won in a poker game years before I'd arrived and now a convenient hideout for me. And, sadly, Guillermo. He was in my apartment, and I very much did not want him to be here, because Dornan had arrived.

'Jealous?' I asked, smiling sweetly as I slammed two coffee cups down in front of me.

Guillermo, Latino and thirty-something, was attractive in an unkempt, rugged sort of way, but he wasn't my type. One of Dornan's thugs, he was also a fully patched member of the Gypsy Brothers and a skilled drug trafficker. He knew everything about me. Almost everything. He knew as much as Dornan and Emilio. As far as I could tell, Murphy was still the only one who knew for sure the details about my son.

'Nah,' Guillermo answered. 'Just thinking should I get my earplugs before you two start fucking like dogs in here.'

I scowled. 'You could always *leave*,' I suggested helpfully. 'Don't you have something to do? Somewhere to be?'

'Yeah,' he replied stonily. 'At the clubhouse. Church is about to start, and if you make me late—'

'I hardly think they'll notice if you're there or not,' I interrupted. 'You're not the president or anything.'

He laugh-snorted, shaking his head. 'Your man ain't the prez, either, cholita.'

I looked around the apartment, as if he were talking to somebody else. 'Since when do you call me cholita? That's Emilio's thing.'

He shrugged lazily. 'Whatever. Don't make me late.'

I glared at Guillermo. He glared back, until his face broke, and he started to laugh. I tried to remain stony-faced, but something about the way Guillermo laughed was contagious. I might have wanted my own space, but his sense of humour was a lifeboat in my lonely existence. I'd never tell anyone that, though.

The front door opened, and I turned eagerly. *Dornan.* He stood in the doorway, his silhouette illuminated by the bright sun outside. He was dressed in dark blue jeans and a black T-shirt that hugged his defined chest, a black leather jacket over the top. He dropped his helmet on the ground and it landed with force on the hard floor, before rolling into the corner, forgotten. His dark eyes gleamed with anticipation.

'You're late,' I said, but I was grinning like an idiot. Guillermo dragged a cigarette out and lit it, breathing a cloud of smoke in my face.

'Guillermo,' Dornan growled in warning.

'I'll see you later,' Guillermo said to me. '*Woof.*' He sauntered past Dornan, who looked on in amusement.

As soon as the door slammed shut, Dornan turned to me. 'What was that about?'

I shrugged. 'Just Guillermo being his charming self.'

Dornan smirked, almost barrelling into me as he closed the space between us. Impulsively, I jumped and wrapped my legs around him, our mouths locked together in a dance we'd rehearsed plenty of times before. It seemed we were always being reunited after long stretches apart, even though I saw him all the time, even though he lived in Venice Beach, only a few miles from the apartment in Santa Monica. But at the strip club there were always people, always Emilio hovering, or Murphy, or John giving us disapproving glances. Plus, Dornan spent most of his days at the Gypsy Brothers clubhouse, which was only a few blocks from the strip club, but we weren't exactly the kind of couple that did lunch. No, he was usually mopping up blood or burning evidence from the sounds of it, and I was usually trying not to flip out and lose my shit if Emilio decided he was going to show up and ruin my afternoon with his wandering hands and outlandish demands.

Dornan pressed me up against the hallway wall, his mouth devouring mine.

'I missed you,' I said, something catching in my throat as I spoke.

He must have heard that waver in my voice, because he stopped kissing me, pulled back to look at me. 'Everything alright?' he asked quietly, his low voice vibrating in my chest.

I nodded. I hadn't seen him since the night we'd celebrated my twenty-eighth birthday together, in this very apartment, with a lone candle and an impossible wish murmured as I cut my cupcake in half.

He frowned, like he wanted to press me further.

'We'll be late,' I whispered, tracing the outline of his mouth with my index finger. His stubble scratched at my skin, but it was a welcome feeling, familiar.

Dornan groaned, setting me on my feet on the floor. 'Are those the shoes I bought you?' he asked, taking a step back and whistling. 'Goddamn, they look even better than I thought they would.'

I gave him a wicked smile, stepping out of the apartment in my brand new black patent heels. 'I'll wear them for you later.'

His hand closed around my wrist and he pulled me back inside, slamming the front door and shoving me against it. His fingers curled around my arms with pressure that bordered on pain, pressure that would probably leave bruises. My stilettos screeched on the tiles, and I laughed. 'We'll be late ...' I warned him again, shivering as he pressed me into the door and began to kiss a trail from my neck down to my breasts. He bit each nipple through the material of my dress, pain and pleasure merging deliciously as one, stopping only to tug my dress up around my hips and kick my legs wider with an insistent foot.

He dropped to his knees, and I watched in anticipation, pressed against the door. Dornan's stubble against the insides of my thighs was fucking torturous, brushing so close to my pussy I wanted to scream.

'Wider,' he demanded, taking hold of my right leg and hooking it over his shoulder. The moment he tugged my panties to one side and his greedy mouth descended on my clit, I yelled, 'Oh, *fuck*!'

He chuckled against my sensitive flesh, sending vibrations through me that made me shudder involuntarily.

'Your father is going to kill us,' I gasped, rocking my hips against his face.

Suddenly, the tongue disappeared. He stopped. I made a small sound of surprise in the back of my throat, opening my eyes to see what he was doing. He lifted his head long enough to glare at me. 'Don't ever mention my father when I've got my mouth on your pussy again, you hear me?'

He put his mouth on me again, and I whimpered as I heard Guillermo's motorcycle start downstairs. 'Don't stop,' I whispered, threading my fingers into Dornan's hair as his tongue did dirty, delicious things to me. My legs started to shake under the pressure of trying to hold myself upright on one stiletto while being tongue-fucked against a door. Just as I started to get close, he took his mouth away and stood upright, yanking his jeans down and palming his cock. 'I've been thinking about fucking you against this door for weeks,' he ground out, putting his hands on my bare ass and lifting me so that his cock was pressed against my wetness.

I wrapped my arms around his neck, crying out when he thrust into me in one rough stroke. 'Don't wear panties to this meeting,' he said against my neck. 'I want to feel your pussy on my back when we ride.'

Oh, I wanted that, too. I barely went on the back of a bike these days because I barely left my apartment, but when it was just Dornan and me flying down the highway, it almost felt like we were free, just the two of us. And the thought of being naked against him, rubbing against the leather of his cut while his Harley sent vibrations through the both of us – it was almost enough to make me come on the spot. He thrust into me slowly, forcefully.

'I want you to come,' he demanded, gathering my hair in one fist and pulling hard enough to force my head back. 'You're going to touch yourself. You're going to come with your mouth around my cock.' And just like that, just as he'd gotten me close again, he pulled out of me without warning.

My mouth watered at this suggestion. There was something so completely carnal about coming with your lips wrapped around a cock, your moans being muffled by someone fucking your mouth. He let go of my hair and I fell to my knees, opening my mouth and teasing the head of his cock with my tongue. I tasted myself on him. 'Make yourself come,' he groaned, bucking his hips until his cock hit the back of my throat. 'I'm about to explode.'

I reached into my lace panties and started making shallow circles around my clit. I was soaked from my own wetness and Dornan's tongue, and my finger slipped a few times before I found a rhythm. It didn't take long. Already perilously close, I crested that wave, moaning loudly around Dornan's cock as I orgasmed.

'Oh, fuck,' he whispered. 'That looks so fucking good.'

He thrust against the back of my throat one last time, coming across my tongue and down my throat as he cupped my face in his hands.

Guillermo was waiting on his bike when we finally made it downstairs, his engine purring loudly, helmet secured. He was ready to go. He took in my slightly dishevelled appearance and made a tsk-tsk noise.

'You two are like fucking animals,' he said, shaking his head in mock disapproval.

Dornan, who'd killed other men for saying less, laughed as he started his own bike. I fastened my own helmet under my chin and straddled the seat behind Dornan as delicately as I could, using my hands and the hem of my dress to shield the fact that I wasn't wearing any panties.

Dornan tore out of the parking lot and I had to hold on tight to make sure I didn't fall off the back of the bike. The man liked to go fast.

Seeing Dornan had sated me, but the closer we got to the clubhouse, the more anxious I became. It was always the same fucking shit with these people, and after nine years I was growing weary of it all. I wondered how much longer Emilio planned to keep me around.

I wondered if he'd ever decide that I'd paid my father's debt and was free to leave.

Ha. When hell froze over, I'm sure. I knew deep down that he never had any intention of letting me leave.

CHAPTER FOUR

MARIANA

Ten minutes later, we were pulling up at the Gypsy Brothers clubhouse. One of the young prospects manning the entrance waved us in, and Dornan steered his bike through the razorwire-topped gates, parking in the lot.

I climbed off the bike, smoothing my black dress down. I'd already checked my make-up in the mirror and made sure my cleavage was on display. See, I didn't want any attention, but more than that, I needed it. I needed to appear non-threatening. When I'd first started work in the cartel, processing accounts and siphoning money offshore for Emilio and his counterparts, I'd dressed plainly to avoid roving eyes. I thought it was the best course of action, to blend in, to be invisible. But I'd quickly learned that the prettier I looked, the less suspicious people were of me. It was a lesson I'd learned from my predecessor, Bella. She'd been the cartel's chief accountant before me, and she'd ended up in landfill somewhere, a bullet in her head and a swathe of stolen cash to her name. Collateral damage, Dornan had called it.

I had vowed not to meet the same fate.

She wasn't all that good at embezzling – creating fake receipts and paying ghost vendors twice. When Emilio had tasked me with investigating the shoddy paper trail Bella had left in her dim-witted wake, I'd encountered a mess the cartel should have noticed a lot earlier.

I was much smarter with the way I stole from them.

Technically, it wasn't even stealing; it was keeping my options open. Because although I loved Dornan, there was still the ever-present possibility that one day my existence would become too much of a liability and I'd be snuffed out. So I kept my own collateral in the form of offshore accounts. Nobody ever needed to know that I was a required co-signatory on most of them, not unless it came down to a situation where my life was at stake and I needed a bargaining chip. It wasn't even about the money. It was about being smart, about realising my gig with the Il Sangue Cartel and their offshoot branch, the Gypsy Brothers MC, could be terminated at any moment. Because although Dornan had shepherded me away from his father and Il Sangue, the reality was that the Gypsy Brothers weren't exactly any safer.

The Gypsy Brothers weren't even a one-percenter club.

They were worse. They were the one percent of the one percent, a toxic wasteland that chewed up and spat out everything they touched.

They'd chewed me up nine years ago, when I was taken from my family.

I was still waiting for them to spit me out: kill me, sell me, *destroy* me.

In the office, I sat in my chair, rigid, as Emilio circled around behind me. I flinched minutely as he sifted his hands through my long ponytail, tugging lightly on the ends.

His touch – his very presence – was nauseating.

Across from me, Christopher Murphy, one-time federal air marshal and now a top-ranking DEA agent, was smirking as he held my gaze with his cold blue eyes. In another person's skull that hue might have been beautiful, but in his, it was freakish. He'd barely changed in nine years – tall and built like a weed, with shaggy brown hair he'd cut a little shorter and an imposing stature. Someone, somewhere, found him attractive enough to date, because he'd backed off from all the eye-fucking he'd been giving me since we met. Not me, though. I couldn't get past the fact that he was a total fucking psychopath.

'The figures are up this week,' Emilio murmured, tracing light fingers across my shoulders and down each of my bare arms. I swallowed thickly, not daring to move, not daring to recoil from his touch. I'd done that once, back in the early days, pulled away when he reached out. That earned me two black eyes, a face full of cuts and a bruised ego, since he'd beaten me to a bloody pulp while Murphy sat and watched with a cruel smile. And then probably went home and jerked off to the image, knowing him. Sick fuck.

I never knew exactly where Il Sangue's money came from, and I kind of preferred it that way. I knew they dealt in coke and weapons, but I didn't see the particular transactions, didn't know what was what. A hundred grand here, twenty grand there. Sometimes it came in as cash. Sometimes as numbers on a statement, deposited into the bank accounts of any number of front businesses the cartel controlled. I didn't like the cash. Often it was marked with cocaine, or blood. Sometimes both. I didn't enjoy peeling apart and drying what was, quite literally, blood money. The smell always reminded me of death.

Mostly I just did my part, funnelled the majority of Emilio's funds out of the United States and into offshore accounts. Kept my mouth shut and my head down. I managed Murphy's money as well, made sure it didn't look suspicious when he was living a caviar lifestyle on a government agent's salary. Needless to say, Murphy had some very generous fictitious relatives.

I hated that part more than anything, the fact that I was enabling the two people I despised the most in the world to live lives of affluence and grandeur. I spent many an afternoon daydreaming about making their cash disappear and burning their houses down.

It was better than the alternative. Better than being dead in the ground.

Most of the time.

Moments like this, I wasn't so sure.

'You're doing an excellent job, Mariana,' Emilio murmured, placing his hands on my breasts and squeezing them. It hurt, so much that my eyes watered and I had to bite down on my tongue to keep from crying out, but I didn't move. Fighting was futile. Besides, it would be over soon. It would be over, and then I could be with Dornan again. And everything would be okay until the next week, when we'd go through this all over again.

'Thank you,' I replied, my gaze matching Murphy's, my gut twisting with impatience. Hurry, I wanted to say. Just get this over with so I can wash my hands of the fucking filth you two make me feel.

'Alright,' Emilio said, taking his hands away and motioning for me to move. 'Get up. We'll keep going now.'

'See you next week, Annie,' Murphy crowed as I passed him on my way out.

The first time Murphy had called me Annie, nine years ago, he'd been trying to hold me down and rape me on my dining room floor. The only reason he hadn't succeeded was thanks to John and Dornan arriving at my apartment unexpectedly and kicking the living shit out of him. Dornan had almost killed Murphy, would have if John hadn't stopped him.

I swallowed down my disgust and eyed the sharp butcher's knife in Murphy's hand, the one I'd been silly enough to think I had a chance of using on him that day.

He flashed a wide smile and pointed to his pants. 'Well then,' he said, tipping his head to one side and fixing those weird blue eyes on me, 'I suggest you get on the floor and get naked.'

I gritted my teeth and stared as he squeezed his cock through his pants, then started to stroke it slowly, as much as the material would allow. He didn't take his eyes from mine the entire time.

He looked at me in mock despair, using his free hand to gesture down to his hard-on. 'Well, come on,' he said. 'I don't think it's going to suck itself, Annie.'

My skin crawled as I was thrown headfirst into the memory of him on top of me, his insistent hands grabbing at my thighs, his gaze pinning me along with his arms that he'd used to cage me in. *Annie*. His mouth curled up a little on one side. I knew he was thinking about the exact same thing as me, only he was clearly enjoying the memory. He wrinkled his nose up and smiled, winking.

Rage and nausea bubbled up in my stomach, but I swallowed them down. I didn't bother replying. It wouldn't make a difference, it never had. I'd already used my daily dose of polite on Emilio, and nobody ever seemed to care if I was nice to Murphy or not. So he didn't even get my wasted breath on a snarky comeback or a meaningless goodbye.

CHAPTER FIVE

MARIANA

Sunday afternoons were like rituals. Dornan would talk business with his men – sometimes I heard shouting, sometimes laughter – and then he'd finish, find me in the rabbit warren of rooms that made up the Gypsy Brothers HQ, take me home and fuck the life out of me.

I had my own responsibilities to attend to while the Gypsy Brothers convened in the great room at the front of the clubhouse. While they spoke business and made plans, I was tasked with a meeting of my own.

With Emilio. And Murphy.

Every single Sunday.

But now that meeting was over, and I had another hundred and sixty-seven hours before I had to endure it again. Seven whole days before I had to endure Emilio's touch and Murphy's roving eyes. Today had been tame. Some weeks, the things Emilio did to me ... He'd never actually held me down and raped me, but it had gotten close a few times. Who knew if the old bastard could still even get it up? Maybe that was the only saving grace that had stopped him from raping me. Or, like he said, maybe he just preferred blondes. Who knew?

I wasn't exactly dwelling on if or when he'd consummate our owner/slave relationship. Mostly, he just liked to threaten to hurt me. It was all part of his sick, twisted mind-fuckery.

I wandered down the long hallway that ran through the centre of the Gypsy Brothers clubhouse. It always made me nervous, being alone in there. Although Dornan was a formidable VP, and would no doubt kick the living shit out of anyone who dared touch me, it still didn't feel right, being in this place. It was obvious the warehouse conversion was for men, and men only – no women graced its hallways, except the club whores. And me. Walking into the place was like disappearing down a dark hole, a hole that smelled like beer and gasoline. The slivers of sunlight that did manage to get in were framed by barred windows that you'd never be able to escape through in a fire.

I made a sharp right at an intersection in the hallway, turning into the large communal kitchen and dining area. The Gypsy Brothers had many, many members, and they demanded to be fed and watered and liquored to keep them tough and at the ready. The place was deserted, a sign that the club meeting hadn't finished yet. I crossed the room briskly, my heels making sharp clicks on the polished concrete floor, threading through tables and chairs as I made my way to the fire escape. That was our place to convene, Dornan and I. Our safe haven, if only for a couple of hours.

'Hey,' a voice called out to me. I stopped in my tracks and turned slowly, looking for the source.

Caroline Portland, John's wife, sat at one of the tables that was partially hidden from view by a half-wall. I hadn't seen her when I entered the room, but I could see her now, and what a sight she was. Her hair stringy and dishevelled, she was wearing jeans and a checked shirt that swam on her emaciated figure. I hadn't seen her in months, had counted myself lucky to avoid the displeasure of crossing her path, and now here she was in all her junkie glory.

I smiled thinly at her, but didn't offer a response.

'Where the fuck you think you're going?' she slurred, leaning her head in her hands as she slumped over the table. I was about to turn and walk away when I saw her teenage daughter walk out of the kitchen, a glass of water and some graham crackers in her hands.

Juliette didn't notice me as she walked towards her mother. An image of my own father danced before my eyes as I watched the young girl try to rouse her mother from something that she was obviously in too deep to shake off.

'Mom,' she said softly, setting the water down in front of Caroline. But Caroline ignored her. She could hardly focus, her eyes were rolling around in her head so violently.

'Mom!' More forcefully this time. Caroline's eyes fluttered shut completely and she sagged forward on the table.

The girl looked around, noticed me for the first time. 'Do you know where my dad is?' she asked quietly.

Something stabbed painfully in my chest. She was only a little older than my son, and I wondered if he would be taller than her, if he had his father's dimples when he smiled.

I nodded. 'I'll get him.'

Walking towards the front of the clubhouse, I veered into the hallway and back out, a set of double doors in front of me not the only barrier to finding John. There were two club prospects eyeing me like I had an AK-47 in my hands and a belt full of ammo. Great.

'Nobody goes in until they're finished,' the older of the two said. He must've been eighteen at most, his hand on the gun at his hip.

'Get out of my way,' I said, my voice saccharine sweet, 'unless you want Dornan to shoot you in the face.'

'You a Gypsy Brother?'

I stared down the younger one, his eyes squinting at me as he tried to appear larger than me. Which he was, easily, but for some reason he hunched when he stood. I, on the other hand, did not. I stood ramrod straight, looking him directly in the eye. I was the furthest thing from a Gypsy Brother. 'Do I look like a Gypsy Brother to you, boy? *Move.*'

It worked. They both parted, looking at the ground as I opened the double doors and entered the sacred space reserved only for Gypsy Brothers.

Sixteen pairs of eyes turned towards me as I looked past Dornan's inquiring frown to John, sitting at the head of the long table, and waited to be addressed. Nobody spoke. John raised his eyebrows as if to say, *What do you want?*

'You're needed,' I said to John. 'Family business.'

Fifteen pairs of eyes averted as John stood, following me out of the room. I ignored the prospects as they closed the doors after us and resumed their spots. I'm fairly sure they were only there to keep them out of trouble. I mean, if someone really wanted to get through those doors, a couple of punk kids with revolvers tucked into their pants wasn't going to stop much.

'Is it Juliette?' John asked, matching my stride as he followed me down the hallway.

We reached the kitchen/dining area and I stopped. I didn't need to explain. It was all clear as day: his daughter, growing more frantic as she shook her mother, the puddle of vomit beside Caroline's head on the table making a nauseating *dripdripdrip* as it cut a path from the tabletop onto the ground. *Idiot.* She had a husband, a child, a career and a life, and she did this so regularly, it was no longer shocking to see her almost at death's door. Usually the kid wasn't a part of it, though. That irritated me. If I had Luis, he'd never have to do anything like that for me. I would love him and take care of him and make him happy.

The fact that Caroline Portland eschewed her freedom while I fought for every minute of mine made me want to grab her by the hair and grind her face into the vomit.

'You want me to call an ambulance?' I asked John flatly, watching the scene unfold in front of me. Some might say that I had no empathy, but if it had been anyone else dying in front of me like Caroline was right now, I would have reacted differently. The problem was I'd seen it all before, and whether she lived or died was irrelevant to me. In fact, if she died it would only make life less difficult.

It's funny how nine years in hell hardens you.

John was shaking Caroline when I felt a hand at my elbow. I whirled around, expecting to see Murphy's freakish blue eyes staring back at me, but I softened when I saw Dornan.

'What'd I miss out here?' he asked, raking a hand through his dark hair, peppered with grey. He'd let it grow just long enough to have that perpetual mussed-up look, and it definitely suited him.

'The usual.' I spoke quietly enough so that John wouldn't hear me. The poor bastard had it hard enough being married to that opiate-soaked waste of space, without hearing us pass judgement.

I don't know why I hated her so fervently. Maybe because, even then, I sensed something about John. I saw his kindness, the very thing she rejected, and I seethed with jealousy at their beautiful child. Mostly because mine existed as nothing more than a worn photograph and an image in my head that faded more each day. Sometimes I couldn't remember what he looked like without looking at the photograph, and that frightened me.

But this whore had everything I would never have, everything I had always wanted, and she chose to space out on heroin every fucking day.

Yeah, that's why I hated her.

'Time for the cold water?' I interjected. I'd had the delight of pouring water on the bitch to wake her up more than once.

John shook his head. 'I'm taking her to the hospital. Her pulse is barely there.'

I turned to Dornan to tell him to help, but he was already stepping forward, car keys in hand, as John took Caroline in his arms. He looked back at me.

'Can you ...?' He jerked his head in his daughter's direction.

I nodded. 'Yeah, of course. Go. I'll take her back to my place.' I didn't much care if Caroline met her maker, but I didn't want John to suffer. We'd worked together for the better part of nine years. I spent more time with him than I did with anyone. I knew he was a good man. I knew he still carried my secret with him, and I believed he'd never divulged it, not even to Dornan, his best friend and VP. It's funny – John hadn't asked me about that crumpled baby photo he'd found in my apartment once in nine years. He'd never asked if the baby was my son. And I'd never volunteered the information. I'd already perfected a lie in case he did ask. I'd tell him, and anyone else that asked, that the baby was my brother. And if Murphy got involved and spilled the truth – that I had a son, who was now somewhere in Colombia with adoptive parents – well, I'd burn that bridge down if I ever arrived at its edge.

Dornan didn't look at me again as he left, following after John. I knew he'd be disappointed. Angry. He hated Caroline at least as much as I did, and probably more.

I thought of the prospects again, their cocky little grins and know-it-all attitude. 'Come on,' I said to Juliette. 'We'll let the new boys clean up this mess.'

Juliette looked tired. 'I should clean it up. My mom will get mad.'

I will pound your mother's face into a fucking wall if she gets mad at you for not cleaning up her vomit. That's what I wanted to say, but I refrained. 'Nonsense,' I said, extending my hand. 'Those boys need to prove their worth.'

Almost as if on cue, bikers started to pour into the room. They all looked at me openly as they passed, but no one said a word. They wouldn't dare. I felt itchy all of a sudden, needed to leave before Emilio and Murphy came out of their own meeting and noticed I was still around. Murphy had a bad habit of trying to corner me, and I'd developed a sixth sense around his impending approach.

Several of the bikers greeted Juliette. Most of them had known the girl all her life, saw her as one of their own. But she was coming up to fifteen, and she was a beautiful girl. I'd seen girls who looked younger than her around this clubhouse. I wasn't stupid. I closed the space between the girl and myself. 'Come on,' I said to her, putting a hand on her shoulder.

Two young Gypsy Brothers appeared in front of me, blocking our path to the door. I looked between the young men with thinly veiled disgust. Dornan's two oldest sons, Chad and Donny, seemed to find Juliette the way … well, the way Murphy seemed to find me.

'Move,' I said. Saying 'excuse me' didn't do any good in a place like this.

Chad, the older and burlier asshole of the two, folded his arms across his chest and leered at me.

'What's the hurry?' he said, reaching out and dusting imaginary lint from my shoulder. Chad's eyes slid down to my chest. And stayed there. He licked his lips, making a suggestive sound in the back of his throat.

'The accountant,' he said, chuckling. I noticed Donny, the younger, weedier brother, edging closer to Juliette. 'Seems like we need to get you to more parties, sweetheart.'

Parties were when they all got their dicks wet with whoever they pleased. Probably in this very room. I wrinkled my nose up in distaste.

'What are you, twenty? I think I'm a little old for you, kiddo,' I said, taking Juliette's arm firmly in my grip as I spotted Murphy enter the room to my left.

Fuck. I was surrounded by idiots. Horny, moronic idiots.

At least I knew I could handle Murphy. I pulled Juliette in the opposite direction, making a beeline for the DEA agent who I despised with a passion. I didn't even look back at Chad and Donny as we made our way out of the room and into the hallway.

'Need a ride?' Murphy asked, falling into step beside me so I was flanked on one side by him, and Juliette on the other. The girl didn't speak, and I had to wonder if she was doing okay. Something struck me as odd. How did they get here? I looked down at Juliette's balled fist to see a set of keys peeking out from her grip.

'Did your mom drive here?' I asked her, knowing I wasn't going to like the answer.

'No,' Juliette said. She didn't elaborate, and I didn't press her. I already knew. She was fourteen, and *she drove her fucking mother here*, through busy LA traffic, because Caroline had taken too much heroin. Again.

I stopped short in the hallway, deciding I didn't need Murphy to drive us, after all. Sweet baby Jesus, that was a relief. The price of a favour from that motherfucker was always way too high.

I wondered, briefly, where Guillermo had gotten to. He'd probably hightailed it to the strip club to get a piece of ass on his one afternoon off, since Dornan and I usually spent Sunday afternoons alone at the apartment.

'Emilio was looking for you,' I addressed Murphy, a blatant lie. 'We'll wait out front.'

Murphy stopped beside me, his mouth curled up into an unimpressed smirk.

'Liar,' he murmured, his eyes flicking from me to Juliette, and then back again.

I smiled sweetly. 'Wouldn't want to be wrong, and keep him waiting, would you?'

Murphy muttered a stream of expletives as he left us, and I started walking briskly towards the front doors of the compound-esque building, Juliette right beside me.

'Which car?' I asked her, once we were past the guys on the door. She pointed to a silver Caprice that had seen better days. I held out my hand for the keys. 'Come on,' I said, aiming for upbeat and probably failing miserably. 'Let's blow this joint.'

Juliette smiled at me, dropping the keys into my hand.

CHAPTER SIX

MARIANA

John and Dornan arrived at my apartment a couple of hours later. Both had bloodshot eyes, which I suspected were for very different reasons. As soon as John walked in, his daughter ran to him, her blonde hair streaming behind her as she rushed to the front door and hugged her father tightly.

I retreated into the kitchen, still in earshot, but I busied myself making coffee. I didn't want to interrupt their moment. Juliette had sat on my couch for the past two hours, mute, resisting all of my attempts to coax something out of her until I gave up and let her be.

I heard steps approaching and poured steamed milk into two espresso-filled cups, setting the jug down and turning when I felt a hand on my elbow. I was expecting Dornan. My smile was a secret just for him, but as I turned, I saw John instead.

My smile dropped. All of a sudden I didn't know what to say. So I went for the first thing off the top of my head.

'Is Caroline okay?' I asked.

John threw me a sceptical look. 'Do you care?'

Nope, not at all. 'Of course I care. I care for you. I care for your daughter. She's spoken five words to me in two hours, John.' I almost added in the part about her driving the car to the clubhouse, but I bit my tongue. The last thing I wanted to do was get the girl in trouble.

He looked over his shoulder. I shifted slightly to the right so I could see the front door. Dornan was talking in hushed tones to Juliette, and she was smiling.

I don't know what it was about seeing them like that, but something stabbed painfully inside my chest. He was a good man, underneath all the bravado and the leather. He had made Juliette smile in moments, whereas I couldn't even elicit a single one from her in two hours, not since she'd handed me the car keys back at the clubhouse. But with Dornan she beamed. Under that gruff exterior, he had the capacity to put you at ease ... but only if he wanted to. It was clear he loved Juliette, and I remembered him telling me stories about how he'd been there when she was born, how he'd brought her home from the hospital afterwards and he and his wife had looked after her as their own, since John was in prison and Caroline went MIA soon after the cord had been cut.

'You know she drove the car to the clubhouse,' I said quietly, changing my mind. He needed to know this shit. I wished he'd just leave his wife, or that she'd finally get it right and take enough heroin to die and release him from their hellish marriage. Yeah. I wasn't a very nice person, wishing people dead, but she didn't give me any reason to wish differently.

John turned back to me, his mouth set in a hard line. He raked his hand through his hair, staring at the floor.

'Caroline ...' John shook his head, meeting my gaze again with his magnetic blue eyes. Intense, like Murphy's, but nothing alike. John's were clear and bright, and trusting. Compassionate. Kind. They were like windows to his soul, turned down ever so slightly at the edges, the stress making them look older than his forty-odd years.

I liked his eyes. They reassured me.

'Caroline used to be well,' John continued. 'She was never like this.'

You've been saying that for nine years, I wanted to say to him. But instead I said nothing.

'Where is she?' I asked.

John's face twisted into a grimace. 'Rehab.'

I knew the mounting costs of his wife's continual cycle – overdose, emergency room, rehab centre – were killing John. I did his finances. I knew he was fighting to keep his house and pay the bills. It always struck me as odd that he had no money, because he was always in possession of so much of the stuff. But he was stone broke.

I nodded, chewing on my lower lip. 'You think it'll stick this time?'

He didn't answer. He didn't need to. His expression told me everything.

'Thanks for watching Julz,' he said, patting me on the arm. It was meant as a casual gesture, but it almost made me jump it was so unexpected. A thrill coursed down my spine as I turned around and collected the cups of coffee, offering John one.

'Do I smell coffee?' Dornan asked, interrupting our ... I don't even know what it was. It wasn't small talk. It wasn't awkward, exactly, but it was something. John was always asking me questions, innocuous enough – things like *how was your weekend* and *did you get out to see the fireworks at the pier* and *are you going home for the holidays?* I managed to answer vaguely enough, but I knew there would come a day when he got sick of those non-answers and would demand to know the entire truth about me. It was written all over his face every time I was with Dornan. John knew that Dornan and I had a relationship, but he liked to pretend we didn't. Despite his terrible choice of life partner, John Portland still, at least then, believed in the sanctity of marriage, and strongly disapproved of Dornan having both a wife and a mistress. I'd heard them arguing about me once. John had been demanding to know why I wasn't allowed out of the apartment, and that was when Dornan had installed Guillermo as my housemate. Nobody outside of Emilio and Murphy knew the full truth about me, about *us*, even after all this time. But I knew John wanted to know about me, in the way he phrased his questions, always seeking more information. Where did I come from? Why was I still under lock and key and 24-hour guard after almost a decade? I saw the question in his eyes, the bewilderment, and the resentment that, even as president of the Gypsy Brothers, he was powerless to extract the information he so clearly craved from anyone.

'Coffee,' I said, handing Dornan the second cup after he drained his whiskey and set the empty tumbler on the counter. John, who hadn't touched his own cup of coffee, handed it back to me.

'I should take Juliette home,' he said, looking between Dornan and me. 'It's been a long one.'

Dornan nodded in response, not moving from his spot, leaning against the counter and tipping coffee down his throat. He finished the cup in one go and dropped it in the sink.

I opened my mouth to say something, to offer some kind of help or reassurance, but then I closed it again. What was I going to say that could ease the pain of a man with a burden like Caroline Portland?

After they'd left, and the door was securely shut, I shifted my attention to Dornan. 'Somebody should just put her out of her misery,' I said.

Nine years in this life and I was starting to talk like him.

'You're saying what I'm thinking,' Dornan said, passing me as he opened the freezer and dropped a handful of ice cubes into the tumbler he was holding. The coffee had been merely a formality, something to keep us awake after a trying day.

I took the opportunity to drink him in: dark jeans, tight black T-shirt that hugged his hard chest in all the right places, his tattoos peeking out from the sleeves and neckline. The Ross family crest on his neck always bothered me for some reason, maybe because it was inked proof that he belonged to Emilio. The revolver down his left forearm was better. And the Gypsy Brothers tattoo that adorned his back curled up enough in the middle that it edged up above his collar. Dark hair that he'd let grow a little longer recently, peppered with grey, like his permanent three-day stubble.

I'd been waiting for him. I had missed him terribly.

I *hungered* for his touch.

But with everything that had happened with Caroline, what I really needed right now was a stiff drink. I sipped at John's untouched cup, always loath to let good coffee go to waste, and watched Dornan pour whiskey over the ice cubes and take several gulps.

'That bad, huh?' I asked.

'That woman is a fucking train wreck,' he mused, cracking ice cubes between his teeth. He wiped his mouth with the back of his hand, setting his whiskey down and stepping over to me. A small smile tugged at the corner of his mouth as he stood over me, his hips pressing me into the counter as his dark eyes gleamed. The edge of the counter bit painfully into my back, but it didn't matter. I was wholly focused on *him*.

'You have no idea,' he said, threading a hand into my hair and pulling me into him. His stubble was rough but his lips soft, sweet and tangy with the remnants of the whiskey. As his tongue found mine, I melted into his grip, relishing the cold of his mouth from the ice cubes.

'I missed you,' Dornan murmured against my lips. My stomach flipped nervously, anticipation building within me. I wanted him. I needed him.

His kisses grew deeper, more urgent, and I felt the unmistakable line of his rock-hard erection pressing at my waist. I reached down and squeezed his hard length through his jeans, smiling when he knocked my hand away.

'There's plenty of time for that,' he said, taking my wrists and pulling them behind my back. I shivered as his mouth, rapidly losing the coolness of the ice cubes, kissed a rough, wet trail down my neck.

'I missed you so much,' I whispered, tensing as I felt his hands curl around my ass and lift me up. I wrapped my arms around his neck, kissing him long and hard as he carried me through the kitchen and deposited me on the end of the dining table, all without breaking our kiss.

But then he did break it. He pulled away and looked at me, really looked at me, one of those moments when you feel like your soul is laid bare. When you wonder what somebody sees in you. Do they see the lies you've told? The people you've left behind? Or do they just see what they want to see?

He pressed a palm against my chest, pushing me down until I ended up on my back, staring up at the ceiling, my legs bent at the knee and my feet – still clad in the black patent stilettos –braced against the edge of the table. I watched as he went back over to the counter and leaned over, collecting his whiskey and taking a sip.

He didn't speak; neither of us did. I watched him with great interest and barely controlled lust, my chest rising and falling quickly in anticipation. I wanted him. Now.

But he loved to make me wait.

He placed the whiskey between my feet, the ice making a clinking noise as it shifted in the glass. My dress was long, past the knee, and tight. It didn't seem to hinder Dornan's hands, though; he hooked a thumb underneath each side of the skirt and pushed it up, over my knees and up my thighs, until it was bunched around my waist. Just like he'd done several hours ago, but with more patience this time, more control. He took hold of my knees and pulled them apart, the sudden movement making me breathe in sharply.

Touch me. Just touch me. It's been too long. I could already feel wetness building at my core.

I still wasn't wearing panties. Dornan made a small sound of appreciation in his throat as he trailed a hand up my inner thigh and over my bare pussy. He smiled as his fingers slid along my wetness.

'You've been waiting for me,' he murmured, his voice low and gravelly. I nodded, bracing my palms against my thighs.

He leaned in, his head between my legs, so close to me that I could feel his breath on my pussy. It drove me wild, that waiting, that feeling, hoping he was about to dart his tongue out and lick my willing flesh. He stayed there for a moment, just breathing, his fingers digging into the backs of my thighs. *Please do it, just hurry up and do it—*

His tongue found my clit. *Holy mother of God.* It felt good. I arched my hips towards his mouth, greedy for more. I groaned when he took his mouth away and stood straight, picking the whiskey up again and taking another sip.

'What do you want me to do?' he asked, an ice cube still in his mouth, a mischievous glint in his dark eyes.

I looked at the ceiling. I couldn't look him in the eye when he asked me what I wanted him to do.

'You know,' I replied.

In my peripheral vision, I saw him shake his head, a smirk spreading across his face. 'Words. I want words.' He rounded the table so he was at my side, crouching so we were eye to eye.

He leaned in, kissing me deeply. His mouth was cold from the ice cube, refreshing. He tasted so fucking good. His free hand went down to my clit and drew slow, shallow circles that made me moan into his mouth.

He broke the kiss, smiling as he took a chair and placed it at the end of the table. He sat down and dragged it closer, so that he now had unrestricted access to me.

Hands gripped my ass cheeks and pulled me down so I was hovering half-off the table. I heard the clink of ice cubes again and braced myself for the cold.

'Say it,' he ordered.

'Fuck,' I muttered. 'I want your mouth on me. I want you to lick me.'

He raised his head, his smile contagious. 'Lick you where?'

'My pussy,' I begged. 'Please.'

We might have done this only hours earlier, but it had happened so quickly, it was almost as if it hadn't happened at all. And let's face it, I was addicted to this man – too much was never enough.

His head disappeared again. I moaned as Dornan's cold tongue touched against my sensitive nub, pressing the ice against me. I bucked involuntarily, trying to close my legs. The cold was overwhelming. It was too much.

'Don't move,' Dornan hissed, before returning his tongue to my clit. It was slightly warmer now. Sighing, I rested back on my elbows and prayed like hell that he'd finish what he was starting.

More ice. More protesting. The heat and the freezing cold stirred within me, Dornan's hands gripping my ankles like twin vices, the unspoken message perfectly clear: Don't. Move.

'Holy ... Jesus!' I cried, as he dragged an ice cube against my opening. It was freezing cold. It stung, but in a good way.

Then he pushed it inside me, along with a finger.

It burned. The cold cube slowly melted within me, ice turning to water, Dornan's tongue collecting the excess as he licked me. It felt so fucking good, it was almost unbearable. He repeated the action with another ice cube, his fingers sliding down from my pussy to the pucker of my ass.

'You want it here?' he asked, his voice humming against my soaking pussy as he took his thumb and circled the small opening. A thrill shot through me as his finger gently probed at my ass.

Oh God, did I want it there.

'Yes,' I whispered, delighting in the glazed sensation that draped over me, the total submission, the anticipation of what was to come. I tried to relax as he pushed his thumb into my ass, stretching me, opening me up, but I tensed anyway. It was a natural reaction to being entered there.

'Relax,' Dornan growled, pumping slowly as he placed his mouth back over my swollen clit and sucked. Discomfort became pleasure as I got used to his thumb sliding in and out of my ass, and my nerves started to fray.

Under his skilled hands, my ass began to burn.

It was fire and passion and fucking all bound into one ticking time bomb. I didn't want him to stop, didn't want him to leave my ass or my pussy as my legs began to shake and I bucked into his tongue faster.

I thought to reach out and grab his head between my hands, to make sure he finished what he'd started, but he anticipated my move. Before I could thread my hands into his hair and pull him closer into me, he took his finger out, took his mouth away, and stood so fast, the chair behind him flew backwards, crashing onto the tiles.

'Don't stop,' I moaned.

He grabbed my hips roughly, his pants already unbuttoned and his cock standing proudly to attention, the smooth head glistening with pre-come.

'Turn over,' he growled, picking me up and doing the work himself. My hands and knees smacked against the table as I pressed my ass backwards into him, looking back and watching as he pumped his rock-hard cock in his palm.

Ice cubes clinked again, and I gasped as I felt the cold breach my pussy again. A finger pushed one ice cube inside me, then another, until it was all I could do not to scream.

My skin broke out in goosebumps as my teeth began to chatter; it felt like I was simultaneously being frozen and set on fire from within.

I felt the head of his dick trail up and down my pussy, pushing gently, but not enough to gain purchase. I whimpered, pressing back into him, as my hand went to my clit and started circling it. I gasped when he fisted a handful of my hair and pulled.

'You want to come?' he asked, tugging on my hair so he could speak into my ear.

'Yes,' I cried, dropping my hand back onto the table to balance myself.

'The only way you're coming,' he growled, pressing his cock against me, 'is with my dick in your ass.'

Holy fucking Christ, those words were the biggest turn on.

'Do you want me to fuck your ass?' he asked, continuing to press against it.

'Yes,' I moaned, pushing back into him. 'Please.'

I braced myself as Dornan released my hair, his hand going to my hip as he coated the head of his dick with my slickness. Then, wet and swollen, he pushed against my tight hole. It burned a little, but it felt so fucking good.

'Relax,' he urged, one hand coming around to rub my clit. I did, letting myself melt back into him, my ass wanting to resist the breach. I concentrated on stilling that urge to tense, and his dick pushed into my ass.

I moaned loudly, swearing under my breath as he pulled back and sank into me, over and over again. His fingers on my clit, together with his dick in my ass coupled together to form an orgasm that ripped through me like fire and ice.

I screamed. *Dornan*. I'm pretty sure I screamed his name over and over again, even as he continued to fuck me. As I came back down to earth, the aftershocks of my climax made every touch agonising. He didn't stop, though, driving into me relentlessly. I felt his body tense up as he grew even harder, and then he was coming inside me, his chest curled over me as he sank his teeth into the tender flesh of my back.

'Missed you too,' he murmured against my skin, the indents where his teeth had pierced my flesh humming with a pleasant pain.

CHAPTER SEVEN

MARIANA

Afterwards, we showered, holding each other as warm water washed us clean. We didn't speak.

We didn't need to.

He was here. That was all that mattered. And I intended to drink in every single moment of our time together.

When I had dried off and dressed, I poured myself a glass of red wine and headed out to the balcony, wearing one of Dornan's shirts. It was like a dress on me, but I liked the way it wrapped me up in him, even when he wasn't with me. It was late afternoon, and the sun was just reaching that low point in the sky where it shone directly into the apartment. I closed my eyes, basking in the golden rays, warm against my face as I listened to the waves crash onto the shore below.

I sensed him behind me before I saw him. I turned my head and opened my eyes to see him standing there in a pair of jeans, no shirt. Even in his forties, and despite the fact that I'd seen him like this countless times over the years, the man was still fucking irresistible.

He reached a hand behind my ear and then opened his palm in front of my face, a mischievous grin plastered on his face as he held out a coin. 'Penny for your thoughts?' he joked.

I laughed, taking the quarter. 'I was just thinking.'

He stood beside me and I turned back to the ocean, the breeze whipping my hair around my face.

'Thinking happy thoughts?'

'You make me happy,' I said plainly, taking one of his hands between mine and playing with his fingers. They were warm and rough, a working man's hands.

Dornan glanced sideways at me, the breeze picking up his hair and making it dance. 'Are you? Happy?'

I swallowed thickly as he took his hand away, feeling the smile die on my face as I looked out to the water. I wasn't happy and I was. Stolen moments, away from everyone else and their demands. In those, I was happy. Outside of that? The nothingness was a yawning chasm. It hurt. It *ached.*

'I'm happy when I'm with you,' I said finally. I reached out again and took his large hand in mine, squeezing it tightly.

'You did good with the kid,' he said, pulling me under his arm.

It felt safe, here. I felt loved.

'That girl needs a mother, not that fucking thing that pretends to be one,' Dornan added.

I shrugged. 'I didn't do much,' I said softly, enjoying the sting of the salt breeze on my bare arms. 'She wouldn't even talk to me. I don't think children like me, somehow.'

'You'd be a good mother,' Dornan said seriously, drawing me closer.

And I didn't mean to, but I froze. I felt my mouth open a little as I screamed inwardly. The mask slipped, just for a second. And in that moment, the man I loved? I hated him.

'What?' Dornan asked, turning me so we were facing each other, the ocean ebbing and flowing below us, just like it had done for countless years, just like it would keep doing long after we were both bones and ash. In that moment, I felt so inconsequential, so unnecessary, so *deprived*. Because I was somebody's mother. And it wasn't fucking fair.

It wasn't Dornan's fault. He didn't know. And I would never tell him, not unless Emilio was dead and buried and we were free. The problem was I didn't even know if Dornan wanted to be free. There were some things we wouldn't talk about, and his father was one of those things.

'Nothing,' I replied, feeling my chest tighten.

You'd be a good mother. He didn't know the significance of those words, how deep they cut into me, leaving bloodied ribbons of my soul in their wake.

I had been somebody's mother, once upon a time. And now, I was nothing. A piece of property. A mistress. A money launderer. A whore.

'Hey,' he said, taking my chin between his thumb and forefinger and turning my gaze towards his.

I saw the haunted look in his eyes, like a deer in headlights, about to be slammed. 'Don't worry about me,' I said softly, gripping his wrist tightly. 'You worry about your kids, okay? I'll be fine. I'll be right here.'

It wasn't fair of me to ask anything more of him than I already had. He'd already saved my life, kept me alive, kept me safe. All this time. And he'd saved me from myself on the darkest nights, without even realising it.

'I'll leave her,' Dornan blurted out. 'When they're grown up. When she can't control them. I'll leave her.'

I stiffened. He'd never said anything remotely like that before. I was his mistress, and nothing more. I knew he loved me. It wasn't ideal, but it was all he'd ever had to give me, and I had taken it gratefully. Every time I thought of the alternative, I remembered that, even though I felt trapped and smothered, it could always be worse. So. Much. Worse. Emilio could have sold me at that auction nine years ago. And, as Murphy had so chillingly assured me, nobody made it out of that shit alive. If I'd been bought, and used, and raped, I'd be dead by now.

'You don't have to say that,' I protested, breaking eye contact. 'You don't have to make promises to me, Dornan. I don't expect them.'

I thought more about that, turning his words over in my mind. *When she can't control them.* An admission of vulnerability from a man like Dornan Ross was a shattering revelation. Was he meaning to say that there was someone even more powerful than the all-powerful Gypsy Brothers and Il Sangue Cartel royalty?

I fingered the collar on his shirt. 'Did you love Celia? When you got married?'

Dornan tensed.

'Sorry,' I said quickly. 'You don't have to answer that.'

'It was a business decision,' Dornan said, his tone suddenly clipped. I was losing him. I could feel him shutting down right in front of me.

'I spoke to Anthony the other day,' I said, swiftly changing the subject. Although I despised Dornan's oldest son, Chad, with a passion reserved for people like Emilio, there was something about Anthony, or 'Ant' as everyone called him. I saw his father in him. A tough exterior, but an instinct to protect instead of exploit. Whereas Chad, on the other hand, was just a younger American version of his grandfather, Emilio.

'Yeah?' Dornan's pride was evident.

'He's a good kid.' I tried to think of something to say about the rest of them and drew a blank.

'He's smart.' He smiled proudly, then the smile faded slightly.

'What?' I asked.

Dornan shrugged, tucking loose hair behind my ear and giving it a soft, almost playful tug. 'I wonder what these boys would be like if they had a choice.'

'Everyone has a choice,' I said.

Dornan raised his eyebrows. 'Like you had a choice?'

'I had a choice,' I said boldly. 'I chose you. And you chose me.'

His smile looked pained. 'I'd spend every moment with you if I could, you know that?'

I nodded, smiling sadly. I knew that more than I knew anything. It was a truth that burned inside me, kept me going when the demons in my mind tried to convince me otherwise.

'Do you ever think about the future?' I asked softly.

'Sometimes,' Dornan replied. Any trace of lightness was gone now, replaced by the weary reality of our collective fates.

'And?' I pressed.

He let his hand drop from my face and turned back to the sun, squinting as it slid lower against the orange and blue horizon.

'And it doesn't do any good,' he said gruffly. 'So I think about something else, instead.'

'Oh,' I said softly. I thought about what he'd said about leaving Celia, about how remote that possibility even was. How could I marry him, anyway? Legally, as far as anyone was concerned, I was a dead woman. Dead women couldn't get married.

I didn't want to be a member of the Ross family. I might have loved the son, but I hated the father. No, even if it was ever a possibility, I'd never marry into Emilio's family.

'I have to go,' Dornan said abruptly, wrapping a hand around the back of my neck and pulling me to him. He kissed me on the forehead, his lips lingering for a long time before he pulled away. I didn't move, not wanting him to break away and return me to this unbearable loneliness.

'Don't go,' I murmured against his chest. 'You just got here.'

We played this game far too often, these days.

He kissed the top of my head again, his soft lips leaving a small damp mark against my skin, and then he left. I stared into my empty wine glass, tears forming in my eyes, jolting a little when the front door slammed.

Alone again.

A tear found its way out, dropping into the glass, followed by another, and then another. My chest constricted painfully as my weeping turned to all-out sobs, my eyes blurring as salt water overcame them.

I was happy in brief moments of time, but I was sad the rest of the time.

I lifted my head, blinked away tears. Saw children on the beach across from where I stood, their happy shrieks like blunt knives being driven into my heart. I saw the Ferris wheel on the jetty come to a stop, collect new passengers, and then start turning again. I heard the front door open and Guillermo's sneakers squeaking on the tiles.

You'd be a good mother.

I wondered if my son liked Ferris wheels.

I wondered if he knew that I existed.

I felt someone behind me, but I didn't turn. I didn't want Guillermo to see my tears.

'She die?' he asked, crossing his arms and leaning on the railing beside me.

I shook my head. 'Nope. Still kicking.'

Before he could do any more talking, I turned and pushed past him, walked down the hall and closed the door, shutting myself in my room. I sat on the edge of my bed, pulling Dornan's shirt around me. I was pathetic. I was in love with a man who could never be mine, and I hated myself for that.

***

Later, in the bath, I took a disposable razor and snapped the plastic with my fingers, releasing the sharp blade within. I kept the hot water running and the plug a little loose to make sure the tub was continually refilled with hot water. I laid out underneath a blanket of fluffy bath bubbles until they shifted under the pressure of the running water, revealing the body I worked so hard to keep fit.

Going to the gym was one of the few freedoms I had – not that it was really a freedom with Guillermo in tow, but it was something to break the monotony. Something to focus on as I ran miles and miles on the treadmill, longing for fresh air on my face. They had these fans you could point at your face as you ran, but the air smelled of sweat and socks, not salt and water.

There was a soft knock at the bathroom door, and Guillermo poked his head in.

'You want a drink, girlie?' He made a tipping gesture against his mouth and I allowed a small smile.

'Sure,' I said, placing the razor on the cold tiles that edged the deep tub. I wasn't worried about Guillermo seeing me naked – there were now enough bubbles covering me that the only things visible were my head and the tops of my knees as they stuck out of the water. And I wasn't worried about him trying anything. Over the years, Guillermo had become one of the few people that I could trust to some degree. He'd shared parts of his life with me, stories from his past, and he'd become a constant in my daily life. And, as much as I hated to admit it, I actually felt safer with him around. There were no more random visits from Murphy like there had been in the beginning of my captivity, no worries about coming and going as I pleased. I got my fresh air, and Guillermo was the price I paid.

Guillermo was a murderer. He'd gone to jail for blowing up his house while his wife slept inside with the guy she was cheating on Guillermo with. The cartel had gotten him a light sentence in a plea deal, since Guillermo was one of the power-players with Mexican connections. Even with those connections, he was still in the minor leagues compared to Dornan and John, which was probably why he'd been assigned to me. We had an odd relationship, almost like brother and sister. He reminded me of my own brother in a way, minus the homicidal tendencies, and I wasn't afraid of him trying anything on me.

Guillermo left, returning with two tumblers of what looked like vodka on the rocks. He handed me the one with a slice of lime and took his over to the vanity, leaning against the countertop as he looked at me questioningly.

He nodded his head towards the naked razor on the edge of the tub. 'If you die, I'll kill you,' he said jokingly.

I shrugged, a wry smile touching my lips. 'I'd never die,' I replied, lifting my foot out of the water and watching rivulets of water stream down, back into the tub. 'Who'd make your coffee in the morning?'

He groaned.

'What?' I asked. He was distracting me from the urge to stick my head underwater and drown myself.

'It's just like when I was married,' he said, shaking his head. 'Pretty little wife fucking somebody else in my house, and I have to visit the clubhouse to get any.'

I grinned, staring up at the ceiling. 'This isn't your house. But sounds like a marriage, alright.' I sobered, my grin slipping as I remembered Dornan telling me what Guillermo had done to his cheating wife. Forensics hadn't been able to separate her tissue and bones from that of her lover's without DNA testing every last little piece. I reminded myself to never get on his bad side.

'Don't blow me up, okay?' I drained my vodka and set the glass on the lip of the bath, chewing ice loudly. 'I know exactly how much half and half to put in your coffee. Those bitches at Starbucks have nothing on me.'

He chuckled. 'You're dangerous,' he said in Spanish, closing the door and leaving me alone.

My smile vanished the moment he closed the door. I sat up, my nipples hardening against the cool night air. I drew my knees up out of the water and took hold of the razor blade with one hand, stroking my skin with the other. I hadn't changed. As I pressed the tip of the sharp blade into the wet flesh of my thigh and watched blood rise to the surface, the dull sting that reminded me I was alive brought a smile to my lips once more.

Sometimes the loneliness was too much. Sometimes it broke my soul. When you're all alone for weeks at a stretch, the only touch the one of your enemy and owner, it becomes a daily struggle not to sink into the darkness and be swallowed, whole.

Guillermo was in the apartment, but he hardly qualified as a person I could bare my soul to. I had nobody in the quiet hours of the night. Every secret I shared was a potential weapon that could be turned against me, and I already had enough of those floating around without exposing more.

But I had a sharp razor blade, and a penchant for spilling my own blood, and so I whiled the hours away carving marks into my own skin. The cuts weren't all that noticeable – tiny, deep gouges into the flesh above my knees.

Back when I'd first been taken by Emilio and his men, I had been a cutter. I'd favoured my wrists then, the way I could draw a knife or a piece of glass against my bare flesh and see my blood spring up, something to make me feel. One of the first things Dornan had done for me was tend to my wounds after I'd gouged my wrists, stuck in a windowless room in Emilio's compound and going crazy with claustrophobia and grief.

My nasty little habit had served me well over the years. Kept the demons at bay, the ones that told me to *just call my mother* or *track down Luis in Colombia* or throw myself off the goddamn Sixth Street Bridge.

Because I couldn't do any of those things, not really. If I tried to contact my family, they'd be killed, me along with them. If I tried to track down my son, what good would it do? It would be good for me, to hear his voice, to see his face. But for him? It'd be confusing, dangerous, and we'd both end up in the same predicament. Dead.

The first two options – contacting my family, or committing suicide – weren't all that appealing. The third option, the cutting, was harder to stave off. More difficult to avoid contemplating, because it was the thing that got me through. I loved Dornan, I did. The work I did wasn't particularly hard. I got to spend most of my day listening to music as I did the accounts for Emilio. I even took a sick pleasure in seeing how much money I could launder each day. And I was good at what I did. Despite the fact that I was doing it under duress, I was actually proud of how well I did what I did.

But none of it was real, see? It was all an illusion. I wasn't the accountant. I could lull myself into believing that truth six days out of the week, only to have it cruelly snatched from me under the weight of Emilio's moist palms on my neck, his reptilian eyes. The way he squeezed my nipples so hard it felt like he was going to rip them off, the constant reminder that I was a piece of property that only he controlled. The ever-present threat of Murphy, lurking in the background, licking his lips as he watched me get humiliated.

So I compensated. I cut into my flesh regularly, and it made me feel better. The sight of my own blood made me remember that, despite the world believing I was dead, I was actually very much alive.

CHAPTER EIGHT

DORNAN

They say drowning is a peaceful way to die, but Dornan Ross wasn't so sure about that. He'd been drowning in blood and lies his entire life, since the moment he'd been wrenched from his mother's womb, thrashing and howling in protest.

He'd even been conceived by force, he learned one night when his mother had drank too much and started yelling at his father. She was crying. Her words were stilted, but the meaning was clear: Dornan Ross hadn't been created out of any semblance of love, but out of his father's vicious need for power and dominance over his mother.

He was twelve when he heard that conversation, and nothing had ever been the same for him since. It wasn't sadness for his mother – she'd chosen this life, and she'd married the motherfucker. It wasn't anger at his father – Dornan was too terrified of the man to feel any particular rage towards him.

No, it was the dragging feeling in his gut, the voice inside his head that said *you should never have been born*.

The age of the internet had changed the flesh trade forever – human trafficking operated under Il Sangue's stronghold. They sold anything you desired – women, body parts, children, even newborn babies. There was a demand for everything in this world, and Dornan's father, Emilio Ross, intended to fulfil those needs and make himself a very, very rich man at the same time.

He rarely bothered himself with the details, leaving that delightful job to his son.

And today was fulfilment day.

Dornan walked through the massive warehouse his father owned in San Pedro, on the Port of Los Angeles. Today it was full of packages and deliveries, stacked high to the roof with pallets. They delivered anything and everything. Wine. Furniture. Appliances.

Kidneys. Whores. Newborn babies.

There was a buyer for everything, and the beauty of the internet age meant the cartel could hold auctions every week with prospective bidders attending via their computer screens. Since they'd harnessed the worldwide web for their devious exploits, business had boomed. It meant they seldom had to dress the girls up and auction them live anymore – they just dolled them up in their holding cells, drugged the bitches up, spread their legs wide and took a couple of photos and videos for prospective buyers. Money changed hands seamlessly, was tucked away into offshore accounts, and one of the only people who had to deal with the human face of the entire thing was Dornan himself.

He dreamed about killing his father. About taking a knife and slaughtering him. Emilio had given him life, but he had damned him in the same instance. But Dornan never did it. Too many people relied on his complicity for him to do anything so brash. His sons. His wife. *Mariana …*

Monday morning. It was the day he always dreaded the

most. Sundays were the best, because he got to see Mariana without fail, and fuck the hell out of her. He got to forget for a few precious hours what came the next morning, what horrors would await him. Only last night, they'd barely seen each other at all, and now he was here, and she was not.

He finally reached the back of the warehouse. There was a large machine – an automatic envelope sorter and stamper. It was perpetually broken, and for good reason.

It never got used.

It was a door.

A door down to hell.

Dornan looked around the warehouse, ensuring nobody saw him, then stepped behind the large machine. There were minimal staff working the cover business on a Monday, for this exact reason. They had no fucking idea what happened downstairs in the lead-lined basement.

No idea that their tasks were pointless, their efforts futile, their delivery business barely profitable. Designed, in fact, to run at a loss. They existed purely to deflect attention from everything else. The real business.

The flesh trade downstairs.

Dornan swallowed back bile as he made his way down the three flights of stairs, past the sub-floor and into the depths of a fucking nightmare. The place was a huge, cavernous limestone and concrete bunker dug deep into the earth. It was located close enough to the docks to be convenient for shipping their wares, yet far enough away to avoid undue suspicion.

They weren't exactly FedEx.

There were several large trucks already backed into the massive expanse, an industrial lift bridge responsible for dropping them below the earth and into the real warehouse, where the action was. Dornan took his clipboard from the place it always sat, at the beginning of the rows upon rows of containers, and began his grim routine. The list had forty-three today. A busy day, but not the busiest by any means.

Number one. The code that took up the first line was deceptively simple. It told him, in a matter of letters and numbers, that inside the first container made of plastic and steel and no larger than a single shower cubicle was a cooler, and inside that cooler was a pair of human kidneys on ice. Bad, but at least kidneys didn't have eyes. Dornan reached up and slid a panel of plastic aside to reveal a small viewing pane. The blue cooler sat innocently on the floor. Container number one got a check mark next to it, and the viewing pane was covered again.

Line numbers two and three weren't surprising. Females, bound for new owners who would keep them locked up for their own pleasure. Sometimes they kept them as maids, but as Dornan peered inside containers two and three, he could clearly see that these women weren't going to be cleaning house. They were going to be on their backs, probably screaming, definitely chained up until they learned that escape was futile.

He moved to container number four, his heart sinking into his stomach with a thud. Fuck. These were some of the hardest ones, children notwithstanding. There was much money to be earned from newborn babies – some could fetch in the realm of a hundred grand or more, if the baby's mother was white enough.

You could call them cells, but that would be too generous. You could stand in them. Turn around in them. They were about the size of a portable toilet, minus the toilet itself, and completely soundproof. Air was piped in through a series of one-way vents. The damned things were even air-conditioned for transport, because nobody liked trucking a horde of slaves across the United States, only to open the doors and find they'd all died of heatstroke en route.

That shit used to happen. Not anymore. His father was a clever man, and he'd commissioned an engineer to design the cells a few years ago. The death rate during transfer had gone down almost one hundred percent. There was still the odd girl who'd have a heart attack, literally frightened to death of where she was headed, but apart from that, they did just fine. The buyers appreciated it. They received their goods in working order, on time and discreetly. No longer was it necessary to arrive in the dead of night and herd screaming, crying women out of the back of a truck under the threat of machine-gun fire.

Because, let's face it, they were almost always women.

Now, all they needed at the other end was a forklift. The truck opened, the allocated package was located – all having been stacked in order of drop-off, of course – the forklift took the container, and so it went on, until every single soul had been exorcised from one of the massive trucks they ran weekly from coast to coast.

Sometimes, they even couriered overseas. They were that good.

No longer did Emilio, as kingpin of the entire operation, have to worry about valuable virgins being covertly deflowered en route by his men, or escaping when the doors were opened and sweaty bodies poured forth like an avalanche of sadness and fright.

It wasn't the dirty, crowded shipping container job it had once been. No, these days it was practically fucking clinical, the way they traded and delivered humans like refrigerators.

Practically fucking civilised. The guys drove the trucks, delivered the goods, and only the buyer had the code to open each large container that housed their human transaction.

The guys never saw the girls they were delivering, and so there was no problem. There was no temptation. Nobody saw a thing.

Except Dornan.

Dornan saw every single soul, stared into every pair of eyes, heard the agonised begging of every single slave they bought and sold. He knew his father did this on purpose, but he'd sold his own soul a very long time ago, and he was indebted to his father for the rest of his life for the favours he had asked and the things he had done.

He hated it. Sometimes he thought about how good it would be to disappear, to slip underneath the surface of the ocean and just swim away.

But it was a briefly indulged fantasy, because he had sons, and *he had Mariana*.

Dornan ticked off the last piece of merchandise on his list. The whole process had taken less than thirty minutes, but it felt like a lifetime. Dornan took the stairs two at a time, not caring that his boots thudded loudly on the metal as he ascended as rapidly as he could. He was a grown man, and the pit – the name he'd given to the basement warehouse of horrors – terrified him.

Lighting a cigarette outside, Dornan wondered briefly if he was turning into his father. He didn't think he was, at least not yet. But his father didn't look into the eyes of the prisoners before he sent them to their hellish fates, and so maybe Dornan was already worse than his father had ever been.

CHAPTER NINE

JOHN

John Portland's morning was fucking splendid. As the president of the Gypsy Brothers MC, there was always something urgent that needed attending on a Monday morning. By 10 a.m. he'd already beaten a guy's front teeth out, sent half his crew on a run, and coordinated the shipping of a new haul of machine guns across to Mexico. His hand was throbbing from where the guy's pointy canine tooth had gouged into his skin, and he had a case full of damp cash to dump at the strip club to be counted and processed.

He stormed into the strip club and was immediately bailed up by Riviera, one of the dancers. Bleached blonde, and with enough fake tan for an episode of *Baywatch*, she thrust her jewel-encrusted tits at him and smiled.

'Hey, John,' she cooed.

'Not now,' John shot back, shouldering her out of his path. His hand was really fucking hurting. Maybe he'd broken something. That guy's face had been like a brick wall. He'd slept in, just had enough time to drop his daughter at the school gates, and then found his fist in someone's face. He hadn't even had a goddamn cup of coffee yet to give him a kicker.

In his good hand, he held a suitcase full of bills. They were supposed to be clean. But when he looked inside, the piles of greenbacks were damp, and some were marked with a fine sheen of blood.

Fucking excellent start to the morning.

He opened the door to the small office on the second floor and dumped the suitcase onto the first of two desks that filled the small, airless room.

The woman behind the desk scooted her seat back and smiled wryly. 'Really, John,' she said. 'You shouldn't have.'

He eyed the suitcase dubiously.

'Please tell me these ones are clean.'

His mood lifted immediately at the sight of Mariana Rodriguez. Pretty, smart and sarcastic as hell, she always managed to distract him from the shit-kicker muscle work he invariably did from day to day. Being Prez might look good on a leather jacket, but in reality it wasn't so fucking special. Plus, being under the thumb of Emilio Ross and his cartel didn't exactly bolster his enthusiasm. Most days, lately, he'd been phoning it in for the sake of keeping the peace. It wasn't like MC President looked great on a resume. The last time he'd held down a legitimate job that wasn't at a front business for Il Sangue was back in high school, fixing bikes at his uncle's garage down in SoCal.

John grimaced. 'I could tell you that, but I'd be lying.'

Mariana stared at the suitcase, resting her chin in her hands. When she leaned forwards like that her dress dipped a little and he could see the outline of her cleavage, and what a welcome sight it was on this particularly shitty morning.

'Do you think if I stare at it long enough, it'll clean itself?'

Her words jolted him out of his breast-worship, and he raked his good hand through his short blonde hair. He'd woken up too late for a shower, and he felt like shit. He must have looked pretty average, too. He'd looked at himself in the rearview before he got off his bike, and his blue eyes were so bloodshot they were practically on fire.

John couldn't help but laugh. 'You know what they say about wishes and horses.'

Mariana frowned. Her American accent was flawless, so he sometimes forgot she wasn't from here. That she didn't always know American sayings.

'Never mind,' he said. 'I picked this up from Enzo. He still owes another payment next week.' He didn't mention how he'd charged extra interest with his fists. Somehow, mentioning that in front of Mariana wouldn't be a good thing, he decided. She might be Dornan's – he wasn't entirely sure – girlfriend? Mistress? Yeah, mistress sounded about right. He didn't really want to think any deeper about where she had come from and why she'd been kicking her own shit in the back office of a seedy dance club for almost a decade, because when he had added things up, they looked very troubling, indeed. He knew Dornan was obsessed with her. He knew that she was Colombian. He knew that she had a baby son, or he'd been a baby once, anyway. He'd seen the photograph.

Aside from that, he didn't know a damn thing about her, except that she was fucking beautiful. Long dark hair that reached past her shoulders and curled ever so slightly at the ends. A tiny waist, high cheekbones and those dark blue eyes – they'd make stunning-looking kids together, with their DNA. He shouldn't even think about that, because he had a wife, and she had Dornan, and they barely even knew each other.

Still. He liked any excuse to come to the burlesque club to see her. Even if it meant fucking his hand up by punching someone whose bone structure was more like a cliff face.

As John was about to explain the contents of the suitcase, Guillermo barrelled into the office.

'I need fifteen grand,' he said, looking at Mariana.

John frowned, reaching over and tugging on Guillermo's leather cut. 'Good morning, Guillermo. Mind telling me why you need fifteen thousand dollars on a Monday morning?'

Guillermo shrugged, stuffing cold pizza into his mouth. 'Oh, hey boss. I don't know,' he said around a mouthful of pizza. 'I just do what Dee tells me to do. And he told me to get fifteen grand for him.'

Mariana looked from Guillermo to John. 'How much is in here?' she asked, patting the suitcase.

John fought back a smirk. 'Ten.'

She smiled, swivelling in her chair and unlocking the safe at her feet. It opened with a *thunk*, and she withdrew a stack of hundreds before closing the safe again and spinning the wheel to lock it.

She unzipped a corner of the suitcase and shoved her stack of bills inside, closing it again and pushing the case across to Guillermo. He wiped his greasy fingers on his jeans and grabbed the suitcase, holding it by his side.

'What's for dinner?' He asked Mariana.

She rolled her dark blue eyes at him. 'I'm not your mother. Order a pizza. *Again*.'

He shook his head. 'I'll get fish tacos from that place you like,' he said, leaving as abruptly as he had arrived.

Mariana turned her attention back to John. 'I swear, he's going to die of a heart attack before he's forty,' she said. 'You got anything else for me to bank today?'

John shrugged. 'Maybe something this afternoon. I just need you to make my regular transfer. Can you put half in this account?' He passed her a piece of paper with a series of numbers and she wrinkled up her nose.

'I need a name,' she said. 'For the banking records.'

'You've never needed a name before.'

She shrugged, picking up a ballpoint pen and twisting it between her fingers. 'It won't work if I don't have an account name to attach to it.'

John stared down at her, his cheery mood gone. 'There is no name,' he snapped. 'Just make it happen. Wire it.'

She threw the piece of paper down on his side of the desk, her smile gone, too. 'New regulations,' she said coolly. 'The bank won't accept the transfer unless I have the name of the bank account.'

John took a deep breath and tried not to lose his shit. It wasn't her fault. She was just doing her job. But how the fuck was he supposed to get money to where it needed to go if he had to use a name? Names were dangerous. Even with the fake alias she was using, they could potentially track her down. Shit.

'Look,' Mariana said, finally meeting his gaze. 'I can wire transfer if the person can collect the cash on the same day. You don't need a bank account for that. You call them and give them a code, and they can go to Western Union and take out the money. They still need to show a driver's licence.'

John nodded, his frayed nerves cooling somewhat. 'Thanks,' he said gruffly, sliding the piece of paper back to her.

He needed to find a better way to get money to Stephanie. He wasn't sure how, but he was going to have to rethink the way he supplemented her before it became impossible.

He thought of Dornan finding out what he'd been doing behind his back, and his stomach knotted. No. He couldn't allow that to happen. Dornan would never forgive him.

'What's wrong with your hand?' Mariana asked, standing up and leaning across the desk to get a better look. Before John could step back, she'd reached out and taken his hand in hers. 'Did somebody bite you?' Her dark blue eyes flashed with concern as she looked from John's injured hand to his eyes.

Jesus, those eyes of hers were dangerous. You could get lost in them. He couldn't afford to get lost in anything that belonged to Dornan. He pulled his hand away. 'It's fine,' he said, brushing off her concern. 'You should see the other guy.'

She shook her head, opening her desk drawer and producing a small first aid kit. 'Let me fix that before it gets infected.'

John shook his head, stepping back towards the door. 'It's fine, really—'

'John!' she said insistently. 'You right handed?'

He nodded.

'How are you going to deliver me money every day without your right hand? Come on. Sit down. Here, have a coffee. Guillermo got an extra one.'

She passed him a Starbucks cup and pointed to the other desk. 'Sit. If I have to look at your hand for much longer, I might puke.'

He laughed, leaning against the second desk, his ankles crossed as he sipped lukewarm coffee. It was sugary and strong, just what he needed. As sugar and caffeine travelled to his brain, he started to relax a little. He wasn't used to anyone taking care of him. His wife was a walking disaster and he'd never expect or want his daughter to take on all the household responsibilities that Caroline ignored, so he did most everything himself. It wasn't so bad – there was worse, he remembered as he looked at Mariana's concentrated expression – but it was nice to have a woman take care of him, for once.

He tensed when she touched a pad of rubbing alcohol to his wound, but didn't pull away or protest. She smiled slightly at his reaction, waiting a moment before she continued cleaning the wound.

He couldn't help it. As covertly as he could, without her noticing, he ran his eyes over every part of her that he could see. She had some sort of make-up on that made her eyes pop, and they looked stunning against her light brown skin and dark silky hair. She was wearing her hair out, and it fell loosely around her face. When she moved, he caught a whiff of her perfume, or maybe it was the shampoo she used. Whatever it was, it smelled of coconut and lime and sex.

He breathed her in deeply, and she looked at him quizzically. 'You feeling okay?'

Oh, he felt better than okay. She smelled so good, he wanted to lean over and take a bite out of her. He smiled. 'Yeah. Better now. Thanks.'

His Monday was looking up.

CHAPTER TEN

MARIANA

Christopher Murphy was a blight on my existence: a man I'd not cared to meet and wished I would never have to endure the misfortune of seeing again.

Sadly, my wish wasn't granted.

I saw him exactly once a week, unless he was away on a job. He needed plenty of money stashed, and I was very, very good at distributing the illegal finances for Il Sangue and its associates. Every Sunday afternoon I was expected to give Murphy and Emilio a rundown on the finances for the week. Safety deposit box numbers, bank accounts, the lot. I memorised everything, didn't write a single thing down that could incriminate anybody. The cartel couldn't afford to be careless, not when they were selling coke and whores and God knows what else. One surprise raid, and it'd all be out in the open. Most of the money was sitting in offshore accounts, numbering into the millions by now, but it was all blood money.

When we'd met, Murphy was a federal air marshal, but he'd since traded that job for a better one, as an agent high up the food chain with the Drug Enforcement Agency. Ironically, he'd scored a position with the drug trafficking unit that was supposed to help stop the cocaine flow across the US border, but his real job, the one Emilio paid him hundreds of thousands of dollars for, was funnelling coke from South America onto North American soil. His connections were spread like tentacles through the law enforcement channels that presided over the illegal drug and human trafficking trades that plagued the gulf; and he was making bank.

He was Emilio's right-hand man.

He'd been the one who had brought me to this godforsaken place.

And now, nine years after I'd returned home one night to find him standing over my father, a gun in his hand and a bored look on his face, Murphy was back in my face. This time he was alone and looking smug as he kicked the front door closed behind him. His gun was on his hip, and he looked smarmy rather than bored. Christopher Murphy was scum dressed in a suit and tie. And he was in my apartment.

'Oh,' I said, feeling my face fall as I watched him from where I was sitting on the couch. 'It's you.'

'Don't look so excited,' he deadpanned.

Guillermo had gone on a run with the club and left me here, a rare event. But sometimes it happened. He'd only left five minutes beforehand. Murphy must have been watching, waiting for him to leave.

I rolled my eyes, feigning disinterest as alarm began to rise within me. It was Monday night. I never saw Murphy outside of our Sunday afternoon meeting, not unless there was a large amount of money to shift. If that were the case, though, we'd do it at the office under Emilio's watchful eye.

Murphy being here in my apartment, alone, could only mean very bad things.

'How'd you get past the alarm?' I asked casually as I calculated the distance between myself and my gun. As luck would have it, it was underneath the couch cushion I was sitting on. I'd still probably get my head blown off before I'd be able to reach it, but it was comforting to know that underneath my ass was a weapon with six bullets in the clip, each with Christopher Murphy written on it.

'I bypassed it,' he said, smiling smugly. 'The perks of working for the DEA. They've got all kinds of things to break through your little locks and codes.'

Great. He now apparently had an all-access pass to the one place I felt safe in the world. I wanted to throw up.

There was a knock at the door. I froze, my eyes darting between Murphy and the door.

'I'd ask you if you brought a friend with you,' I said quietly, 'but I know you don't have any of those.'

I stood, mainly because I didn't want to be a sitting duck. Murphy reached back and opened the front door, while I shifted my balance onto my toes, ready to move quickly if I needed to. I was fucking stupid for not having my gun right at my fingertips! But after nine years you get complacent.

A figure entered through the front door. A woman. She wore black pants and a gun holster that sliced a criss-cross over her white shirt.

'This your partner?' I asked. 'Should have called ahead, Murphy. I would have gotten out the good china.'

The woman, who'd not spoken yet, eyed me. Judgey fucking eyes they were, too. From her appearance, I could see she had some Latina in her, maybe Mexican. She had long, dark brown hair that was swept up into a messy ponytail and caramel-coloured skin, like mine when I went out in the sun. Her almond-shaped eyes were lined with black make-up, and they were narrowed at me.

Yeah. Murphy definitely had a type.

'Mary-anna,' she said, mispronouncing my name on purpose. 'I've heard so much about you.'

'That's funny,' I said, my hands burning to grab the hidden gun. 'I haven't heard a single thing about you.'

She chuckled. 'She's mouthy,' she said to Murphy, but looking at me.

'*She's* right here,' I replied. 'And she's busy, so if we could get to the point ...'

Murphy smiled. 'Allie, I'll meet you in the car. Give me a call if that shit-kicker comes back.'

Allie looked put out. 'We'll hear his bike,' she protested, angling herself so that I couldn't hear and placing a hand on Murphy's chest. Only, she was three feet in front of me, and I had excellent hearing.

A wry grin spread across my face as soon as she touched Murphy. Gross.

'Oh, you two are fucking. Sorry, I'm a little slow tonight. I wasn't expecting you to let yourselves into my house, *Allie*.'

She snorted. 'That's Agent Baxter to you, bitch. And this is *your* house?' Allie repeated, turning back to me. 'Really? You own this place?'

I didn't respond.

'How many bedrooms?' she asked, looking around the hallway and lounge room. 'Two? Three? Still holding out hope that they'll let you bring your little bastard to live here?'

My grin vanished. All I saw was red. My fingers tingled impatiently, anxious to wrap them around her throat and squeeze until she begged me to stop.

Seemed I'd absorbed some of Dornan's violent tendencies in the past decade.

As my grin vanished, hers grew.

'You should probably leave,' I said coolly. 'Your boyfriend likes to try and fuck me when we're alone, and I think you're putting him off his game.'

There it was. *Snap.* I could practically see the rage rush through her veins, it was so instantaneous. Her entire demeanour changed, and she lunged for me. Murphy, who'd been silent thus far, reached out and closed his long fingers around the top of her arm, wrenching her back.

'I'm going to kill this bitch,' Allie said, trying to pull her arm from Murphy's grip.

'I could have your ass thrown in jail, and your precious fucking Gypsy Brothers couldn't do a thing about it,' she seethed. 'Who the fuck do you think you are?'

I snorted. 'Someone who looks a lot like you, apparently. Funny that.' Seriously, though. The resemblance was uncanny. We could have been sisters, for Christ's sake. *Eww.*

She lunged again, and Murphy made a growling sound, pulling her roughly towards the front door. 'Go wait in the fucking car,' he fumed. 'I wouldn't touch this filthy whore if you paid me.'

I put a hand to my heart in mock disappointment. 'You're breaking my heart,' I said.

Allie continued to stare at me, trying to kill me with her eyes, and Murphy bundled her out through the front door and slammed it in her face.

'She seems lovely,' I said, my tone sickly sweet. 'Has she met your parents yet?'

'My parents are dead,' Murphy replied stonily.

'What'd you do, kill them for their retirement fund?' I thought it was funny.

Murphy didn't seem overly amused, though. He seemed antsy. I wondered if he was actually worried about what she'd say when he got back to the car. She looked like she'd probably beat him up or something.

'She's fucking crazy,' Murphy replied. 'Lucky she gives good head.'

I expected him to approach me, to do something, but he didn't. He walked *past* the living room, holding a paper bag in one hand, a pair of aviator sunglasses in the other. I reached underneath the couch cushion, quickly locating my gun and flicking the safety off before I hurried into the hallway after him. He strode into the kitchen, dumping the paper bag on the counter as I raised my gun and aimed at him.

I had a gun now. *I was allowed to have a gun*, and it was because of Murphy. It was something Dornan had given me, not long after Murphy had tried to rape me on the dining room floor. Murphy had even brought a syringe full of drugs to make sure I complied. Dornan had beaten him almost to death. The only reason he hadn't was because of John pulling him off Murphy and talking sense into him. Truth be told, I wished that he'd just let Dornan finish the guy off.

Murphy turned and raised his eyebrows in amusement, tossing his sunglasses on the counter. 'Oh, put that away,' he said, pandering, his smile wide but his crazy blue eyes devoid of warmth. He rounded the counter and began opening cupboards and drawers, pulling out cutlery and napkins like he knew the place intimately.

I didn't relax my aim. 'What do you want, Murphy?' I asked impatiently. ''Cause I'm kind of busy right now.'

He looked around. 'Busy doing what?'

I rolled my eyes. 'Staring at the walls.'

He didn't respond.

I cringed as a streak of blood threaded out of one of his nostrils and down over his lip.

'Did the rest of your brain cells just explode?' I asked, gesturing towards his nose.

'I get nosebleeds,' he shrugged, wiping his arm across his face and creating a bright red line of blood on his white shirt. 'It's the heat.' He pressed a napkin to his nose to staunch the bleeding.

I raised my eyebrows. 'Uh, I think it's all the coke you put up there.' Idiot.

He looked unperturbed. Satisfied that the blood had stopped, he threw the napkin in the trash and washed his hands in the kitchen sink.

'What is this?' I gestured to him as the smell of Chinese food hit me.

'Here,' Murphy said, taking several boxes from the bag and placing them on the bench. 'I got your favourite. Egg rolls and lo mein.'

How the fuck did he know what my favourite Chinese takeout was? I was about to issue some witty retort when I swallowed my words. Egg rolls and lo mein *was* my favourite. Sometimes Dornan would surprise me with it.

He hadn't done it in a very long time.

'You brought dinner?' I asked, my tone scathing. 'You want to date me or something, Murphy? While your girlfriend waits in the car?'

He grinned, his tongue sliding across his top teeth as he chuckled. 'I don't think you're exactly *dateable*, honey. Fuckable? Yes. Dateable? Debateable!'

He laughed at his own ridiculous joke, and that made me mad. It made me livid.

Still grasping the gun, I crossed my arms, rooted to the spot in the hallway. Murphy continued to dig through my kitchen drawers, clattering plates and assembling spoons next to each cardboard container.

I won't lie, my mouth was watering. I wanted to shoot that motherfucker dead in my kitchen and step over his bloody corpse, just to eat that takeout.

'Eat,' Murphy commanded.

I stood my ground.

'Tell me why you're here,' I repeated. 'Tell me why your crazy girlfriend knows about my son.'

He took his plate, loaded with steaming hot food, and shovelled a spoonful of lo mein into his mouth. Seemed our Murphy was too retarded to eat with chopsticks. No great surprise there. He started walking towards me, towards the living room. Fuck that. When he was within arm's reach, I raised my gun towards him again.

I pressed the barrel into his forehead, stopping him in his tracks. 'I. Will. Shoot. You.' I said through gritted teeth.

He didn't drop his smile, despite the fact that he had a gun to his head, held by one extremely volatile, pissed-off Colombian woman with a tendency to snap and make bad decisions. No, he licked the grease from his lips and stared me right in the eye, calm as day.

'Don't you want to see your son again, Mariana?'

I'd like to say his words didn't affect me. That they rolled off me, unbidden.

But it would be a lie.

I backed up, felt the sting of tears building in my eyes. Refused to let them out. He didn't deserve my tears.

'Get out,' I demanded. It hurt to talk around the lump in my throat. 'Take your fucking food and get out of my house.'

He moved slowly, our eyes never leaving each other's. I watched, mesmerised, as he pressed his palm towards me in a sign of peace, then ever so slowly reached his right hand inside his suit pocket, balancing his plate in the other.

I watched, my finger ready on the trigger to take down the son of a bitch if he so much as sneezed. He pulled out a piece of paper. A photograph. And held it up to me.

'I can get you what you want,' he said casually, like I wasn't holding a gun to his head.

My heart broke in an instant as I looked at the photo he was holding up.

I swallowed thickly. It was *him*. My baby. Only, he wasn't a baby anymore. This photo was recent. How could I tell it was my Luis and not just some random kid Murphy had plucked off the street and asked to pose? His eyes. They were like mine, dark blue, and inside them I saw my own soul. I knew without a doubt that Murphy was not bluffing. I knew that he had somehow gotten a photograph of my son.

My heart started to beat wildly.

'Where did you get that?' I whispered. *Thudthudthud*. My heart was about ready to beat out of my chest.

'I took it,' Murphy shrugged. 'I'm not exactly a pro at photographing children, but I think I did okay.'

I wanted to take the photo from him. I wanted to shoot him. 'Why?'

'There are plenty more of these,' he said, opening his fingers and letting the piece of paper flutter to the ground. 'Why do you think I took them? I can't very well buy your cooperation with just the one.'

I remained silent; it wasn't easy. My skin was crawling, just from being alone with him. I just wanted to know what the hell Murphy wanted from me, so I could either acquiesce, or shoot him between the eyes.

I kind of hoped I'd get to shoot him. I'd try to aim so that none of his blood would splatter against the photograph that lay on the floor between our feet.

'Ask me,' he said.

'Ask you what?' I sighed.

'Ask me what I need your cooperation with.' He took an egg roll between his fingers and bit into it, hot sauce running down his chin. 'But ask me while I'm sitting down eating. I'm fucking starved.'

***

Ten minutes later, we were sitting at the dining table. Murphy had proceeded to bring a stack of photographs out of his suit pocket and place them face-down on the table beside his hand, but hadn't let me see any more. I'd since collected the one he'd let fall to the ground, and I held it in front of me, my food untouched. I'd also poured myself a vodka, no mixer. No ice, either. After the fucking I'd taken from Dornan on this very dining table, I couldn't think of ice cubes without blushing and getting very, very turned on. Being turned on didn't really match being stuck with Christopher Murphy.

'You're not gonna eat?' Murphy asked around a mouthful of food.

'Just get to the point,' I said.

'Alright.' He stopped eating, looking at me seriously as the snark vanished from his face. I swallowed nervously.

Snarky Murphy I could handle. When he got serious, it scared the living shit out of me.

'In approximately—' he paused to check his watch, 'one hour, your father and the rest of your family will be entering the United States government's witness protection program. The DEA are on the ground in Colombia, moving in to take them to a safe house.'

I raised my eyebrows; inside my heart was thundering.

'Why should I believe anything you say?' I replied tersely. *Witness protection? Bullshit.*

He didn't smile, didn't smirk. In fact, this Christopher Murphy was entirely normal, concerned even, and that made him even more terrifying.

'You don't have to,' he said, sitting back and wiping his hands on a napkin. 'But you have two options right now. You run and tell loverboy Dornan and give him the tip-off. Or we make a deal, and you get to see your son again.'

I saw the corner of his mouth twitch, a suppressed smile.

'It's a very good deal.'

I didn't say anything for a moment, my head whirling. I remembered sitting at a similar table in Colombia nine years ago, swallowing packages of what I believed to be cocaine, only to find out later that I'd couriered eighteen pellets of baker's-grade flour across the border as a test.

Was this a test? Were they testing my loyalty after all this time?

'You think you can mention a son I gave up for adoption over eleven years ago and I'll just do whatever you want?'

Murphy eyed me confidently. 'That's exactly what I think.'

Well, I didn't know what to say to that. I pressed my lips together. 'He doesn't even know me,' I said, but my words came out weaker than I'd planned.

'You might think you're covert, and you're clever, but my dear Mariana,' Murphy paused and leaned across the table, smiling smugly, 'you're also *very* fucking predictable.'

'If Emilio heard you talking like this, he would kill you.' I said. 'Slowly. Painfully. I heard what he did to Bella. I'm sure he's done plenty worse since then.'

Murphy's eyes lit up at the mention of her name; the accountant who had been there before me, the girl who had been tortured, piece by piece over the better part of a week, until Dornan shot her and put her out of her misery.

'I *saw* what he did to Bella,' Murphy said. 'Did you know if you drill into the right part of a person's skull, you can see their brain while they're still conscious?' He pretended to drill into his forehead with two fingers, a *zzzz* sound coming from between his teeth.

I was suddenly convinced that he'd played an active part in her grisly demise.

'Anyway,' he said, running his tongue over his teeth, 'your father's actually stopped drinking and gambling. Crazy, right?'

'Unbelievable,' I answered. 'Just like the rest of your story. Why would the DEA help my father go into hiding? It's ludicrous. He's a criminal.'

Murphy waved his fork dismissively. 'He's small fry compared to Emilio and Julian Ross. We're talking about smashing an international drug syndicate here. You think I'd have stuck around for this long if it wasn't worth something huge? My entire career has been devoted to taking these fuckers down.'

I huffed incredulously. 'Murphy, you have a bank account in the Bahamas with hundreds of thousands of dollars in it. Drug money.'

'Drug money,' he smiled. 'That's a cute name for it.'

'It's the truth!' I insisted. 'What the hell are the DEA going to do when they realise you're in on this whole mess?'

He shrugged. 'I'll lay low for a couple of months, then charter myself a plane straight out of Dodge and into early retirement abroad. The government pension isn't exactly enough to pay for all my ... *hobbies*.'

'Emilio will know it was you,' I countered. 'He'll empty your accounts quicker than you can snort a line of coke off your desk.' I'd seen him do it before.

He pursed his lips and stared at me like I was a moron. 'Why do you think I came here?' he responded. 'You're going to make sure that doesn't happen. And in return, I get you your son.'

'What about Dornan?' I asked, dazed.

'What *about* Dornan?' Murphy rebounded.

I searched his face for an indication of how this could go but got nothing. 'I'm not participating in anything that would hurt him. He saved my life.'

Murphy sneered. 'He took you to be his own personal whore. He used – uses – you for his own perverted pleasure. Does he make you say *thank you* after you swallow?'

Wow. That hurt. Even coming from Murphy. *I shouldn't care*, I scolded myself.

'You don't know anything about me,' I answered coldly. 'Or him.'

'I know your son is dying to meet you,' he said, smarmy fuck that he was. 'What else matters? The whole family is in WITSEC, and if you do this one little thing for me, you'll be right there with them.'

'When you say the whole family—'

'He's not included,' Murphy cut me off. 'There's no records of your son even existing. I had the birth certificate and the adoption papers removed from the state office when you started cleaning my money, just in case I ever needed to blackmail you, babe.'

Was he lying? I couldn't tell. The sick thing was, he knew exactly what to say to get me to pay attention, whether it was the truth or not. I wanted to see my son more than I wanted anything in the entire universe.

I'd kill to see him. Die if it meant I could touch his face one more time.

'What do you want me to do?' I asked dully. Dornan's face loomed large in my mind, so distracting I could barely concentrate on what Murphy was saying.

He smiled, and it was like he knew he had me hooked on his bait. Now, to reel me in.

'You're gonna move some money for me, sweetheart,' he said. 'Some of Emilio's money. Don't worry, I'll let you keep a little to get yourself set up. But the bulk of it goes into my personal offshore accounts, are we clear? It costs money to hide.'

I nodded. 'And that's it?'

He nodded, chewing slowly.

'Well, I guess we're done here, then. You need help packing your shit up?' I was acting nonplussed, but inside I was a quivering mess. I needed to be alone so I could figure out what the fuck my next move would be. Some vague feeling in the pit of my stomach told me I had to bring Dornan in on all this, but the urge to investigate a little further myself was too tempting. I still had the burner phone John had gifted me with, and I needed Murphy to leave so I could make some calls.

He threw his fork down, and it made a high-pitched ting against the china as he pushed his plate away. Hurriedly, I closed all of the cardboard boxes and shoved them back into the paper bag, thrusting it at Murphy. He rolled his eyes and removed the lo mein, setting it on the table for me to keep. How thoughtful.

'I can't leave without cracking open the fortune cookies,' he said, standing slowly. 'That would be rude.'

I took a deep breath. 'Open them in the car. With your girlfriend.' I snatched up the two fortune cookies – the romantic motherfucker had brought one for each of us – and stalked towards thc front door.

'I'll call you,' Murphy said, knocking his shoulder against mine as he passed me.

'Can't wait,' I threw back, tossing the fortune cookies at him. He caught them easily, a look of amusement on his face. Bastard. I hated him. I hated him almost as much as I hated Emilio.

He pocketed the plastic-wrapped cookies and reached for the door handle but drew back at the last second. 'I almost forgot,' he grinned, looking back at me as he held up the stack of photographs.

I wanted them. But I knew if I showed how much I wanted them, he'd raise the stakes. I held my jaw rigid and slipped the tip of my tongue between my front teeth, biting down until I tasted blood. *Don't react.*

He held the stack out to me, a smirk on his face. 'You want them?'

I reached for them slowly; too slowly. He yanked them back just as my fingers were about to close around them, dropping the paper bag full of leftovers on the floor as his other hand wrapped around my throat. Squeezing tight, he pushed me back into the wall. My head hit the plaster with a dull thunk.

I gave him a sour look, my voice coming out in a rasp as his fingers hovered at my throat. 'I knew there'd be a price. What is it?'

He chewed on his lower lip thoughtfully, watching my mouth with great interest.

'You want to kiss me, Murphy? Is that it?'

He grinned, letting go of my throat and grabbing a chunk of my hair as he pressed me harder against the wall. He pushed his greedy lips against mine, nine years worth of his pent-up frustration crushing against me. It was bad, but not so bad, until he stuck his tongue in my mouth. Gross. I stilled for a few moments, thinking it was a small price to pay in the scheme of things. When his hand started travelling from my waist up towards my chest, I shoved him off me.

'I think I threw up a little in my mouth,' I deadpanned. 'This was fun, we should do it again *never*.' I snatched the photos from his hand, and he made no attempt to stop me this time.

Murphy sniffed, wiping his wet mouth with one finger. Still sampling the goods, no doubt. I knew he was excited about finally laying one on me after all this time, but his pupils were pinpricks. There was something bubbling in his veins, and I was betting on coke.

'You forgot your fortune cookie,' he said, tearing open the packaging and cracking the cookie in half before holding it out to me. 'Read it.'

'No.'

'Then no more photos for you.'

I snatched the broken fortune cookie out of his hand and pulled out the piece of paper, letting the cookie pieces fall to the ground as I read it.

'Fortune favours the brave.' I dropped the piece of paper, and it fell lazily to the ground.

'How brave are you feeling today?' he asked, tucking a stray hair behind my ear. I pulled away sharply. He'd touched me all he was going to touch me today. My skin was already screaming for me to get in the shower and scrub his prints off of me.

I didn't bother answering the brave question. It irritated me.

'Aren't you going to read yours?' I said instead.

He cracked his open and threw the cookie into his mouth, as he unfurled the quote that had been jammed inside. He laughed, handing the piece of paper to me. I took it reluctantly. What I really wanted was for him to fucking leave so I could see the rest of the photos that were clutched in my hand.

'If you would rule the world quietly, you must keep it amused.'

I handed it back to him. 'Looks like you got the right one. I don't want to rule the world.'

Murphy tilted his head to the side. 'Everybody wants to rule the world, Mariana. Which reminds me. If you tell anyone what we spoke about – Dornan included – I will slit your throat ear to ear and hang you off a fucking bridge. And I'll make sure your son sees you die. Got it?'

A chill ran through me. 'Yeah. I got it.'

I opened the door for him, shoving him out and slamming it as hard as I could behind him.

I didn't want to rule the world. I didn't care about power.

I just wanted to be free.

CHAPTER ELEVEN

MARIANA

It was late. Almost midnight, by the time Murphy had left. I spread the photos across my coffee table, drinking them in as his words started to hit home.

I wanted to believe what he was saying. Wanted to believe it wasn't a cruel trick, a test, as Emilio was so fond of subjecting people to. But I'd known Murphy a long time now, knew his subtle little tells, could pretty much always pick when he was lying.

But, faced with the possibility of seeing my son again, my heart overrode my brain until I was so confused, I had no idea if he was lying or telling the truth. My BS meter was completely screwed in the face of the chance to reunite with Luis.

Murphy wanted me to embezzle money for him. A lot of money. It was a probable death sentence. Emilio had people everywhere – hell, he had Murphy, one of the most senior and powerful officers in the DEA.

But it seemed Murphy had grown tired of playing second fiddle to the Il Sangue Cartel. Seemed he wanted it all for himself. Seemed he was cleaning house, and he wanted me to assist him. Maybe it had something to do with Allie. Perhaps it was true love.

I looked at the photos one by one. Luis riding a bicycle. Luis entering a school classroom, a backpack slung over one shoulder. Luis kicking a soccer ball. His hair was long, his skin darker than mine. Lord, he looked exactly like his father. His eyes were the only thing that said he was mine. He looked exactly as I'd imagined he would, and that was a miracle within itself. It was as if I'd dreamed him into existence. He was exquisite. Greedily, as I examined the photographs, I wanted more. I wanted to hear his voice. I wondered if it still had that high, child-like pitch. He was almost twelve. Soon, it'd get deeper, more mature.

I wanted to hear his voice as a child just once before he grew up. Just one time. I wanted to hold him in my arms. I wanted to look into his eyes and see him looking back. I wanted to be his mother.

My hands were shaking.

I weighed up my options. If I told Dornan, Murphy would deny everything. He'd make sure I died, but worst of all, he'd hurt Luis. I'd heard his threat, and I knew he wasn't bluffing.

Fuck.

If Emilio went down, what did that mean for Dornan? For John, even? For Guillermo?

If Emilio went down, what did that mean for me?

The notion that I might one day be free of the Il Sangue Cartel seemed so ludicrous, I couldn't even picture it. I was a survivor, and survivors didn't live on hope and dreams. They lived on blending in and doing what they were fucking told.

Dornan. Luis. It seemed like I was going to have to risk one to protect the other.

Dornan would understand, I reasoned with myself. He was a father. He knew the ferocity of a parent's love.

I'd always loved Luis above all else, even though I'd never known him, even though he'd never remember a single thing about the precious few hours we spent as mother and son before he was taken away. But Dornan against Luis? One or the other? I'd never had to face that ultimatum before.

I thought of how far I'd be willing to go to protect my son. Would I betray Dornan? Could I?

Of course I could. I loved Dornan beyond words, beyond space and time and every shitty thing that stood between us ever finding freedom. But I loved my son more. He was a part of me. He came from me. And I'd tear the fucking world down to lay my eyes on him one more time.

CHAPTER TWELVE

MARIANA

Murphy was long gone, and I'd looked at each photograph at least a dozen times before I sprang into action. I rechecked the front door, making sure it was locked, and jammed a dining chair underneath the door knob for good measure. Once I was certain the place was relatively secure, I retrieved my burner phone from its hiding spot: a canister of flour that sat at the back of the pantry. Shaking the excess powder from the protective ziplock bag, I took the phone out and dialled.

I prayed for an answer.

'What?' the voice on the line said abruptly.

'It's me,' I whispered, my heart thundering in my chest. Nobody was with me, but if Guillermo arrived home from his ride, I didn't want him hearing my conversation.

'We're not due to speak for two weeks,' Este's older brother hissed. 'Is this a safe line?'

Once a month for the past eight-and-a-half years – ever since John gave me the phone – I'd been speaking to Miguel, my dead boyfriend's brother. Checking on my family. Checking on my son. My family still thought I'd died nine years ago, shortly after I was brought to Los Angeles, and I needed to keep it that way. If they ever found out, my father would no doubt do something stupid and reckless and we'd all be dead inside a week.

Miguel was the only person I could think of who I *knew* would keep the secret for me, and, more importantly, keep tabs on the son Este and I had been forced to give up for adoption when we were teenagers. The family who'd adopted Luis were distant relatives of Esteban, and they lived in the same small village that Miguel had settled in after I left. Miguel was the only one in the world who knew where Luis was – but now Murphy had stripped that secret away and turned it into a liability.

'Of course,' I replied. 'This couldn't wait. Something's happened. A man told me my parents have been taken into witness protection. Is that true?' I closed my eyes and leaned against the cool refrigerator door. My legs shook as I waited for Miguel's response.

He let out a long sigh, and I immediately knew something was very wrong. 'Bambina,' he said, 'I am so sorry.'

Oh God. 'What?' I whispered.

I heard the flick of a lighter and a sharp inhale as he smoked.

'Miguel!' I insisted.

'They're dead, bambina.'

I almost choked on my own tongue. 'What?'

Not Luis. Not my baby, please God, not my baby. 'Where is my son?' I asked through gritted teeth, opening my eyes wide and praying like fuck. Not my boy. *Not my boy.*

Miguel coughed. 'Luis is safe, Mariana. He's alive. But your papa. Your mama. Karina and Pablo. They're gone. Dead.'

I covered my mouth with a shaking hand and pressed my palm into my teeth to stifle the scream that was coming from my chest. I couldn't stop it; the rage and the grief threatened to split me open. And the relief. Luis was alive. He mattered the most. He was just a child.

'It's worse. They're looking for Luis. A man was here, a DEA agent. He offered the children at school pesos for his whereabouts. I've got him somewhere safe, but it's only temporary, Ana. There is nothing left for you there. There is no reason for you to stay. *You're collateral for a debt that has been revoked.*'

Even if Emilio did inform me of my family's murder, he'd still never let me go. There are few things in life that are certainties, but this was one of them.

'How?' I asked, feeling like every piece of air had been sucked out of my body. I couldn't breathe. I couldn't think. This had to be some terrible fucking nightmare that I was going to wake up from any minute. I felt my breath coming faster and faster as panic rose in my chest, suffocating me from within.

I heard Miguel clear his throat. 'Julian's men stormed the house, tied them up and poured gasoline on them,' he said quietly.

Julian's men were Emilio's men. Emilio's younger brother oversaw the Colombian operations in his absence, but there was no disputing who the boss of the Il Sangue Cartel was.

'And then?'

A long silence. 'And then they lit a match, Ana.'

I retched once. Dropped the phone onto the kitchen counter and swallowed hard. *Get your shit together.* I took a deep breath, stood straight again. I suddenly had an overwhelming urge to drink something strong, something that would wash away the shock, or at least dull it.

'Mariana!?' Miguel's voice sang up from the cellphone. I picked it up and held it to my ear again, not sure I wanted to hear anything else he had to say. They'd burned. They'd *burned alive*.

'I'm here,' I said, using my free hand to open the freezer and take out a bottle of vodka. I unscrewed the cap and tipped a good amount down my throat, the cold liquid punching my senses awake.

Murphy had been playing a cruel trick on me, and it had almost worked. I thought of my gentle brother and my beautiful sister, and imagined the flesh melting from their faces, their agonised screams, as fire consumed them.

I took another drink. It was making my stomach flip, drinking straight vodka so quickly, but I didn't care. I needed something.

'Luis?' I asked.

'I have him, Ana. But you need to figure something out. You can't come here – they'll kill you both. He's safe. But we need money, passports. You need to help me get him out of Colombia.'

Relief flooded my weary bones, flowing all the way down to my toes along with the last of the vodka in my bloodstream. It was an unfamiliar feeling, to be so terribly sad yet so relieved at the same time. My son was alive. But how long could he survive if the likes of Murphy were looking for him?

I had to do something.

'Are you sure?' I asked. Maybe it was all a misunderstanding. Maybe it was all a bad dream.

He coughed. 'There were witnesses, Ana. People saw. People saw them storm the house, and people saw it burn afterwards. People heard them screaming.'

Oh Jesus. I wished I hadn't asked.

'Keep him safe,' I whispered. 'Please, Miguel, keep him safe for me.'

Miguel's voice cracked. 'He looks like my brother, but he has your eyes, bambina. He asks for you.'

'He knows about me?'

It was almost too much to bear.

'Of course he does, Ana. He has a photo of you – remember your senior dance?'

I did remember. The milk hadn't even stopped leaking from my breasts in the aftermath of Luis' birth and adoption, but Mama had insisted I go to the dance, get back to normal life. Este had borrowed a suit that was too big and presented me with a corsage I knew his mother had stayed up late the night before making. I'd spent the entire night sobbing in the dark outside the dance hall, as Este held me and promised to find a way to get our baby back. I remembered the photo my mother had taken, just as we were leaving the house. My mother had done my make-up for me. I remembered thinking how odd it was that she was acting so normal, especially when my father refused to even look at me, much less engage in a conversation. In fact, he only said one thing to me that night. He appeared as I was getting ready to leave, slapped me across the face hard enough that I tasted blood in my mouth, and told me, 'Keep your legs closed, you little slut.'

I remember holding my cheek, in shock. I wasn't going to have sex. I'd given birth to a *baby* a week earlier. I was barely walking, let alone the rest of it. And my father was calling me a slut. My mother had pulled me outside and snapped a photo of Este and me. He was squinting at the sun and I was still reeling from shock, a reactionary smile plastered across my face. Karina had a Polaroid camera she'd found at a market, and she snapped a photograph, too, let it spit out of the front of the camera, and gave it to me.

It seemed that Polaroid photo had survived and ended up in my son's hands.

'Mariana?'

I snapped back to the present as Miguel's voice cut through blurry memories of days long gone, feeling the flour dust sticking between my clammy fingers. It was hot in the apartment all of a sudden and I desperately needed some fresh air.

'I'll get money. I'll call you again tomorrow,' I said to Miguel in a monotone voice. I ended the call abruptly, switching the phone off and returning it to the ziplock bag and finally back into the canister of flour. After I'd done that, I took the dining chair that I'd wedged beneath the front door knob and carried it back to the dining table, staring at the surface where Dornan and I had fucked. I loved him. I loved him so fucking much, and I didn't want to hurt him. Nausea rolled through me and I swallowed back bile.

Rushing over to the sliding door, I wrenched it open, stepping onto the patio as ocean air hit me. The cold greeted me with a slap that made my skin sting. I breathed deeply, tasting salt on my tongue, wiping floury hands on my skirt. The sea was torrid tonight, churning. It was going to rain. It hardly ever rained in Los Angeles, barren wasteland that it was, but it smelled like the heavens were going to open and dump water any second.

I wondered if anyone had organised a funeral for my family, if there had been anything left to bury. Fire had a nasty way of reducing fully formed people to bones and ash, inconsequential piles of what used to be flesh and blood.

I thought it odd that I wasn't crying. Maybe the relief of knowing Luis had been spared was making the deaths of my parents and siblings less traumatic.

More likely, I was in shock.

Everything Murphy had said to me, about witness protection and getting out of this place? It had all seemed so good, so of course it was a lie. I felt like a fucking idiot for even daring to consider what he'd fed me as truth. He was a shark, and he'd just tried to convince me he wasn't so he could take me by surprise and eat me alive while I wasn't looking. He'd tried to make me trust him.

When something seems too good to be true, it usually is.

I'd never believed that until now.

My parents, my brother, my sister – they weren't going to be saved. They were already dead. And Christopher Murphy had been in Colombia looking for my son.

I was never getting out.

Murphy's deception unleashed something primal inside me. He had poked a sleeping beast that been lying dormant for nine years, curled deep in my belly.

I ran into the bathroom and reached the toilet just in time to throw up the contents of my stomach. Wiping my mouth with the back of my hand, I caught sight of myself in the mirror, and I saw something alight in the recesses of my dark blue eyes.

A thirst for payback. A yearning for vengeance.

My entire body hummed with the desire to inflict suffering upon Emilio Ross and his minions as I washed my mouth out with cold water. For the first time in a very long time, I felt renewed, invincible.

I was hungry for blood.

The front door slammed shut. Sneakers squeaked on tile and I breathed out in relief. Guillermo. I flushed the toilet, washed my hands, and made my way out to the kitchen.

Guillermo was facing away from me, digging in the refrigerator when I saw him pause.

'Did you go out tonight?' he asked, his tone aiming for casual but hitting suspicious.

'No,' I replied honestly. 'I've been here all night.'

He closed the refrigerator, Murphy's Chinese in his hands. 'I didn't know these guys delivered,' he said, slinging the rest of the lo mein into the microwave and hitting start. The thing lit up, heating the food as two eyes stared accusingly at me.

'Murphy dropped it off,' I said. 'He must've heard about the plans for the club ride at your meeting. He was in here five minutes after you left.'

Guillermo nodded. We shared a mutual hatred of Murphy, something that had actually made me relieved in some small way to have Guillermo around, even in the early days.

'What did he want?' Guillermo asked, staring at the microwave as it counted down.

I shrugged. 'What does he ever want?'

Guillermo nodded, taking the lo mein out of the microwave and placing it on the counter. He stood across from me, fork poised in the air above the steaming container.

'He hurt you?'

I shook my head.

Guillermo stabbed his fork into the food. 'We telling Dornan about this?'

I held his gaze. 'Whatever you think.'

'Is there anything I need to deal with?'

I shook my head. 'Just the usual shit. You know what he's like.'

The silence between us was thick, and it smelled like Chinese food.

'If he comes back again, tell me,' Guillermo said. 'He needs to know his fucking place around here.'

I nodded.

'Hey, Guillermo,' I said, watching him eat. 'Can I ask you something?'

He nodded, his dark eyes watching me in anticipation.

'What did it feel like? When you decided to blow up that house?'

He stopped chewing, his eyes darting around the apartment as he swallowed audibly.

'Why do you ask?'

I chewed on the inside of my lip. 'I've wanted to ask you for years. Guess I finally feel like you won't get mad at me if I do.'

He stared at me some more.

'Forget it,' I said, circling the counter and brushing past him to get to the vodka in the freezer. He turned, grabbing my arm and leaning in close to me.

'It felt good,' he said, the ghost of a smile playing on his lips. 'I knew they'd catch me. I knew I'd go to prison. It was still worth it to me, the risk that I'd be in prison until I died.'

His fingers digging into my arm were hurting, but I ignored the pain.

'You don't regret it? Even now?'

He grinned. 'Never.'

'That's what I thought.'

He dropped the smile. 'Is there something I should know, Mariana?'

Now I smiled. 'No. I was just thinking if I kill Murphy one day, maybe I'll call you first.'

He looked uneasy. Very uneasy. 'Don't get involved in shit above your paygrade, cholita. Leave it to the boys. I swear to you, one day Murphy will lose relevance, and on that day your boy Dornan'll be first in line to end that piece of shit.'

'You called me cholita again.'

He dropped my arm and turned back to his food. 'You're talking like a tough girl. Seemed appropriate.'

I stared at the back of his head and smiled.

CHAPTER THIRTEEN

MARIANA

Tuesday morning greeted me with no sign of rain, but with humidity and lazy grey clouds, heavy and swollen with a need for release as they crawled across the Californian sky.

It was a religious holiday. Normally I'd be expected to work anyway, but this particular day was some big deal for Emilio since he was a good, church-going Catholic. The entire Ross family would be there, including the wives and children, which meant I was spared the indignation of having to sit beside Emilio as a priest talked about God and faith and forgiveness. Guillermo had woken me in the night, frantic. His mother was sick, and he needed to get to the hospital in Mexico. Guillermo's absence meant that I had an entire day ahead of me and nothing to do, something that almost never happened.

So when someone knocked at the door, I already had my gun firmly in hand.

'Get your purse,' the man at the door said.

I was sporting sweatpants and unbrushed hair at 3 p.m., with a scowl to match.

'Excuse me?'

John smiled, flashing a mouthful of shiny teeth, his hands jammed into his jeans pockets. Those shiny teeth were at odds with the rest of him – rough stubble, perpetually messed up hair, those bright blue eyes that turned down slightly at the outer corners, giving him the appearance of melancholy even when he was smiling.

And he was smiling right now.

'Get dressed,' he said. 'We're taking you out.' He tilted his head to the side, his grin fading slightly. 'And maybe do something with that bird's nest.'

I raised my eyebrows, but I wasn't offended. Honestly, I was just happy to see another human being that wasn't Murphy.

John shifted slightly and I saw his daughter, Juliette, standing behind him, eyes closed as she nodded her head to music nobody else could hear. The headphones covering her ears looked much too big for her delicate head.

'Come in,' I said, holding the door open and gesturing for them to follow, shoving my gun into my pocket. The photos of Luis were hidden inside a slit in my mattress until I could find a better place for them. It made my stomach twist to think that the safest thing to do was burn them.

John and Juliette followed me inside, the apartment cooler than the muggy heat outside. My mind was still reeling from Murphy's visit the night before, and from the phone call I'd made to Miguel.

I hadn't cried yet. I was definitely still in shock. I'd spent the day sitting on the floor of my living room, staring into space, trying not to throw up.

'What's the occasion?' I asked John as he headed straight for the pot of coffee I'd just brewed. 'You're not Catholic, are you?'

He shrugged, looking pleased with himself. 'Nope. Still get the day off, though. Thank you, Jesus.' He held his mug of steaming black coffee up and clinked it against another imaginary one.

I put my hands on my hips, amused. 'What's going on, John?' And then my smile faded and I felt my entire body go cold.

Was he here to check up on me? Had Murphy sent him? No, that was impossible. He hated Murphy.

'Hey, Earth to Mariana,' John said, stepping forward and clicking his fingers in front of my face. I blinked, pushing my suspicions away as I glanced at Juliette, who was currently sprawled in one of my dining chairs, her blonde hair fanned out around her head on the glass table top.

'She can't hear a damn thing with that iPod in her ears,' John said, taking a swig of coffee. He made a face, set the coffee down, and opened the pantry, searching. 'You got sugar in here?'

He pulled a canister out and set it down on the counter.

The fucking flour canister. Where I hid my phone. I mean, I knew he'd been the one to give me the phone, but did that mean I could trust him? It had been eight-and-a-half years since we'd had that conversation. To be honest, I was very surprised the phone still worked after almost nine years. I guess because I barely used it.

I reached over and grabbed the canister just as he was going to open it. 'That's flour,' I said quickly, holding the canister to my chest. 'The sugar is in the smaller one. And since when do you take sugar?'

He was perceptive. He studied me and the flour canister for a few seconds, before shrugging and returning to the pantry shelf. He grabbed the sugar and dumped several heaped spoonfuls of the stuff into his mug.

'I need the extra energy today. You want some?' he asked, holding the sugar out to me.

I shook my head. 'I'm sweet enough.'

He chuckled, returning the sugar and closing the pantry, the flour seemingly forgotten. 'What does that make me, bitter?'

I smiled. 'Something like that. But seriously ...' I glanced at Juliette again, who seemed to be in a world of her own. I envied the casual way she could be so happily absorbed in the soundtrack on her iPod, the only thing she needed to entertain herself. '... what are you doing here?' I asked.

John downed the rest of his coffee and rinsed his empty mug out, setting it on the drainer. 'Taking you two out. It's a holiday. We should take advantage of it while we can.' He looked beyond me to Juliette. 'And Dornan called me and asked me to.'

'Oh.' I deflated a little. Of course. My knight in shining armour was with his wife and kids and his reprehensible fucking father at Mass. Dornan had just placed a call to his bestie to occupy me so I didn't get up to anything risky while I was left to my own devices for one whole day.

'I take it that's not the response you were looking for?' John enquired.

Damn, he was perceptive. I had practised my poker face to perfection, but there was something about him, something magnetic that made it feel like he could crack my head open and unravel every lie I'd ever told. Maybe it was because I saw him as an actual human being, instead of the monsters I normally encountered. Donning my poker face with Emilio wasn't a choice, it was a matter of survival.

Either way, I could count on one hand the times I'd seen John act so casually. Usually it was within the confines of the tiny office where he'd do money drops, when his mask would occasionally slip and he'd flash me one of those grins. But over the years those smiles had become less and less common. He always seemed like he had the weight of the world on his shoulders these days.

I shrugged. 'No, it's fine. I just wasn't expecting company.'

He nodded, running his tongue over his perfect teeth as he looked me up and down. 'I know.'

'Screw you, asshole,' I joked. 'On my days off, I am the queen of sweatpants and bird's-nest hair.'

He tipped his head back and laughed. The sound was almost startling. It had been years since I'd heard John Portland laugh. It made his eyes sparkle, something about the way the light bounced off his baby blues. There was always some other biker club to worry about, some transaction to officiate, some police heat to deal with. He. Never. Laughed.

I swallowed thickly, my cheeks suddenly pooling with blood. 'I'll go get ready,' I muttered, hightailing it to my bedroom.

I chose something pretty, a blue spaghetti-strap dress – the exact colour of John's eyes – that fell to just above my knees. It was only later that I realised I'd chosen it because of the colour match and that made me feel kind of jittery. I shouldn't be looking at a married man's eyes long enough to notice what colour they were, let alone get lost in them. Because I had Dornan, and he loved me, and he had always done right by me. Dornan adored me. He worshipped me. He'd risked everything to make sure I wasn't sold to the highest bidder as a slave nine years ago. If my heart belonged to anyone, it belonged to Dornan. More importantly, it belonged to my son.

But the heart is a fickle thing, and my heart was lonely. In John Portland's blue eyes I saw something I hadn't seen in a very long time.

Kindness.

CHAPTER FOURTEEN

JOHN

The boardwalk on Santa Monica Beach was teeming with people when they arrived. John parked in a tow zone. He didn't have to worry about things like that. This was his town, and he took what he could get in the way of favours like free parking and generous discounts. He was less keen on the other perks offered to him on a daily basis, like free hookers and every kind of drug under the sun, even the ones the Il Sangue Cartel weren't involved in.

The ice-cream parlour was packed, but it didn't matter. John's booth was always available. It had a permanent 'reserved' sign on it. The irony of having a booth in an ice-cream store didn't escape him, but it sure came in handy when he needed to take his little girl out.

Only his little girl was getting older, and sweet, frozen dairy products and shiny plastic booths had lost some of the lustre they'd once had. Now she remained quiet when he took her out, barely touched her ice cream, and sulked for eighty percent of the visit.

He didn't take it personally. He remembered being fourteen. Fourteen sucked.

Especially today. His only daughter had just had her heart broken by the local stud and it took every tiny bit of self-control John possessed not to ride over to the boy's house and strangle him to death for making his baby hurt. The boy was a senior, and apparently he'd dumped Julz for an older girl, Shailene, whose loose reputation preceded her. John knew of her reputation because he'd had to personally escort Shailene from his clubhouse on several occasions after finding the underage girl drunk and making a play for some young prospect's cock.

It reinforced John's desire to keep Juliette away from his world, but at the same time she was forced into it, because there were only so many places he could keep an eye on her. And entrusting his wife to watch over their daughter was like throwing chum into shark-infested waters and then expecting the sharks to stay away. Caroline always found some way to endanger their daughter, either through sheer neglect, or by doing something completely inappropriate like taking her on a trip to score some blow and making her wait in the car. In the projects. At three in the morning.

Yeah, Caroline didn't get to be in charge of their daughter anymore, and that was probably the only reason she was still relatively young compared to girls like Shailene.

John was glad for today.

'What'll it be?' he asked Mariana and Juliette. Mariana was across from him, a look on her face that said she was still trying to figure out what was going on, and Juliette was beside him, crammed into the middle of the U-shaped booth.

Juliette shrugged, taking her headphones out. 'Whatever.'

Mariana smiled, looking at the menu. 'Surprise me.'

As John approached the counter, he heard Mariana talking to his daughter. Maybe because she wasn't high like

Caroline, he thought. No. Today was not about Caroline, or about worrying. Today was a goddamn day off from everything, and unless somebody called to say somebody was dying, they could fuck off until tomorrow.

The woman who owned the place knew his order by heart. 'Add in a ...' He surveyed the glass display cabinet, reading each flavour as his eyes passed over the ice cream, 'strawberry, as well.'

He didn't pay for anything here. He'd stopped trying to years ago, after Didi, the owner, had told him his money wasn't welcome. Before John had started frequenting the place, it had been robbed so many times that she was considering boarding the place up and declaring bankruptcy. But John couldn't have that. If they closed, he would have had to take little Juliette to one of those crappy chain stores to buy ice cream, and they sure as shit didn't have a view out to the ocean and the Ferris wheel like this place did.

As Didi bustled off to prepare his order, John couldn't help but listen in to what Mariana and Juliette were talking about. It was quiet in this corner of the store, and the acoustics were excellent. He felt bad for eavesdropping, but he was worried about Julz and her poor broken heart, and he needed to make sure she was okay. She wouldn't speak a word to him about what had happened, and so for her to be chatting up a storm with Mariana made his heart lift.

'Most boys are idiots,' Mariana was saying. 'Especially the popular ones. What was his excuse?'

'He wanted to fuck me,' Juliette said plainly. 'So I dumped him. And he told the whole school he dumped me first.'

John stole a glance at them, his hands balled up into fists, his head about to explode at the casual way his teenage daughter had just mentioned some guy wanting to *fuck* her. John debated getting the club together and cutting the boy's dick off.

Mariana's eyebrows looked like they were about to lift the ceiling off. 'You should get your revenge on this boy,' Mariana said. 'Nothing dangerous, nothing that would lead back to you. But maybe a rumour.'

Juliette leaned in closer. 'What kind of rumour?'

Mariana smiled. 'Oh, you know, something like ... he's got herpes or something. Tell people you had to dump him because you caught him kissing his sister.'

Juliette laughed. Mariana looked directly at John and smiled, as if she knew he'd been listening the entire time. John grabbed the ice creams, which had been sitting in the holder for some time already, and took them over to the booth as if he hadn't heard a thing.

'My mama used to make ice cream from fresh cream and strawberries,' Mariana said, taking a bite of her cone. Almost as soon as the words had left her mouth, she seemed to still, her eyes widening slightly, before she composed herself again.

If John had blinked, he would have missed it.

'Do you see her often?' John asked, his tone casual. 'Your mama?'

Mariana froze like a deer in headlights, bracing for the car that was about to plough headfirst into her.

Juliette poked her father. 'Can I play the pinball machine?'

John reached into his pocket, taking a pile of loose change and giving it to her. Immediately, he felt lighter. He hated carrying shrapnel around. 'Stay where I can see you,' he said softly. Juliette rolled her eyes, but she was still smiling. 'Yes,

Daddy,' she said, climbing out over the back of the booth and heading for the small bank of pinball machines in the far corner of the ice-cream parlour.

John turned his attention back to Mariana, who was staring out of the window at the water, her ice cream starting to melt in her hand, forgotten.

'You know, in all the time I've known you, I've never heard you talk about your family. I've never really heard you talk about ... anything.'

She turned back to meet his gaze; her lips pressed together tightly. 'Yes, I know that.'

John raised his eyebrows slightly. 'How's your ice cream?' Great. She was gonna clam up before he'd even said three words to her.

She smiled, but her eyes remained impassive. 'Cold,' she said, holding it away from her like it was poisoned. 'It's cold.'

John laughed. Mariana remained stony faced and silent.

'Jesus, you really don't get out much, do you?' he said, the humour gone now.

Her lip curled up, an amused smirk. 'It took nine years for you to notice that?'

Nine years. Christ. They'd been working together for nine years, and their conversation had barely gotten past the weather. There had been that one time, when he'd taken the photo from her, and the other time, when he'd given her the burner phone with his number programmed in. He'd wanted to help her, but she hadn't called him once. Not ever.

'You never answered my question. Do you see your mama very much? I know Dornan and Emilio keep you busy in the office.'

'I don't, no. You see your wife very often? I know Dornan and Emilio keep you busy with ...' She paused for a moment. '... whatever it is a president does.' She waved her hand at the tattoo on his neck that marked him a Gypsy, before returning her eyes to the water that lapped at the Santa Monica shore.

Wow. Talk about sucker-punching him in the gut with a dig about Caroline. He went to bite back, but then he realised: she was deflecting his questions, diverting his attention. She was like this ghost that was always around. He spent several hours with this woman every week, and beyond her name, he didn't know a damn thing about her. He knew that she was stuck here, but she'd never told him why. And Dornan wasn't one to offer up specifics, even when John pressed him. It seemed that Mariana Rodriguez was off limits in their conversations.

And that was a shame. Because he liked her. She was funny and kind, not to mention fucking beautiful.

Shit. He needed to not think of her like that. She wasn't fucking beautiful. She was nobody. Christ! Under the table, his cock was straining against his pants again at the mere sight of her tongue running lazily across her bottom lip as she stared into space. Those lips looked so soft, he wanted to reach out and brush his finger across them. *Jesus, you're married, and she's taken.* Cold showers. Emilio. Ahhh yes, nothing made his cock go softer than thinking about his psychopathic boss.

'You don't like talking about your family, that's OK. I don't like talking about mine.'

Mariana got up and tossed her cone in the trash. Sitting back down across from him, she started shredding her paper napkin, making a neat pile on the table in front of her. John observed her as he finished his cone, unsure how to rescue the conversation.

'What do you want to talk about?' John asked. 'I'll give you the floor.'

He watched her face, waiting for a reaction, but there was nothing. As she pressed a hand to the window and continued to stare at the sea beyond, it occurred to John that she wasn't ignoring him.

She hadn't even heard him speak.

CHAPTER FIFTEEN

MARIANA

'Can I go on the wheel?' Juliette asked.

The three of us gazed up at the Ferris wheel. John shrugged. 'Sure. You want me to come with you?'

She shook her head. 'I'm not a baby, *Father*.'

Defiant little thing. If I had spoken to my father like that, I would have been smacked upside the head. Then again, if I'd talked to my father at all when I was Juliette's age, he would have smacked me upside the head.

Thinking of him did nothing to lift my black mood. I should be happy, being out here like this, but I was fretting. Why was it suddenly necessary for John to babysit me? Had Dornan somehow figured out Murphy's plan? Was he waiting to see if I shared what I'd learned the previous night with him? Or was this just a happy coincidence, that the very day after Murphy dropped a bomb on me and I then learned the truth – that my entire family had been murdered – that John had decided to take me out?

And John's questions about my family were starting to irritate me. They made me suspicious. Was he baiting me to see if I'd confess knowledge of their deaths, only to punish me for making the forbidden phone call to Este's brother? Has John been listening to the calls I've made through the burner cellphone, the one *he* gave me, this entire time?

So many questions. I didn't know who to trust. Had he brought me out with Juliette so I felt more comfortable, so I let my guard down?

Well, he wasn't getting anything from me. Not one iota. If I was wrong, and this was innocent, I'd apologise later.

Maybe.

Once Juliette was riding the Ferris wheel, John turned his attention to me again. I'd been expecting it. He was as stubborn as me.

'So, you don't like talking about your family,' he said, lighting a cigarette. 'What do you like talking about?'

I shrugged, not meeting his gaze as I squeezed the metal railing that separated us from the wheel. Did he have to pick at me like I was an open wound, begging to be torn open and exposed?

Sighing, he stood closer to me, so that our shoulders touched. I wanted to jerk myself away in protest, but my shoulder burned pleasantly where it touched his. *I am such a loser*, I thought to myself. *Any tiny bit of human contact and I'm fighting to keep my hands to myself.*

I was so deprived of affection, a casual touch of someone's shoulder against mine sent a thrill through me. Not just anyone, though. There was something about John that did it.

I felt heat rise in my cheeks. I couldn't afford to think like that.

'Tell me something about yourself,' John pressed me. 'Tell me anything.' He'd angled his body so it was achingly close to mine, his hips twisted so that his stomach was inches away from my ass. And he was talking directly into my ear, so close I could feel his breath on my neck.

I shook my head resolutely. 'No.'

Out of the corner of my eye, I could see that he looked almost amused. 'Where are you from?' he asked, stepping back a little as we watched Juliette go around and around.

I eyed him warily, shaking my head. His questions made me mad. I would tell him nothing.

John sighed. 'You had a son.'

I wanted to punch him in the face. Was he part of this, then? Was he working with Murphy? Was he trying to find out where Luis was, so he could kill him? I whirled to face John, jabbing my finger into his hard chest as a look of surprise spread across his face.

'Do you really think if I had a son, I would be standing here with you?' I asked, gritting my teeth. How dare he? He had no right to talk about Luis. No right.

He considered that for a moment. Leaned back, putting space between us as he took another drag of his cigarette. He dropped his gaze, staring at the lit end as if he was pondering something, before levelling his eyes at me once more. His stare was intense, but I didn't look away. I wouldn't back down.

'You carry a photo of a baby around, but he's not your son?' John asked dubiously. 'Okay, whatever.' And I could tell he was offended that I wouldn't tell him anything.

He was hurt. And somehow I knew that he was telling the truth. That he wasn't trying to get information from me to hurt me. I had an overwhelming feeling that he was on my side. Call it intuition, call it gut feeling – but suddenly I felt terrible for assuming the worst of him.

I hated to lie – especially to someone who was trying to be nice. But I did. Because he'd been Dornan's best friend forever, and he'd worked for Emilio almost that long, and one more person knowing about my son was one too many. I thought of Murphy, of the way he used Luis as a pawn against me, and how effortlessly it worked. I couldn't handle Emilio Ross doing the same thing. Not to mention Dornan's reaction if he found out that I'd kept the knowledge of my child from him all these years. He'd never forgive me for lying to him about it, even if it was technically only lying by omission.

'He was my baby brother,' I said, skimming the murkiness of the past to extract and craft a suitable lie. 'He died a long time ago. So don't make things up to try and bond with me, John. Do I *look* like somebody's mother to you?'

He looked disappointed. He didn't respond.

'I'm sorry for your loss,' he said finally, dropping his cigarette butt and crushing it under his heel. 'I just assumed, is all.'

'It's fine,' I said, feeling like a fucking bitch for lying to him, nice, dependable John. 'I can see how you'd think that.'

But I clung to my secrets. My son was already in danger, our future together seemingly impossible. They couldn't have his memory, too.

'Like I said, I'm nobody's mother.' I snorted. 'I'd make a lousy mother, anyway.'

John let out a breath, turning to watch as Juliette's chair descended slowly and she was let off the carnival ride.

'You did more motherly things for her in the past hour than her actual mother's done in years,' he said, and my heart broke a little for the both of them.

'John—' I started.

'It's fine,' he said, echoing my previous sentiments. He started towards Juliette. 'Let's go.'

I followed him wordlessly as he walked away from me. He stopped and touched Juliette's shoulder gently when she stopped in front of him, murmured something in her ear. He was a good father.

Soon we were climbing into John's car, the doors making a dull thunk as he closed Juliette's door, then mine. Our eyes caught as he closed my door, and I attempted a small smile. I didn't know what the hell the outing had been for other than a babysitting gig for John, but I still wanted him to know that I was grateful for the brief reprieve from my apartment. He stared down at me through the car window, and something passed between us. I don't know what it was or even how to describe it. It was something, though, because all of a sudden my throat was thick, my stomach was doing flips and the hair on the back of my neck was standing on end. Something inside me lit up, and I had to look away.

I shifted my gaze to the sky, watching the clouds on the horizon as they continued to roll in above us. Everything seemed to get colder almost immediately, and then the sky burst open.

It rained so infrequently in Los Angeles that when it did, it was almost magical. Back home it rained often and the land was lush and green as a result. Here, it seemed to make everything spring to life and sparkle. It washed away the dirt and dust that clung to everything, a byproduct of existing in a desert by the sea.

John swore, shielding his face as he circled the car and got into the driver's seat. I watched him silently as he started the engine and revved it a few times. Maybe he felt my gaze on him, because he glanced up at me sharply. His eyes looked tired. Bloodshot. I wondered when he'd last had a decent night's sleep. I was betting it was the last time Dornan did. Well before I met either of them.

CHAPTER SIXTEEN

MARIANA

It was late. John had dropped me off at my apartment and called me three times to make sure I'd activated the code on the door correctly. Seemed he took his job as protection detail in Dornan's absence seriously.

If only he knew.

I kicked my wet shoes off and walked through the bedroom into the adjoining bathroom, flicking the light on and leaning over the basin, wringing my wet hair out in the sink. I was freezing cold, the water clinging to my skin in tiny droplets that made me shiver.

I caught sight of my eyes in the mirror and cringed. My mother's eyes, my son's eyes. Dark blue. When I'd been born, the doctors had told my mother that they'd eventually turn brown, just like my father's eyes. Because brown was meant to be the dominant gene. But my eyes had only gotten bluer as I got older, bluer and more serious as the innocence of my youth had ebbed away. And now there was nothing in them, nothing but a vast darkness that stretched as far and wide as my empty existence.

I had the sudden urge to call Miguel again and check on Luis. I wrapped my hair up in a towel and padded, barefoot, through my bedroom and into the hallway. I heard rustling and looked for Guillermo, but – wait – Guillermo wasn't here, was he?

Guillermo was in Mexico.

My heart dropped into my stomach as I realised somebody who wasn't Guillermo was in my apartment.

Nothing was out of place. But somebody was here.

I smelled it first.

Oranges. The sharp citrus smell stung my nostrils. I never bought oranges. I hated the way they tasted. Yet I could smell, as plain as day, the overpowering scent of freshly sliced orange.

I took a few tentative steps down the hall, suddenly on high alert.

I didn't have my gun. I'd left it in my handbag, in the bedroom, and now I was here, defenceless, and somebody was in my house. In my fucking kitchen. And then I saw him, hovering in the shadows beside the refrigerator, and as he shifted the streetlight slicing through the blinds cut across his blue eyes.

'I thought you'd never get back,' Murphy said, not moving.

I backed up a little, debating if I had time to run back to the bedroom. My entire body was alight, rage and fear humming in a steady vibration. I couldn't think properly. It was the first time I'd seen Murphy since learning the truth about what had happened to my family.

But he didn't know that I knew. At least, I hoped he didn't know.

He stepped out of the shadows, holding his palms up in

a supplicating gesture. 'Did you bring me back a chocolate ice cream?'

I changed my mind. He needed me, and even if he'd somehow intercepted the call I had made to Este's brother, he wouldn't shoot me. He couldn't. I had the keys to the city, as far as he was concerned. I was the co-signatory on every single dirty bank account he'd been stashing money in, in this country and the rest.

'You look more like a vanilla man to me,' I replied coolly, rooted to the spot. 'Boring and weak.'

He laughed, swiping at the drink on the counter. 'You're hilarious. Ever since the first time I stuck my finger inside you, I knew you were fucking hilarious.'

'You're drunk,' I realised, a little surprised.

He was soaking wet, from head to toe. The rain that had begun as we were leaving the ice-cream parlour hadn't eased off, instead it had come down in sheets.

It looked like Murphy hadn't been here long, judging by how soaked through with rain he was. It looked like he'd taken a bath fully clothed. And he was drunk?

Never, in nine years, had I seen him even *slightly* intoxicated. High on cocaine, yes, but not drunk. He was always so controlled, so polished. Now, not so much. Something must have happened. Something to make him lose control.

I mean, apart from him killing my entire family and trying to hunt my illegitimate son to use as collateral against me.

'Have fun with Johnny Boy?' he asked. 'Romantic walks on the beach? Did you share an ice cream before he stuck his dick in you?'

Wait. He was *jealous*?

'His kid was there,' I said, still in disbelief. 'He's my fucking babysitter, Murphy.'

'Sure,' Murphy drawled. 'Babysitters don't fuck you.' He snickered. 'Well, sometimes they do. But they shouldn't, nuh-uh.'

'There's only one person who fucks me,' I replied sharply. 'You'd do well to remember that.'

He laughed again, but there was no joy in the sound. It was a guttural noise that rattled in his chest, full of loathing, full of hate. He hated me, I realised. He hated me because I had chosen to align with somebody like Dornan, rather than somebody like him.

I didn't move as he reached up and grabbed an unopened bottle of whiskey from the top of the refrigerator and tore the lid off.

I didn't move as he approached, stopping only to throw back a swig straight from the bottle, wiping the excess that dribbled down his chin with his suit sleeve.

I didn't move, and then he was so close to me, I could smell the whiskey on his breath.

'Had to get liquored up before you came over here, huh?'

My mama always said it was my mouth that got me into trouble, and she was right. Even after all this time, I just couldn't help myself when it came to Christopher Fucking Murphy.

He narrowed his ice-blue gaze at me, pushing his black fringe out of his eyes. And then, before I could react, before I could even step back, his hand was wrapped around my face, and I was slammed back into the wall. I saw stars for a second, blinked as I heard something smash against the wall beside me, and then drew in a sharp intake of breath as the jagged teeth of a broken whiskey bottle taunted me. Inches away from my eyes, its sharp edges were still dripping with whiskey.

'Murphy,' I cautioned, 'think about this. You need me. You need me if you want to get your money.'

Fuck!

I struggled to keep my breathing even as I watched his eyes slide from mine, down to my lips, over my chest. A smirk tugged at the corner of his mouth.

'I'm pretty sure there's a way around it, little lady.' The whiskey on his breath burned my nostrils. My mind was whirling. This motherfucker had killed my entire family – or at least been directly responsible for it – and it looked like he was about to kill me, too. I couldn't let that happen. I wouldn't.

You know what he wants, the rational part of my brain screamed. *Give it to him.*

No!

Save yourself.

Jesus.

I reached my hand out, moving slowly in case he thought I was on the attack and he decided to stab me with the broken bottle. I wrapped my hand around the back of his neck and pulled his face closer to mine, pulling even though I wanted to push him away, fighting back the rising panic inside me.

'What do you want, Murphy?' I asked softly. 'Because I'm pretty sure it's not just my cooperation with your little scheme.'

He licked his lips, breathing heavily. He lowered the bottle to his side and seemed to calm down a little, his blue eyes still cold and fucking crazy, but his breathing slower, his urge to stab me apparently in check once again.

'You know what I want,' he breathed. 'I could make your life so fucking sweet,' he brushed a thumb across my bottom lip, 'if you just gave it to me.'

Something violent and dark unleashed itself within me.

'You want to fuck me,' I breathed. 'Fuck me already. I'd be so much better than that little bitch you've been screwing.'

My words were like a green light to someone who's been stuck in a traffic jam for almost a decade. I saw the shift in Murphy's gaze, from predatory but controlled, to completely animalistic. A low growl came from his throat as he fisted a handful of my hair and began dragging me towards my bedroom.

There was a gun in my bedroom. In my purse.

I followed him without fighting. Part of me was screaming inside, trying to convince myself to run, to try and get away, but another part was swiftly concocting a plan.

He threw me towards the bed, where I landed on my side, hard. I rolled onto my back, looking to the left and seeing my purse sitting below the pillow.

I turned my attention back to Murphy, who'd discarded the broken bottle somewhere along the way. His pants were around his ankles and his dick out before I could even blink. I sat up, swallowing back nervous bile that rushed up my throat. I was going to have to fuck him, I realised, my heart sinking at the prospect of him touching any part of me. He palmed his erection, pumping it as he looked down at me.

'You on birth control?' he asked, staring at the space between my legs that was still hidden by my dress.

'No,' I said, almost too quickly. I was, but he didn't need to know that. 'There are condoms in the bathroom. Top drawer.'

He looked pissed, but he pulled his pants back up and held onto the waistband, hurrying into the bathroom. The second he was out of my line of sight, I reached back and into my purse, rummaging around until my fingers touched cold metal. I slid my gun out as inconspicuously as I could, shoving it underneath my pillow with the handle facing me.

The slam of the bathroom drawer made me jump, and then Murphy was in front of me, a foil packet in his hand.

'Put it on,' he demanded.

I looked up at him without taking the packet. 'I think you've got me all wrong,' I deadpanned. 'I don't have a dick.'

His fist slammed into my cheek and I tasted blood. I fell back onto the bed, fighting as he grabbed my wrists.

'You're a very bad girl,' he said, tutting. 'Let's try that again. Put it on *me*. You can suck it first for talking back to me.'

He fisted a handful of my hair and pulled my face closer. I took a deep breath, debating my position. Sure, I could pull the gun out now – assuming I could still reach it – and hold it to his balls, but he could easily just drop down on me and overpower me.

'Open,' he sneered, pushing his erection against my lips. Reluctantly, and out of options, I opened my mouth.

Bitterness coated my tongue as pre-come leaked from his dick and into my mouth. I fought the overpowering urges to throw up and bite down as hard as I could. Death by penis removal – it'd be a fitting end for somebody like him, but I didn't like the idea of potentially being shot in the head as soon as I bit down. Instead, I relaxed my throat, letting him slide in and out of my mouth.

'You like that?' Murphy asked, squeezing my throat painfully with his free hand. His eyes flashed with excitement as he pushed in harder, hitting the back of my throat. I struggled not to gag as he pistoned his hips, driving his dick deep into my mouth again and again.

'Oh, you dirty little whore,' he said, breathing heavily. 'I can feel my cock in your throat. You're my little whore now. I'm taking you with me when we get outta here, you understand?' He squeezed my throat harder when I didn't respond. I nodded, because I couldn't exactly talk with a mouthful of dick.

My fingertips burned, begging me to grab the gun and shoot him. But I couldn't reach, and I couldn't very well just casually lean back, with the way he was holding my head immobile. He sped up, getting rougher as he approached release. Beneath the fear and the rage, I was already getting bored. I'd have a sore jaw after this. It was already screaming in protest.

'Suck harder,' he commanded. 'Suck the come out of me, you dirty whore.'

I didn't change what I was doing. I refused to make it any better for him. At the moment, as it was, it looked like his dirty little long-held fantasy was doing just fine without any enthusiasm on my part.

He let go of my hair all of a sudden, withdrawing from my mouth. I gasped for air as he palmed his wet erection, giving it a couple of tugs. He was close already, and he wanted to draw this out. For fuck's sake.

'I'm about to come all over your face,' he grunted, 'and if you close your eyes, I'll hurt you. You understand?'

I rested back on my elbows and spread my legs open wide, bracing my bare heels on the edge of the bed. 'You're not scared of fucking me, are you, Murphy?'

He sneered, snatching the condom up from beside me. 'Put it on,' he said. 'I wouldn't breed with a dirty little slut like you if you were the last woman on earth.'

Well, the feeling was mutual. I fought the urge to fire off a retort, rage burning in my chest. I needed to get the taste out of my mouth. Now. It was so vile, I was struggling not to puke.

Making my face go blank, I took the foil packet and ripped it open. Dornan didn't wear protection, ever. Murphy didn't know that, though. Thank Christ.

'I don't know how,' I said.

Eyes flashing with frustration and lust, he took the packet from me and rolled the condom onto his erection. Once it was on, he looked at me and grinned.

'Turn over onto your stomach,' he ordered. 'This will hurt, but I promise you'll love it, like the little slut you are.'

Wow, he sure liked the word slut. Wasn't very creative when it came to alternatives.

Again, I thought of the gun. If I laid down on my back, I'd be able to reach it. I wasn't going to flip onto my stomach, not if I could help it. I'd be powerless then. On my stomach, he could capture my wrists, crush me under his weight and I wouldn't even have my arms to fight him off with.

'Don't you want to watch me come?' I pouted. 'That's Dornan's favourite part.'

Mentioning Dornan was exactly what I needed to do to set him off. He launched onto me like a goddamn lion, his lips crashing into mine as he tugged my panties to the side and pushed into me in one hard movement. I wasn't exactly turned on, and my eyes watered at the sudden intrusion.

His skin was cold and damp from the rain. I'd fared better than him, with my umbrella, and so when his freezing cold skin touched mine I jerked back, our kiss broken as he fucked me, rough and fast. He hadn't even undressed me, he was so impatient. I smiled wickedly at him, pushing my hips up to meet his with every thrust.

He closed his eyes, a sigh of appreciation falling from his lips. I kept my own eyes wide open. I thought I'd feel scared at what would come next, but all I felt was the stark relief of knowing I'd soon have one less enemy in the world.

Thrust.

My fingers itched. *Wait.*

Thrust.

Almost.

Thrust.

Now.

I reached up, slid my hand underneath the pillow and curled my fingers around the gun. I located the trigger and kept my index finger on it. Almost.

Thrust.

I rested my free hand on his ass and pulled him deeper. 'Harder,' I murmured.

He liked that. His head fell forward as he used every ounce of energy on making sure he'd bedded himself as deep and as hard as possible with every single thrust. I was mostly numb to it now, too distracted by more devious things.

Thrust.

Wait.

Thrust.

Almost.

Thrust.

Now.

I pulled the gun from its spot under the pillow and pressed the end of the barrel to Murphy's pale forehead.

His eyes flew open, ice-blue and full of What-the-Fuck? He stopped everything. Stopped moving, stopped breathing. The only thing that was happening was in his bright eyes.

They were afraid.

'Pull out,' I demanded. He didn't move. 'Now!' I cried, pushing the gun harder against his pale skin. He jerked his hips back, pulling himself out of me, and I almost cried at the immense relief from knowing he wasn't inside me any more.

It was like I'd floated away and was looking on from above. It didn't feel real; none of it did. I was on the bed underneath Murphy, and his eyes started to become wet and glossy. Tears?

'Afraid?' I asked, unable to wipe the grin from my lips. Something had changed inside me through nine years of hate and pain, and that *something* that lurked in the deepest recesses of my dark soul enjoyed Murphy's discomfort entirely too much. Craved it. Wanted more of it.

'Did you kill my family?' I whispered, and the smile I was wearing faded away. Grim realisation spiked in his eyes, and his entire body tensed. A wave of nausea rolled through me. *It's true. He fucking did it.*

He didn't answer, but the answer was clear as day in his eyes; in the way he looked away for a split second before meeting my gaze again, in the stunned look on his face, in the heavy exhale that came from his chest.

I saw the questions in his eyes.

'How?' he asked, his words tumbling out quickly, with urgency. 'You were tracked. You were fucking watched day and night. You don't take a piss without me knowing, so *how*?' Beads of sweat were starting to gather above his eyebrows, and his anxiety made my heart beat faster in excitement.

'Tell me what happened to them,' I demanded. 'Tell me, and I'll let you walk out of here.'

His eyes dipped to the side. I responded by cocking the hammer on the gun, a loud metallic click.

'You really think I didn't check on my family in nine years?' I whispered. 'How stupid are you? How stupid do you think *I* am? Tell me.' My lips quivered as a single tear escaped from my left eye. Damn it. I didn't want him to see what he'd done to me. The pain he'd caused. I didn't want him to have the satisfaction of knowing how I'd suffered thanks to him.

'Your father killed a school kid in a hit-and-run. He was drunk, and when they arrested him, he turned on Emilio,' Murphy spoke slowly, his words careful, measured. 'The feds realised what an opportunity they'd been given and granted your father immunity in exchange for his testimony against the cartel.'

'The feds? Be more specific.'

Murphy scowled. 'The FBI.'

I made a small sound of annoyance in the back of my throat. 'I want a name, asshole. Give me a name. The FBI's a big fucking agency.'

'Why?'

I applied pressure to the trigger and Murphy blanched. 'Lindsay Price. He's investigating Emilio. You tell anybody I told you that and we'll both be dead.'

'And?' I pressed.

Murphy shrugged, his arms beginning to shake as he held himself above the treacherous nozzle of my gun. 'Nobody testifies against Il Sangue, Mariana. Your father was a fool to think he'd even make it to the FBI's safe house.'

'I can only see one fool now,' I said, 'and he's right in front of me.'

Murphy narrowed his eyes, opening his mouth to reply, and I took that as an invitation to jam the barrel of my beautiful gun between Murphy's lips and teeth.

He spoke angry, unintelligible words around the gun in his mouth, his fingers curling around my biceps and squeezing.

I thought of how I'd been stuck here for nine shitty fucking years. I thought of *them*, screaming as they burned and died. And any hesitation that lived inside me was replaced with a cold, numb nothingness.

'Fuck you,' I whispered.

Before I lost my nerve, I pulled the heavy trigger back.

CHAPTER SEVENTEEN

MARIANA

The blast deafened me, the force of the kick throwing Murphy off of me momentarily. What goes up must come down, though, and he landed heavily on my chest a second later, my grip still firmly around the gun in his mouth as his dead weight knocked every ounce of air out of me. His mouth was not what it had been three seconds ago. My eyes had adjusted to the light enough to see his cold, unblinking blue eyes and the gore the bullet had created beyond his shattered teeth.

He was as dead as they come. I'd just killed a man as he hate-fucked me, and I was pretty sure I was going to be murdered brutally for it.

My senses went haywire. My eyes could see better than ever in the dark, every detail soaking into my brain and lying in wait for later, when they'd become my nightmares, no doubt. I drew in a panicked breath as I tried to push Murphy's bleeding corpse off me, but he wouldn't budge. *Jesus.* I was pinned, blood rushing from his mouth onto my stomach and chest and sliding down my right side, pooling underneath me where it quickly grew sticky and cold. I panicked. I started to scream, clapping a hand over my mouth as I shrieked into it, tasting the heavy, metallic blood that coated my lips and palm. Vomit rose in my throat and I swallowed it down.

I forced myself to stop screaming. The immediate threat was gone. Murphy was dead. I'd just successfully avenged the murders of my family in some small way. There was more to do, further to go, but I'd just taken the first brutal, bloody step towards my own redemption.

And it felt fucking scary, but more than that, it felt exhilarating.

But still my primitive brain was freaking the fuck out. I started to wail again.

Focus.

I let go of the gun, let go of my mouth.

Figure it out.

First things first. Get Murphy the fuck off me.

I braced the heels of my palms against his shoulders and pressed my left knee against his leg, leveraging his dead weight enough to haul him, painfully slowly and inch by excruciating inch, until his body sagged onto the bed at my right. But now his weight was pinning my arm, trapping me. I pulled, hard, my tendons stretching painfully as I wrenched my hand free.

I crawled to the edge of the bed and slid onto the floor, backing away on hands and heels. The smell of blood was so thick in the air, it was like I was swimming in the stuff.

Using the wall for support, I stood, my legs trembling violently. I made it three steps to my bathroom and puked in the basin. Adrenalin, maybe. I'd need a new mattress. Would somebody call the cops after hearing that gunshot? I hoped not. I didn't need any attention.

I leaned against the bathroom doorframe and watched as the remainder of Murphy's blood drained out of the dirty hole in the back of his head and onto my Egyptian cotton sheets.

An angry buzz rang in my ears. I couldn't hear a thing. Maybe I'd blown out my own eardrums when I pulled that trigger.

I turned the faucet on to wash the vomit away and noticed blood running down my bare arms for the first time. Dreading what I'd see, I slowly raised my eyes to the large mirror that hung above the basin.

It was as if the devil stared back at me. A pair of dark blue eyes and a shock of long, tangled dark hair were the only things I recognised. The rest was a garish caricature, soaked in blood from head to toe. Was it really possible for one little bullet to do all that harm? Make all that mess? I looked like something out of a slasher movie.

And the blood wasn't the worst part. As I studied my right arm closer, I noticed a fine coating of gritty stuff. Like grains of sand, but bigger.

His skull. My arm, the one that had been trapped underneath him until I'd wrenched it out, was covered in pieces of Murphy's skull.

Luckily I was already in front of the basin, because otherwise the second puke would have gone all over my feet and the floor.

I retched until there was nothing left in my stomach but a hollow ache. I used a towel to wipe the blood from my face, hands and feet as best as I could. I stared longingly at the shower, wanting nothing more than to step underneath the hot water and let it wash every trace of Christopher Murphy from my skin. But I couldn't. I knew I had precious time left to do something.

I crept past Murphy's still form, my eyes returning to his face. His mouth. His broken teeth and the hole in his head.

I reached for my purse, taking my phone quietly as if making a noise would awaken Murphy. He wasn't waking up. Ever.

I was bloody and dirty, and I didn't want to stain the armchair in the corner of my bedroom. I tiptoed backwards, back into the safety of the tiled bathroom, sitting on the floor as I dialled Dornan on my regular phone with shaking fingers. He answered almost immediately.

'Hey.'

I thought hearing his voice might move something inexplicable inside me, make me cry, make me realise the full impact of what had just happened. *I just killed somebody.*

Nothing.

I felt nothing. I missed Dornan. I wanted Dornan here, to help me.

'What are you up to?' I asked, my voice clear, my tone casual. I must be in shock, I thought. That's got to be the only reason I can't feel something right now.

I could hear commotion. He was at home. I heard his boys in the background, his wife. 'Is something wrong?' he asked me.

'Who is that?' I heard his wife say. My heart sank. Doubt flooded through my mind. He was with his wife. He'd go to bed with her tonight, and he'd wake up tomorrow morning with her, and he was never going to leave her for me, so what the hell was I doing, living like a prisoner, lying in wait six days a week only to have him on the seventh for a mere few hours? He'd told me that he didn't sleep with her any more. He told me he didn't love her, that he only stayed because of his boys. And I'd believed him. But was he lying? Did he still touch her? Kiss her?

'It's okay,' I said quickly. 'We can talk tomorrow.'

The ghost of a smile flickered across my mouth as I stared blankly at Murphy's shiny black shoes. They gleamed as the bright bathroom light reflected off them, showing up tiny specks where blood had misted over them. It seemed to have taken forever for the flow of blood from his mouth to slow down.

'Sounds like a plan,' he said coolly, and he hung up on me.

I stared at the screen, chewing on my lip as I glanced up at Murphy.

What the fuck was I going to do with him? He was heavy. I contemplated getting my hands on a chainsaw and dismembering him in my bathtub. Too messy, and maybe a little too gruesome, even for me. Acid? I didn't know what the bath was made out of, or even what type of acid to use. I was completely unprepared for my initiation into the killer club.

I racked my brain. If I could somehow wrap him up in something, then I'd be able to put him in a car and dump the body far, far away. But he was a DEA agent. His DNA was probably everywhere in my apartment, not just from the fact I'd blown a hole in his skull tonight, but from his previous visit where he'd tried to make it like a fucking dinner date. He'd touched everything in my kitchen, in my living room, the dining table ... No, I had to somehow get rid of his body so it would never be found.

I snapped out of my daydreaming and stood, passing Murphy's dead body as I made my way to the kitchen, leaving smudges of blood where I'd not wiped every smidge of blood from the soles of my feet. I was going to have to Lysol the hell out of this apartment, I realised grimly.

But that would have to wait.

I still had the enormous problem of a *body* to get rid of.

I opened the pantry and shifted a few things, finding the flour canister where I always left it. I set it on the counter and reached my hand inside, the blood left on my fingers mingling with the white powder to create globs of garish pink. I swallowed thickly as my fingers located the plastic ziplock bag I was rummaging for. Shaking free the excess flour, I unzipped the plastic bag, tipping the burner phone into my hand. I switched it on and navigated to one of the three numbers it contained.

***

He answered after two rings. 'I thought you'd never call,' John joked, and I could imagine the cocky grin on his face. It was true, I hadn't used the phone to call him once, and he'd given it to me almost a decade ago.

'I need your help.'

He must have heard the seriousness in my voice, because his response was devoid of the jovial tone he'd greeted me with.

'What happened?'

'I shot Murphy. He's dead. He's in my apartment.' Might as well get to the point.

A long pause. Then, 'Fuck, Ana. *Jesus.*'

He never called me Ana. Always addressed me by my full name. I guess murder cut the need for formalities.

'Does anyone know?' John asked quietly. 'Does Dornan know?'

'Nobody knows,' I said, taking a bag of ground coffee from my freezer and kicking it shut again with my bare foot. Another surface I'd need to scrub clean. Great. I flicked the coffee machine on and left it to heat up, taking two mugs from the dish drainer and setting them beside the bag of Colombian roast. The small photo of lush Colombian jungle on the package taunted me, reminding me of where I came from, of where my son was. 'John.'

'Yeah.'

Fuck.

'Will you help me?'

I hated to ask but it was unavoidable. And of all of them, he was the most trustworthy. It still didn't mean he wouldn't betray me, in the end. It just meant he was most likely to keep his mouth shut for longer than anybody else in the Gypsy Brothers.

'I will *always* help you,' he said, some kind of emotion behind his words, and something about the way he said it made me break inside. 'I'm on my way. Don't move. Don't call anybody. Definitely do not answer the door, you hear me?'

'Thank you,' I said, and the line went dead.

I tidied up the flour as the coffee machine hummed to life, dripping the precious stuff into a pot that served two. I kept the burner phone out, in case John decided to call me back. My thoughts wandered as I moved around the kitchen on autopilot, a deep grief punctuated by an eerie calm. Indirectly, and without planning it, I had in some way avenged my family's murders by slaying the person – at least, one of the people – directly responsible. It made my head spin.

And there was one thought louder than the rest, incessant as it sank its barb into me, again and again. I tried to blink it away, even shaking my head from side to side to try and rid myself of the thought, because it was so insignificant it didn't deserve my attention.

The thought wasn't what you'd expect.

It wasn't *I just killed someone.* Not *I'm a murderer.*

No.

The thought that buzzed around my head like a heavy blowfly was: *I'm going to have to buy a new mattress without Dornan noticing.*

I'd just killed a man, and I didn't even care.

Nine years in hell will do that to a person.

CHAPTER EIGHTEEN

MARIANA

I was worried that John might call back and cancel on me. I didn't know where he was, or what he was doing. Shit, he was a busy guy, with a fuck-up for a wife, a teenage daughter who was too pretty to let out of his sight, and a club that needed to be run like a well-oiled machine to keep Emilio happy.

He didn't cancel. He was at my front door six minutes later, dressed in jeans and a leather jacket, a look of grim determination on his face and a five-o'clock shadow to match.

In the six minutes between him hanging up and then arriving at my door, I'd ventured back into the bedroom and located the gun in between all the blood and brain matter on my duvet. I held the gun loosely at my side and waited for the metallic click that signalled the unlocking mechanism at my front door. The door swung open and I raised the gun slowly, almost lazily.

John eyed me warily. 'Is that a gun, or are you excited to see me?'

He entered the apartment and kicked the door shut behind him. Satisfied that he was alone, and that he was here to help, I dropped the gun to my side.

'Is it still raining out there?' I asked. My throat sounded raw. Probably from having Murphy's cock rammed down it. *Well, you should see the other guy*, I thought to myself.

John shrugged. 'A little.' He didn't look wet. Not like Murphy, drenched through with rain and now soaking in all the blood that had once been inside his body.

I padded to the kitchen with John in tow, my stained feet leaving small smudges of blood, and set my gun on the kitchen counter. Taking the two mugs of coffee I'd prepared, I handed one to John, keeping the other for myself.

He took a sip of the coffee and started to choke. He was staring at my chest, I realised. The hallway wasn't lit, but the kitchen was, casting a bright glow over my current state of mess. John slammed the coffee on the counter, his eyes wide. I followed his gaze down to my dress – of course, I was still wearing the baby blue dress that matched John's eyes – and saw again just how much blood I had on me.

'What'd you do?' John coughed. 'Kill him and then roll around on top of him?'

I crossed my arms over my chest, suddenly feeling dizzy. 'Something like that,' I said.

John was quiet for a moment. 'Where is he?' he asked finally.

***

He studied the scene for a few moments without speaking, sipping his coffee every now and then. His head tilted to the side, he was like some kind of rogue detective, taking in every detail. The broken whiskey bottle. The blood-soaked sheets. I stood beside him, not so close that our arms touched, but almost. I copied his head tilt, wanting to see what *he* saw, trying to observe the scene objectively, as if it wasn't me who'd committed the crime.

Murphy wasn't a pretty sight. It was as if his body had softened somehow, melting heavily into the mattress. And his death hadn't been dignified, not one bit. His pants were still around his ankles, his bare legs a pasty white without any blood circulating in them.

The condom still clung to his flaccid penis, the empty end sticking to his thigh. John noticed it instantly, his eyes darting to mine.

'He raped you?'

I shrugged.

'It's a simple question.'

I responded, perhaps a little too sharply. 'You'd think so, wouldn't you?'

John took a step back and turned to me. 'You know, I'm missing some excellent leftover macaroni cheese and a beer for this.' His mouth quirked, as if he were about to laugh.

I snorted behind my coffee cup.

'Seriously, though,' he said. 'What happened here? I need to know. I'm a part of this now.'

I swallowed bitter coffee. 'He was here when you dropped me off.'

He looked up sharply. 'In your apartment?'

I nodded. 'He killed my entire family, and I'm pretty sure he was going to kill me, too.' I hadn't meant to say that, but fuck it, I might as well tell him.

'*What*?'

I was shaking. Why was I shaking? I was cool. I was calm. I was fine. And then suddenly, I was most definitely *not* fine. I started to suck in great lungfuls of air as the room spun around me. *My family is dead.* The people who gave me life, the ones who raised me. And until the very moment those words had left my mouth – *He killed my entire family* – I had been numb to the reality, refusing to accept it was true.

There was no witness protection for me, or them. There never had been. There was only cruel lies. Murphy had disposed of them, and he had been about to do the same to me, once I secured his stash of hidden money for him. It was all so abundantly clear, and I felt like an idiot for even considering that he'd been telling the truth before.

It was the photographs. He'd baited me with promises of seeing my son and I'd thrown logic out the window. It was terrifying how easily he'd manipulated me.

Well, who was the sucker now?

Yeah.

I stumbled, losing my balance as the room continued to spin, and John caught me before I toppled. I hated being weak, but right now, I'd give myself a hall pass.

I started to cry. Deep, wretched sobs.

'Hey,' John said, his face close to mine. 'Ana. You gotta pull yourself together. I can't take care of you and bury this motherfucker at the same time. Ana!'

I heard a loud, high-pitched scream. I think it was coming from me. I was breaking apart.

'Fuck,' I heard John swear. Clamping a hand over my mouth, he hauled me into the bathroom and into the shower recess. A moment later, freezing cold water drenched the both of us and I pushed him back angrily, my screams vanishing as the shock of the cold forced me back to my senses.

'There you are,' he muttered. He reached across me to adjust the water and soon it was warm. I stared at the drain, transfixed, as Murphy's blood washed off me. My dress. I needed to take my dress off and wash the blood from my skin.

I unzipped my dress at the back and unhooked the straps from my shoulders, letting the material fall to the shower floor in a soggy, bloody heap. John's eyes widened slightly as he looked at me, dressed only in a white bra and panties, marked in places with Murphy's blood, the thin cotton steadily turning see-through under the stream of warm water.

Had I imagined it? Had he even looked at me at all?

Yes. He had looked. He was still looking.

It was bad. It was wrong. There was a dead man lying in my bed, killed by my hand, and yet when John's eyes widened and he drew in a sharp breath, it still excited me. I felt pathetic.

'Clean yourself up,' he said gruffly, turning to go. 'I'll make some calls, get this sorted out.'

Calls? Who in the hell was he planning to call?

I caught the sleeve of his leather jacket. He stared at my hand like it was burning him just by resting there.

'Don't go,' I pleaded. 'He's in there and I can't— I just— Please don't leave me here with him.' My voice rose higher with each word until I was begging. Pleading.

I didn't even know what I was trying to say. I started to gasp for air again, panicking.

'Are you going to tell Dornan?' I asked, clawing at the front of his jacket. 'Are you going to tell Emilio?' I couldn't breathe. 'They'll kill me. Jesus, they're going to kill me, aren't they?'

'Hey,' he said firmly. 'Calm. Down.'

He cupped my face with his palm, not afraid to touch me, even though I was a dirty murdering whore with the blood of a dead DEA agent all over her. I could see myself in the mirror beyond John, and I didn't look pretty. I looked like I'd just stepped out of a warzone.

'You have blood on your face,' he said, his tone lower, gentler this time. 'Here, close your eyes.'

With his hands still cupping my face, he guided me back slightly. I closed my eyes as the warm jets of water hit my cheeks, and smelled soap as his fingers rubbed the blood away.

He had to scrub hard in some places, his rough fingertips moving urgently against my skin.

'Sorry,' he apologised.

I didn't move. I was like putty in his hands, ready to fall to the floor the moment he let go of me.

'Okay,' he said finally, pulling me slightly so my face was out of the water.

I was out of the direct stream, but water continued to dribble down my face and into my eyes. I wiped at them with my fingertips, feeling clumps of mascara come away on my skin. John's hands were still around my wrists from where he'd pulled me out of the water, and they tightened when I met his gaze.

His eyes flicked down to my lips, ever so subtly, and then back to my eyes, pinning me in place. One stolen glance at my mouth.

My heart started to race.

A second stolen glance.

The breath in my lungs started to not be enough, and I needed to breathe faster.

I dared a look at his mouth. His teeth bit down into his lip, as though he was causing himself pain to stop himself from doing something.

Mesmerised, almost as if I were in a daze, I reached my hand up and brushed my thumb over the lip he was biting down on.

He tore his head to the side and ripped my hand away, pressing it back to my side. *Wrong move, Ana.* He looked angry. I had read it all wrong. I might have wanted to kiss him, but it was clear by the way he was regarding me that he didn't feel the same way.

'I'm sorry,' I whispered, turning my head to the side.

I felt his eyes on me. They burned into my skin, but I refused to look at him again. I'd just very, very narrowly escaped making a fool of myself. Touching his lip might be forgivable, but if I'd kissed him? Jesus Christ. He'd probably kill me.

'What do you want from me?' he asked finally. I stole a glance at his face, saw the stricken expression of a man who had seen too much suffering in his life.

'Is that a trick question?' I asked quietly. 'Maybe you should tell me what you want, John Portland.'

He tipped his head back and let out a frustrated sigh. Dropping his gaze back to mine, he took a step forward, forcing me back against the cold tiles of the wall. His hands were like cuffs on my wrists, but I wasn't struggling to break free.

He opened his mouth, as if to say something. I could tell he didn't trust me, and I didn't trust him either. I mean, he could be setting me up.

I could be setting him up.

This could all be one giant set-up that went far wider than the two of us.

You never could trust anyone in this Gypsy Brothers world.

He shifted slightly, and my cheeks flushed with blood as I felt hard steel against my hip. *He wants me.* The shock must have been written across my face, plain as day, because he moved back, averted his eyes. He dropped my wrists and went to turn away.

'Stop,' I said, my tone cutting through the tension like sharp glass through flesh. I darted my hand out and grabbed the front of his jacket, yanking so he was forced back around to face me. Poker calm descended upon his expression, and I fixed mine to match.

We stared off.

'You're trying to trick me,' I breathed.

'Why do you immediately assume I'm trying to fuck you over?' he growled.

'You know why,' I snapped. 'You don't get to be a fucking stranger to someone for nine years and then suddenly change your mind after bonding over murder for five minutes.'

His poker face disappeared, morphing into something that looked equal parts lust and rage. His hands found my wrists again, pushed me roughly so my back settled against the tiles once more.

'What do *you* do when you want something you can't have?' he ground out. His blue eyes were bright, a dead giveaway about the state of his mind. When he fired up, they spoke loud and clear. I knew because I'd been looking away from them for years, afraid that if I stared too long I'd get lost in them. And I could absolutely, definitely, categorically, not get lost in John Portland's eyes for even one second.

He. Was. Dornan's. Best. Friend.

'I wait,' I whispered, my own convictions sliding away like melted butter as he rested a hand on my hip, just above my panties, and squeezed.

'And then?'

I thought about the money I'd stockpiled over the years. Emilio's dirty money. My escape plan for a rainy day. And it was pouring with rain right now.

'When nobody's looking, I take it.'

His eyes burned into me.

'Nobody's looking, Ana.'

Something inside me snapped, like an elastic band that had been pulled and pulled until it broke apart. I was starving. Not for food. For affection. For understanding. For the touch of a man who wasn't trying to hurt me.

We came together in a frenzy, lips crashing on lips, hands everywhere. I pulled him close to me, sighing into his mouth as I felt how hard he was against me, only his jeans separating us. Jesus Christ, he tasted exactly like I thought he would, a combination of the coffee we'd just drunk and something sweeter, something undefinable but delicious. I devoured him, unable and unwilling to stop, to come to my senses, until I remembered the reason why he was in my apartment in the first place.

Murphy.

I broke the kiss and pushed a hand against the middle of his chest. I wasn't rough about it, but I was firm. I covered my mouth with a shaking hand, my knees like rubber, my nipples hardened to twin points, clearly visible under my barely there lace bra. I didn't let go of him, though. I held onto him like my very life depended on being in constant physical contact with him, this man who'd pushed me away for nine excruciating years. Because he'd been attracted to me, too? God, the hours upon hours we'd spent together in that tiny office, breathing the same air, working the same jobs, numbers and accounts and with enough sexual tension to make me think of him when I touched myself at night. John Motherfucking Portland, the guy who'd carried a photo of my secret son around with him for months, until it was safe to return it to me. John Motherfucking Portland, who had barely looked into my eyes for nine whole years. The things Emilio did, that he couldn't control.

The dark pleasure Dornan carried and tucked away in an apartment like a dirty secret. A sin. All of those things were what I'd assumed John had thought of me, but now, as I looked at the tight expression on his face, the stricken eyes and the sad, resigned air he wore like a second skin, I realised how utterly wrong I had been.

I opened my mouth, and what I meant to say was, *I thought you didn't really like me.* But that didn't come out. What came out was something else entirely.

'He killed them all,' I said in disbelief, my knees no longer holding me up. John caught me, slowed my fall to the floor. He wrapped his arms around me, getting soaking wet under the shower spray. I closed my eyes, sagging into him as my legs curled around me on the hard tiles.

I cried like I'd never cried in my life. I cried nine years worth of tears, worth of lonely nights, worth of longing. I cried until I couldn't breathe, and then an exhausted calm descended upon me. I was empty. I was broken. The most ironic thing of all was that I had somehow managed to be the only one who'd survived out of all of us.

My mind went to that cool, dark place where it retreated when it couldn't cope any more. The place I'd been when they first took me, the place where I didn't have to be afraid. My tears had soothed me enough to allow me to enter that detached sort of depersonalised state, and I sank into it with relief.

He didn't let go of me, not once. He held me, and he stroked my hair, and he shut off the water when it finally ran cold.

CHAPTER NINETEEN

JOHN

Nine years is a long time to watch somebody from the shadows.

He did it, and he wasn't proud of it. He had a wife and a daughter, and he'd never betrayed them. Not once.

But he'd wanted to.

And now what had he done? Put his hands on another woman. The woman he'd been watching for nine fucking years, picturing in his head as he jerked off in the shower or, less frequently, while he made love to his wife, on the rare night when she was her old self.

'Mariana,' he murmured.

She was falling apart right in front of him, and it scared the shit out of him. He didn't know what to do, so he just held her. She looked so small, so fragile, and so despondent. He was almost certain she'd shatter into a million pieces if he didn't hold her together. He washed her hair with a bottle of shampoo he found in the shower, being careful not to make a face as he picked small pieces of Murphy's skull out of her long tresses.

The water went cold and he shut it off. All the while, his thoughts bounced between two things: the dead body in the bedroom and *that kiss*.

That kiss, the one that set his veins on fire and made him feel like he was losing his fucking mind. Maybe he was going crazy. She was Dornan's woman, and if he ever found out that anyone had so much as touched her, he'd kill them.

Dornan had almost killed Murphy once, for trying to do just that.

Pride swelled in his chest as John thought of Mariana shooting Murphy. He knew he should probably feel dread, but he didn't. Christopher Murphy had been the worst kind of scum, and John couldn't wait to dispose of his body and pretend like he'd never existed. Somebody else would spring up in Murphy's place, some corrupt asshole with their own agenda. Maybe they'd be better than Murphy. Maybe they'd be worse. But Murphy was finally gone.

The body. The pressing task, the thing that needed to be actioned.

'Mariana, hey,' he tried again. He reached for a clean towel and wrapped it around her shoulders. Her teeth were chattering, and her underwear was still specked with the drops of blood that had sunk deep into the fabric, but she was mostly clean apart from that.

Mariana wasn't looking. She was staring into space, not answering him. He shook his head, got up and went back into the bedroom. The smell of death was overpowering, even though Murphy had probably been dead less than two hours. It was the large amount of blood in such a confined space, and he was hardly going to open a window and alert the whole world to the stench.

John found jeans and a black T-shirt for Mariana in the large closet, and then went in search of a change of underwear for her. He hesitated upon opening her dresser drawer and seeing the lace and cotton neatly assembled into sections that seemed to scream 'functional' on one side and 'fuck me' on the other. Shaking his head, he grabbed black panties and a bra from the functional section and took them to her, along with the jeans and shirt.

'I have some clothes for you,' he said. She didn't respond. She was practically catatonic, and that worried John deeply. Fuck! How was he supposed to deal with her mental breakdown *and* find a way to dispose of a fucking DEA agent without a trace at the same time?

Time to stop worrying about being inappropriate and just get on with it.

'Come on,' he said gently, helping her to stand up. 'Come on,' he coaxed her onto the fresh towel he'd put down on the bathroom floor. She stood there wrapped in her own towel, her dark blue eyes fixed to the floor, shivering violently.

She was in shock, John knew that much. He needed to get coffee into her, coffee and sugar and probably some kind of food. He'd never hit a drive-thru on his way to dispose of a body, but there was a first time for everything, right? And he found himself unable to be annoyed with this exotic creature who had broken down in front of him. He was too conscious of who – of *what* – she was, even though she'd never come out and said it to him.

She was one of the ones that had been destined for a basement somewhere, a sex slave for somebody's sick whims. Only for some reason, she'd been spared. Not that you could exactly call this spared, but at least she was still alive. John liked to pretend that that shit didn't go on, but he knew the world he was a part of.

'Come on,' he said. He took the towel from her and started to remove her underwear as discreetly as he could, without looking at the magnificence that lay beneath. He dressed her in clean clothes and then he led her past the grisly reality of the man she'd just killed and down to his car outside.

***

That fucker had been heavy, even with the majority of his blood on the mattress. John contemplated calling a crew to pick up Murphy's body and dispose of it, but once he'd safely wrapped Murphy's lifeless form in the thick comforter and hauled his ass into the back of his pick-up, he'd come to the reluctant conclusion that it would be too risky to involve anyone else. He'd have to come straight back after he ditched Murphy and get someone to help with the mattress disposal.

He picked up McDonald's for Mariana on the way to the county morgue. He ordered her fries, black coffee, lemonade and an apple pie, trying to cover all bases: sugar, salt and fat. She'd perked up a little bit since downing the coffee, the caffeine and fresh air bringing a little colour back into her cheeks.

They got to the morgue soon after Ana had started in on her large serving of fries, John backing the pick-up into the crematorium entrance. She looked up, alarmed, brushing salt off her fingers onto her jeans.

'Where are we?' she asked, looking him in the eye. And just like that, she snapped out of it.

'Stay here,' John said, hopping out of the car. He'd changed from his leather jacket into a black hoodie while they were waiting in the line at the drive-thru, and he flipped the hood over his head before he stepped into the open. 'I've got to speak to somebody. Do not get out of the car. You hear me? Last thing we need is for both of us to show up on the security footage.'

She nodded, and then he was speaking to his buddy, who fetched a steel gurney.

'You want to hang around for the remains?' the attendant asked, as John slipped him an envelope fat with cash. John briefly contemplated taking the ashes home and pissing on them, but decided against it.

'Nah,' he said. 'Just make sure they're gone.'

Less than ten minutes later, Murphy – along with the bloody sheets, towels, Mariana's blue dress and comforter – was roasting nicely in the crematorium furnace. And within the hour, the man who'd caused Ana and everybody else so much grief was nothing more than a pile of ashes and dust.

While John was waiting for Murphy to be pulverised into ash in the furnace, he placed a call to one of his contacts who cleaned crime scenes for a living. He was also a guy who was very fond of cash, and extremely discreet. John gave him the passcode for Mariana's apartment and the guy promised to have the whole place sparkling in two hours. John didn't see how that was possible – she'd tracked blood everywhere – but he didn't argue. If the guy did it that quickly, he'd get a fat tip in his envelope when John dropped off the payment.

When John got back to the car, she was still there. *Thank Fuck*. The last thing he needed was a crazy woman running around with traces of Murphy's blood on her. He'd washed her as well as he could, but there'd still be traces of blood and DNA in her hair, under her fingernails.

'Someone's cleaning your apartment right now,' John said to Mariana. 'He's a pro. He'll wipe every surface, take away every trace of DNA. If the cops come tomorrow, they could turn the place upside down, and the only place they'd find evidence is under your fingernails.'

'Thank you,' Mariana said quietly, looking at him with a sense of wonder.

John shrugged. 'It's kind of what I do. Nothing to be proud of.'

He hated what he did. Despised it.

Still. There were worse things. At least he didn't have to have any part with those poor fucking girls they trucked across the country—

'John,' Ana said, breaking his thoughts.

'Yeah?' he replied gruffly, pulling out of the county morgue parking lot and making a sharp turn onto the service road.

'What happens now?'

He glanced over at her. Her hands were clasped in her lap, and her arms were covered in goosebumps. 'Here,' he said, tossing his leather jacket at her, still a little damp from the shower. 'Put this over yourself. You're shaking.'

She took the jacket wordlessly and draped it across the front of her like a blanket.

'What happens now,' John repeated, watching as headlights whizzed past in an endless succession. Before he knew it, he'd pulled onto the I-5 and they were racing down the freeway.

'What happens now is that we kill some time until they get all that pesky blood out of your apartment.'

'My bed—' Mariana started.

John held up a hand. 'Trust me. When we get back in a few hours, you won't be able to tell the difference.'

She settled back in the seat. John saw the exit he was looking for up ahead, the one that would take them to a secluded spot where he liked to go and sit when he didn't want to be bothered. As he pulled off the road and up a narrow, unpaved track, Mariana tensed beside him.

'Don't worry,' he said, 'I'm not going to kill you.'

CHAPTER TWENTY

MARIANA

John stopped the car in a small clearing of trees and cut the engine. In front of us was a small man-made lake. It was nothing special, and it looked neglected and overgrown, but it was deserted out here, and that was the whole point.

My mind was struggling to catch up after the night's events. What the fuck had just happened? I'd killed Murphy.

Murphy was dead.

I was freaked the fuck out, but I couldn't pretend that I wasn't also feeling victorious in some strange way. He'd committed the ultimate sin when he killed my family, and I'd returned the favour in all its bloody glory. He'd died vulnerable and afraid, and that brought me a small measure of relief, knowing the way my parents and siblings had endured their final moments.

'So,' John said, his hand resting on the steering wheel, 'I think you owe me an explanation.'

It was the least I could give him.

'How do I know I can trust you?' I asked softly.

John laughed. 'I think we're beyond that, don't you?'

I nodded. 'I suppose so. But it's a long story.'

He turned to me and smiled, his perfect teeth glinting in the weak moonlight. 'Honey, I've got all night.'

I licked my lips and rearranged the leather jacket so it was covering every bit of my exposed flesh.

'Have you got a cigarette?' I asked suddenly.

John nodded, pointing at the glove compartment. I opened it, took out a lighter and a pack of cigarettes, and lit up. The smoke burned my chest, and I had to resist the urge to cough. But I liked the feeling. It reminded me that I was alive.

I wound my window down a few inches and blew the smoke out.

'I can't tell you,' I protested, but I was tired and my words lacked conviction.

'Why not?' John pressed. 'What do you think I'm gonna do? Do you think I'm going to use it against you?'

I shrugged. 'Maybe. I have secrets that nobody knows, John. Not Dornan. Not Emilio. Nobody.'

'Like secret sons?' He raised his eyebrows.

I nodded my head in resignation. 'Didn't buy the baby brother story, huh?'

'You don't react like that over a photo of a child that isn't your own,' John said softly. 'I'm a father. I know a mother when I see one. And I swear on my fucking life, I will never tell anyone what you tell me. You can trust me, Ana. I just helped you get rid of the body of a DEA agent. Not any DEA agent, either. The one that happens to work for our boss. I could be killed for that. So let's start hearing some of these secrets so I can understand what the hell I've just gotten myself into.'

He had a point. And I was tired of keeping everything locked up inside. It was lonely and exhausting.

I told him everything. I started with the night Este and I were confronted back in Colombia, how he'd been murdered in front of me on the ground in a dirty alley. How I'd offered myself up in exchange for Emilio letting my family live. How Dornan had saved me from a certain fate as a slave at an auction. How I'd do it all again if it meant my little blue-eyed son would be safe. I told him every last detail, the way my father took Luis from me, how Murphy had killed my family, and now how I'd exacted the ultimate revenge against him, luring him into my bed with promises of a dirty fuck and instead blowing his brains out.

I told him everything, until I was empty, and in the end there wasn't a single word left inside me.

CHAPTER TWENTY-ONE

JOHN

She told him everything, and as soon as she'd finished, all John wanted to do was bundle up every word that she'd uttered and hand it back to her. Because there was power in knowledge, but there was danger, too. And now he was a very real part of it. By helping Ana to dispose of Murphy's body, and now hearing about her family, about her son, he was a pawn in whatever game she was playing at.

He didn't respond. Didn't ask questions. Didn't say anything for a very long time.

'Did you burn the photos?' he asked finally.

She shook her head. 'Not yet.'

'Burn them all.'

'John—'

'Stop. Stop talking for a minute. I need to think. *Fuck.*'

He yanked the car door open and got out, his mind going crazy. So his suspicions about her had been right the entire time. Emilio fucking owned her. Dornan had 'saved' her in some way, but she was still the property of the Il Sangue Cartel, and, to a lesser extent, the Gypsy Brothers.

And he'd fucking known that kid was her son! But he guessed she had reasons to distrust him. He was a Gypsy Brother. And he was Dornan's best friend.

He heard Mariana's door open and close, and then she was approaching him, in front of the pick-up. He'd left the headlights on, and they cut a stark line across her midsection.

'John. I just want to go home, okay?'

He twisted his head to look down at her, this beautiful, exotic creature he'd been watching from the wings for the better part of a decade. He remembered the way her mouth had felt, the tight buds of her nipples hardening without him even touching them. His cock stirred painfully at the memory of lusting after a woman who could never be his.

Her dark blue eyes were bloodshot. She looked incredibly tired. And yet she was still exquisite.

'You want to go home?'

She nodded. 'I'm sorry. Maybe I shouldn't have told you all of that.'

He raised his eyebrows. 'It's a little late now, isn't it?'

'Why did you kiss me?'

'What?'

She looked at the ground. 'Never mind.'

He stomped back to the car, not taking his eyes off Mariana as he dragged his door open. She stood immobile for a moment, and then followed, sliding into the passenger seat. He folded himself in behind the steering wheel and jammed the key into the ignition, but didn't turn it.

'Let's just go,' she said softly. Almost like she was pleading.

He pulled the keys out of the ignition and pocketed them, turning on her. He was frustrated. He was pissed.

'You should have told me,' he said finally.

'Told you what?' she asked, but her expression said that she already knew what he was going to say.

'You lied to me. You told me that photo was of your brother. I *knew* I was right. I knew he was your kid. What am I supposed to do with that? What am I meant to do when Dornan finds out? What do you want from me?'

Panic registered in her eyes. She freaked the fuck out and jumped out of the car again. Christ, it was like they were going in circles. Why couldn't she just trust him?

She stood in front of the car again, looking left and right. Was she going to try and run? It seemed absurd, but he'd seen his fair share of runners before. When people panicked, they either froze, or they fled.

And judging by the way Mariana was twitching at the front of his car, she was getting ready to flee.

'Fuck,' John muttered under his breath, jumping out of the car and cutting her off before she could head into the thick trees. He reached for her wrists, found them, and used his body weight to press her against the hood of the pick-up. She was crying. He'd never seen her cry before tonight, not in all the years he'd known her, and now it was like she couldn't stop. Killing someone for the first time would probably do that to you, he surmised grimly. He could barely remember anymore, he'd done it so many times.

'There's nowhere to run,' he murmured in her ear. 'Never has been. You know that, Ana. Don't be stupid.'

She whimpered against him, struggling against his grip before going limp.

'Fuck you, John,' she whispered weakly.

He wrapped his arms around her. 'Shhh,' he said. 'We all go a little crazy the first time we kill somebody. You're gonna be okay. Everything is gonna be okay.'

He didn't believe that, of course, but he'd never tell her that.

CHAPTER TWENTY-TWO

MARIANA

It was almost dawn when we finally got the call to go back to the apartment. I walked tentatively up the stairs, stopping short when I reached the door. John glanced around, checking out the surrounds. Weary, and still sporting mascara-streaked cheeks and puffy eyes from all the crying I'd been doing, I went straight to the scene of the crime, to find it ... sparkling.

Seriously, the place was spotless. Someone had brought in a new mattress, made it with fresh sheets and a duvet I normally kept aside for winter nights. The pillows were plumped, new towels hung over the rail in the bathroom beyond.

They'd even sprayed air freshener – not too much, just enough to mask the cloying smell of congealed blood – and lit a scented candle on my dresser. I stared down at my new mattress, almost expecting to find a chocolate on my pillow or something, but it seemed the service stopped there. My heart lurched when I realised the photos of Luis had been hidden in the mattress. Fuck!

'My photos,' I muttered. 'Shit!' I started opening drawers randomly, praying that whoever had cleaned up had thought to put them somewhere instead of destroying them along with the mattress.

John entered the room, alarmed. 'What's wrong?' he asked.

'You mean apart from the obvious?' I replied, rummaging through sweatpants and pyjama shirts in my bottom drawer.

'What are you looking for?' he asked.

I closed the drawer and straightened, scanning the room as I tried to think of other potential hiding spots. 'Photographs,' I said quietly. 'They were hidden in the mattress.'

John nodded, handing me an A4-sized envelope. I peered inside, breathing a sigh of relief when I saw the photos were all intact. 'Thank you,' I murmured.

'Don't mention it,' John replied, shifting from foot to foot as he glanced into the bathroom. *Oh yeah, the bathroom where we'd just groped each other like horny teenagers while a man lay dead six feet away.* An awkward silence descended upon us, and I wasn't sure where to look. Eventually, my eyes landed back on his lush lips.

'I don't feel anything,' I blurted out, going to sit on the side of my new/old bed. 'Shouldn't I feel something?' I put a hand to my chest and imagined the barren heart that beat beneath my ribcage. The heart of a killer now. And instead of feeling remorse, I was too busy imagining kissing Dornan's best friend again. My life was a fucking mess.

'I think all the feels happened in the car,' he said, and I didn't know whether to laugh or cry at that.

'Right,' I replied.

'I was kidding,' he added. 'I'm sure if you killed someone you actually cared about, you'd be feeling something. But right now, based on your track record with Murphy, I'd be feeling pretty fucking relieved if I were you.'

I nodded. 'You're right. That must be it.'

Neither of us spoke for a beat.

'What happened to your family?' he asked, and I heard the caution in his voice. Fresh tears sprang to my eyes, and I blotted them away with the sleeve of my T-shirt before they could roll down my cheeks.

'Somebody tied them all up and poured gasoline on them,' I said flatly. 'There was a fire. Nobody made it.'

'And your boy?'

'He's safe.'

'Where is he?' John pressed.

I stared openly at him, keeping my mouth shut. I'd never tell.

'So you let me dispose of a DEA agent for you, but you don't trust me?' He looked affronted.

I shrugged. 'Would you tell me where your daughter was, if the tables were turned?'

John nodded. 'Yeah, okay. I get it. So what are you going to do?'

I looked around. 'What do you mean, what am I going to do? I'm going to do nothing. I'm going to lie low and figure out what the fuck my next move is.'

'You gonna run?' John probed.

'Of course I'm not going to run,' I replied. 'Running means dying. Besides, like you said, there's nowhere to go.'

John nodded again, deep in thought. 'When's Guillermo due back?' he asked finally.

'A few days, I think. I'm not sure. Depends if his mother gets better or goes downhill.'

'I'll sleep on the couch,' he said.

When I raised my eyebrows, he gave me a look that said it was out of my hands.

'It's almost five,' he said. 'I'll crash for a few hours, have some coffee, and leave.'

'Suit yourself,' I said, not moving from my spot.

He left the room, and I lay down on my side, rolling myself into a ball. I didn't mean to fall asleep. I wanted to stay awake, and try to process the last several hours, but before I knew it, I was out like a light.

***

I woke to hear a fist beating on the front door. I jerked awake, sitting straight up in my bed. John appeared, looking tired as fuck. He hadn't slept then. He had a gun in one hand, gesturing for me to stay put.

'Open the fucking door!' a female voice yelled outside.

Allie. That hadn't taken long.

'Murphy's girlfriend,' I whispered.

John's eyebrows shot up as he looked at the front door, apparently undecided.

'Let me answer it,' I said.

John reluctantly moved out of my way, training his gun at the door.

'She's DEA too,' I murmured, pushing his gun gently to his side. 'Let me deal with this.'

I opened the door just a crack, to find a very irate Allie Baxter standing on my front stoop, dressed in jeans and a black Ramones T-shirt. She was off duty. Still packing, though, I could see, judging by the gun holstered on her hip.

'Do I know you?' I asked.

She laughed bitterly. 'You know who I am. Where's

Christopher?' she said, barging past me into the apartment. I followed her in, closing the door warily behind me.

'Who the fuck are you?' she asked John, who was sitting at the dining table. He had one hand under the table, and I was ninety-nine percent sure he was aiming a gun at Allie, waiting for her to make one wrong move.

Great. I didn't need another dead DEA agent in my apartment. I'd just gotten rid of the last one.

'I could ask the same of you,' John snapped, resting one palm on the table.

She looked from me to John, disgusted. 'I'm looking for my partner,' she said, scanning the place casually. 'DEA Agent Chris Murphy. Have you seen him?'

I shrugged. 'He was here for maybe ten minutes last night. He needed a favour.'

Her eyes lit up at that. 'Oh, he did, did he?'

'Yeah,' I said slowly. 'And then he left.'

She looked dubious. 'What kind of favour?' she pressed.

I shrugged. 'I can't tell you that. It's confidential.'

She rolled her eyes. 'Oh, come on,' she said. 'You're not even a real accountant.'

'She is, actually,' John interjected. 'Four years at night school. So client confidentiality stands, and it's something we take *very* seriously.'

I looked back at him, surprised. He was pulling this out of his ass. I'd never be allowed to go to something like night school. What point was there in official certification when, on paper, I'd died nine years ago in the Californian desert and been buried for my family to find?

'We? As in the Il Sangue Cartel? I see you're wearing a Gypsy Brothers patch. Maybe I should bring you down to the station for questioning.'

'I'm sure that would be really helpful for your partner,' John replied coolly.

'Allie, we haven't seen him,' I repeated, going back to the front door and holding it open for her. *Get the fuck out of my house, you corrupt bitch.*

She glared at both of us one last time before storming out. Before I could close the door, she stuck her hand out.

'I'll be watching you, Mariana,' she said. 'One false move and your ass is mine.'

I slammed the door in her face so hard it echoed, staring at it for a long while before I made my way back to the dining table. John was looking at me expectantly, waiting for some sort of explanation.

'What was that?' he asked.

I filled him in on her last visit, and on the things Murphy had said to me before I killed him.

John whistled. 'So, they were about to take off together, huh? And take Emilio down in the process?'

'Something like that,' I confirmed. 'He didn't really give me anything specific to go on. Just wanted me to transfer a lot of Emilio's offshore cash into an account for him. And the way they were acting, she was in on it, too.'

John rubbed his hand against the stubble on his chin, seemingly agitated. 'She's a liability,' he mused. 'She'll keep coming back to you until she finds him. And he's in little pieces in the bottom of a crematorium somewhere, so we need to deal with her before she gets the DEA officially sniffing around.'

'Huh,' I said, an idea forming in my mind. 'How hard do you think it'd be to get her bank account details?'

***

We drove in silence to the strip club. In less than twenty-four hours, I'd gone from being a numbers girl to a part of the action. Blood and bullets, all in a day's work.

John had what I needed within an hour. I didn't ask him how. He was the president of the Gypsy Brothers, a motorcycle club controlled by the most powerful drug cartel along the west coast. He could pretty much get whatever he wanted.

'We doing this now?' he asked.

I shrugged. 'Sure.'

The beauty of working for Emilio was that he had all sorts of safeguards already in place when it came to the money laundering business. For instance, he'd had someone install an IP address blocker in my laptop, so that if any heat ever came down on the finance side of things, it couldn't be tracked from our location inside the club. I didn't understand a lot about the intricacies of it, but I did know that if Emilio thought that it was good enough to hide the staggering amounts of money he was channelling out of the country, then it would surely be good enough for what I planned to do.

'That's a lot of money,' John said, watching over my shoulder as I set up three transfers that equalled more than a hundred thousand dollars, from three of Murphy's bank accounts into Allie's. They'd appear as cash deposits, and with over a hundred grand sitting in her bank account by tomorrow, we might just be able to avoid both her wrath and the DEA's attention. It wasn't the nicest thing to do to somebody, but that bitch had threatened my son, and if she was Team Murphy, then she had to be stopped.

John pulled out a burner phone he'd just purchased, along with a voice-altering device, a small box that he taped to the handset and plugged in using a small cord. He punched in a number and let it ring.

'Yes, hello,' he said to whoever answered. 'This is Timothy at First National Bank, West Hollywood. I'm calling in relation to a large deposit one of your staff has just received. We've had this account flagged as being connected to an international drug cartel run by Emilio Ross.'

The person on the end of the line said something I couldn't hear, and John smiled. 'Of course. Her name is Alexandra Baxter.'

He ended the call and broke open the back of the phone, pulling the SIM card out and snapping it in half.

'You want to get some breakfast with me?' he asked. 'I'm starved.'

I smiled.

CHAPTER TWENTY-THREE

MARIANA

Another Sunday.

I was sitting at the end of a long conference table where the Gypsy Brothers normally held church. This week, however, they were convening in the dining room, and Emilio had commandeered the large boardroom. Across from me, Emilio looked at his watch, and Dornan paced. That was unusual. Dornan was normally in his own meeting with the rest of the Gypsy Brothers, not in here discussing finances with his father, myself and Murphy.

'Are we waiting for Murphy?' I asked finally, looking at the door. He'd been dead less than a week, but neither Dornan nor Emilio seemed to know this.

Emilio unbuttoned his suit jacket and sat back against the large conference table that took up most of the room, so that he was painfully close to me. I wished he'd just sit across from me like any normal person would.

'That's why we're here,' Emilio said, studying me carefully. 'I'd like you to check on something for me. Did you bring that computer?'

I nodded, patting the bag at my feet.

'Get it out,' he said impatiently. 'I don't have all day, girl. Pull up Murphy's bank accounts. The offshore ones.'

So they were missing him already. I was glad we hadn't waited any longer to transfer money from Murphy's accounts into Allie's.

I took a measured breath and reached for the laptop, pulling it from its protective bag. I placed it on the table in front of me and fired it up, navigating to a browser and looking at both of them expectantly.

'Wi-fi password?' I asked. Dornan and Emilio stared at me like I was speaking another language.

'I need an internet connection to log on,' I explained. Seriously, how had these two gotten this far? With people like me to take care of the details, I realised. Great. I loved enabling rich assholes to get richer. My job satisfaction was at an all-time low.

Dornan disappeared, coming back a few moments later with a post-it note. He stuck it to the desk in front of me, making a concerted effort not to touch me at all. He never gave me the silent treatment. I keyed in the wi-fi password, waited for it to connect, and navigated to the website we used for our offshore trade accounts. Within a few moments, I'd pulled up all six bank accounts that I had set up for Murphy in various places in the Caymans and Europe.

I turned the computer to face Emilio, and watched his face with great interest. He sucked a breath in between his teeth, tapping the screen. 'What's this?' He angled the screen so I could see it, pointing to the last transaction on Murphy's account, from only days ago.

I moved closer. 'It's a transfer,' I said. I tilted my head, feigning confusion. 'A few.'

Emilio looked at Dornan, an eyebrow raised. 'Who the fuck is Alexandra Baxter?'

I'd had her pegged as an Allison. Alexandra was much too refined for that woman.

I shrugged.

'Wait,' Dornan said. 'Alexandra. Allie?'

Emilio ran his tongue along his teeth. 'His partner?'

'I'm pretty sure she was more than that.'

Emilio looked pointedly at me. 'Can you find out where she's spending this money?' he asked.

'Not unless I have her online banking details,' I replied. 'I'm not a hacker. I don't even know who we're talking about.'

Emilio waved his hand dismissively. 'We'll go over the figures tomorrow,' he said, turning back to his son. 'You think he's skipped town?'

Dornan lit a cigarette. 'I told you not to trust that motherfucker.'

'Oh, really? You got someone else in the DEA who we can use?'

Emilio glared at me. 'Go.'

I stood and pointed at the laptop, and he placed a hand on it. 'I'll get this back to you,' he said, staring at me until I had the urge to squirm.

I looked at Dornan, but he wouldn't even meet my gaze. Slowly, I turned and left the office, half-expecting one of them to pull out a gun and shoot me in the back.

CHAPTER TWENTY-FOUR

MARIANA

'Your boy left early today,' Guillermo said, as we walked down Santa Monica Boulevard together. I shrugged, worry churning in my stomach. Something was up, and I didn't know if Dornan suspected me of cheating on him with his best friend or murdering his associate. Something was definitely not right and the stress was eating me alive. After the meeting, I'd hung around outside, waiting for Dornan to drive me back to the apartment. It was what we always did on a Sunday. And, sure enough, he had driven me home. He'd pushed me down onto the bed (complete with brand new mattress), fucked me and left without saying more than two sentences to me. I was feeling adrift.

'You miss me while I was gone?' Guillermo asked, teasing me.

'Always,' I replied, smiling. 'Your mom okay?'

'She'll be dead if she doesn't stop eating so much fucking fried shit. I tell her, Mama, you're diabetic, and then I catch her eating cookies and shit behind my back.'

I cleared my throat. 'Who does that remind me of?'

He rolled his eyes. 'Ha ha, very funny. I work out, don't

I?' Guillermo pointed to the large gym we were approaching. 'So I can eat whatever I like.'

'I don't think that's how it works,' I replied. 'I'm pretty sure fried chicken every night is going to kill you, regardless.'

'Whatever. I've got arms today,' Guillermo said as we walked into the gym, referring to his workout. I nodded, splitting off into the female changeroom as he entered the male one. I threw my bag in a locker, grabbed my towel and headphones and headed out to the cardio area. I wasn't feeling particularly energetic after the way Dornan had literally come and gone, and so I stepped onto the easiest piece of equipment – the treadmill. The great thing about our gym was the view – like my apartment, it overlooked Santa Monica Beach. The treadmills had prime position, up against the floor-to-ceiling glass windows that framed the beach like a postcard. It was a beautiful day, so I cranked the treadmill up to an easy jog and started running. Back before the gym had opened, Guillermo and I had always run along the path that stretched along the beach, but nowadays he was more concerned with bulking his arms up and talking with his dude friends in the weights section.

I closed my eyes for a moment. I pretended I was running along the beach, instead of on this treadmill. The beach I could always see, but not touch. I imagined there was sand underneath my sneakers, instead of a rubber belt that looped endlessly around and around. I imagined dark blue eyes, a small boy's hands reaching out to me, the warmth of the afternoon sun on my face.

'Excuse me,' a male voice interrupted my daydream.

'Jesus Christ!' I muttered, standing on the sides of the treadmill and holding my chest with one hand, panting, as I stopped the treadmill belt with the other.

I looked to the source of the voice, my eyes landing on a clean-shaven face belonging to a guy with a short crew cut and thick arms that Guillermo would be envious of. *He looks like a cop* was the first thing I thought. Maybe a marine. His hair was the dead giveaway. No one as attractive as this guy would willingly shave their hair that short. He was tall, with striking green eyes that were circled with light brown at the edges of the irises. You'd call them hazel, except that the two colours were completely separate. The green and brown didn't intersect.

'Nope. I'm not Jesus Christ. Sorry if I startled you there.'

My treadmill had slowed to a stop, and I stepped off the edge. Bad idea. I hadn't realised how tall this guy was and now he was towering over me.

'Look,' I said, 'I'm flattered, but I'm kind of busy.' Before he could open his mouth again, I turned and hightailed it over to Guillermo, who'd been oblivious to the entire exchange. Some bodyguard.

He was lying on a bench, sweat pouring from his face as he did chest presses.

'You here to spot me?' he asked through gritted teeth, a vein bulging on his forehead as he lifted again.

'I don't think I'd do it justice,' I said, stealing a glance at Not Jesus Christ. He was talking to the woman at the front counter, flashing his white teeth at her.

'I'm going to shower,' I said, leaving Guillermo to his workout.

I was washing my hair in a shower stall when a voice cut through the silence and almost made me scream.

'Mariana Rodriguez?'

I opened my eyes, which was stupid, because shampoo-laden water flooded them straight away. Fuck! I pulled my head away from the stream of water, my hand searching for my towel.

The hook was empty.

If someone had taken my towel, I'd murder them. I knew how to do that now. I rubbed the water from my stinging eyes and opened them again, gasping when I saw the guy from the treadmill, Not Jesus Christ, leaning against the wall outside the shower, my towel dangling between his thumb and forefinger.

I snatched the towel from his grip, pressing it to my chest.

'Don't worry, I wasn't looking,' he said. The cocky bastard then proceeded to give me a once-over, from head to toe, an amused smile plastered across his face.

'This is the women's changeroom,' I said emphatically, still holding onto the hope that he'd come in here by accident. 'And I think you've got me confused with someone else.'

'You ran away from me,' the guy said. 'We could have done this out there, when you weren't completely naked.' He looked like he was about to dissolve into laughter. 'And I know the name you're going by now, but that's not the name your parents gave you, is it?' As I opened my mouth to argue, he held up a xeroxed copy of my old Colombian driver's licence, complete with my photo.

Shit.

'How do you know my name?' I asked. 'Are you a cop?'

He grinned. 'Maybe. Are you a friend of Christopher Murphy's?'

I wrapped the towel around me. 'No.'

'Do you know him?' The man pressed.

'Maybe.' Fuck. Motherfucking fuck. Was he going to arrest me? Great. I was going to get arrested, and I wasn't even wearing clothes.

'He seems to be missing. You haven't seen him around, have you, Mariana?'

I shook my head. 'Nope.'

He nodded, as if we were sharing a secret or something. He reached into the pocket of his sweatpants and pulled out a business card. 'In case you see him anywhere,' he said, 'or if you want me to take you out to dinner. You eat too many microwave meals with that Mexican schmuck who lives with you.'

How did he know what I ate? Who I lived with?

I took the card, every nerve in my body screaming at me to run as I turned it over.

My eyes just about bugged out of my head when I read the name that was printed on the thick paper.

Agent Lindsay Price, FBI. The name Murphy had given me before I shot him. The same man who was investigating Emilio and the entire cartel.

Jesus Christ.

I looked up from the card, but Agent Lindsay Price was gone.

CHAPTER TWENTY-FIVE

Three weeks later

I locked eyes with Dornan, his smirk eliciting a small smile from me as he squeezed his erection, dropping to his knees on the floor in front of me. I saw a bead of pre-come glistening on the head of his cock and my mouth watered at the thought of licking it up. *Later.*

Now it was my turn to receive.

It was difficult to lie on my new mattress, legs spread, a tongue dragging on my clit and not enjoy it. I was a sexual being. I practically lived for these moments. But lying on this bed, all I could think about was Murphy and the look of sheer terror on his face as I shoved a gun between his teeth and pulled the trigger.

Focus. This is your time with Dornan! And it was bonus time, too. It was a Monday night. He never showed up on a Monday night.

An orgasm was building inside me, much slower than normal, not through Dornan's lack of effort. I gasped, squirming as he pushed one finger inside my tight slit, then two. When he added a third finger, I started to moan. The feeling of fullness was overwhelmingly satisfying, and it was enough to send me up over that elusive edge as I fisted the sheets and cried out, my pussy clamping around his fingers as I came.

As I crested down the precipice of my afterglow, a delicious warmth settling in my belly and limbs, Dornan stood over me, thrusting into me in one fast stroke so that I cried out. He didn't last more than a few seconds before he, too, was spilling himself inside me.

I imagined John taking his place for a split second, how his face would look as he came, and blood rose uncomfortably in my cheeks. *Don't think about him. Do not think about him!* What was wrong with me? Suddenly, after nine years with Dornan I was thinking of somebody else just because we'd shared one stupid kiss?

No. I refused to give in to those treacherous feelings that had been gnawing at me ever since I'd kissed John in the shower.

But it raised an interesting question.

If I had a choice, who would I choose?

'Goddamn, that was hot,' Dornan said, pulling out of me and handing me a towel.

I cleaned myself off as well as I could, kissing Dornan's stubbled cheek as I headed for the shower. He responded by grabbing a handful of my ass and squeezing, sending little shooting pains through my body that felt oddly good. I pushed him away playfully, knowing if I wanted to get a shower and some dinner I'd have to avoid another round of our lovemaking.

Standing in the middle of my bathroom, I stared at the empty shower cubicle as the image of John continued to taunt me. What the hell was going on with me? Was I hell-bent on self-destruction? Was I just looking for something to distract me from the memory of Murphy's death stare?

Turning away from the shower, full of self-loathing and arousal, I ran myself a bath instead.

The water pressure was excellent in the building, and it didn't take long for the tub to fill. I dumped a good amount of lavender body wash into the warm water and sank my weary body into the bubbles, sighing in appreciation as my limbs were caressed by liquid heat. It felt divine, and I reminded myself to take more baths.

I grabbed a rolled-up towel from the stack next to my head and nestled it under my neck. I wouldn't be long. I'd have a quick dip, a wash off, and then get dried and join Dornan out in the kitchen, where I could hear him banging and crashing things. I thought of Murphy, of how he'd died here in this very apartment and nobody had even mentioned his absence to me, yet.

I thought of John, closing my eyes as I let my mind drift. I barely ever relaxed, always too tightly wound, but grief and killing had numbed me in some small way. I was too exhausted to be strung out. I was too devastated to be anxious.

It felt good to let go a little. I skimmed my fingertips over fresh self-inflicted wounds on my thighs, the ones I'd been able to hide from Dornan despite what we'd just done. It wasn't too hard. I was good at redirecting his attention to other parts of my body.

The ends of my long hair floated loose around my shoulders, weighed down by the water, as I remembered John's hands on my head, on my face. I licked my lips and thought of kissing him. I shook my head from side to side, trying to rid myself of thoughts of somebody I'd never be able to touch like that again, and remembered the way he'd cradled me.

I opened my eyes and sat bolt upright in the bath. Fuck! I just wanted to zone out for a while, but all I could think of was John.

CHAPTER TWENTY-SIX

DORNAN

He resisted the urge to join her again in the bath. He'd fuck her all night if it were up to him, but he'd heard her stomach growling. The woman needed sustenance. So instead he lit up a cigarette and went searching in Mariana's kitchen.

He had one go-to dinner recipe: Italian breaded chicken and tomato salad. His mother had made sure to teach him at least one recipe before he'd married his first wife. He'd been such a kid when he left home, but at least he'd been able to cook a meal.

He was looking for breadcrumbs in the pantry when his eyes fell on a tub of flour. That'd work. He could use some egg and flour and smash up some of the stale bread he'd found in the freezer.

He reached for the cream-coloured canister but paused when he saw what looked like spaghetti sauce smeared along the side.

Or blood. Dornan had a way of judging situations. He got gut feelings about things and they almost always turned out to be correct. And his gut wasn't thinking about pasta sauce when he looked at that red smear.

He was thinking about who'd been bleeding in his apartment, and why.

He took the canister out carefully, focusing on the tiny red smear. His senses were in overdrive, his nose conditioned for such macabre things. He scratched his fingernail against the dried red substance and took the cigarette from his mouth as he brought his fingernail up to his nose.

Blood. It was blood. But that wasn't the only thing ringing alarm bells in his head. He shoved the cigarette between his teeth again so both of his hands were free.

Christ, how heavy is this flour? The canister weighed a ton, strange since it was made of plastic. Dornan set it down again, prised the lid off and, on a whim, stuck his clean hand into the white powder.

His fingers hit something solid.

He stopped for a moment, his heart rate increasing in excitement. But it wasn't the kind of excitement that was, well, exciting. It was the buzz of a thousand angry bees, settling in his chest, demanding to know what the fuck was hidden in this container.

No secrets, that was one of his cardinal rules. It was the thing that kept their dysfunctional relationship from completely imploding, from being eaten away by bitter distrust.

He got a grip on the solid thing hidden underneath the flour and pulled it out, sending a plume of white dust around his face.

It was a ziplock bag, wrapped around something about the size and weight of a cheap, disposable cellphone and a charger. He unfolded the layers of plastic, his temples throbbing with the weight of the possibilities.

He glanced towards the bathroom, hearing movement, and tipped the hard rectangular weight into his palm.

Well, what do you know. It was a fucking cellphone.

A rage that presented as cold indifference began to build in his body, the humming of the angry bees only drowned out by the desire for an explanation. But his gut said there was no explanation. She'd deceived him. She'd probably been talking to her family this entire time, risking everything he'd built so carefully. He located the power button and pressed it with a clean thumb, turning the phone on. It immediately demanded a passcode. Dornan jumped as his own phone began to ring, sending the long spike of ash that had been holding on to the end of his half-smoked cigarette onto the ground by his feet. He glanced down at the phone, hearing Mariana as she moved around in the bedroom. He dropped the phone back into the bag, and shoved it back into the flour canister, giving it a good shake to bury it properly. He replaced it in the pantry and swept the small bits of flour that had powdered the counter onto the floor.

Dornan braced against the counter with one hand as he took his cellphone from his jeans just as it stopped ringing. One missed call from Viper. Dornan's stomach dropped as he remembered what had happened earlier in the day.

Another day marked another round at the fulfilment centre, another assortment of women boxed up, sold and ready to be delivered.

Only today had been different.

The cells that contained the prisoners were soundproof, part of their brilliant design. X-rays couldn't pierce the boxes they'd had constructed to herd people like cattle through secure checkpoints and border crossings. But when you moved that little swatch of plastic to the side, sometimes the screams got out.

Today had been one of those days.

Cell four. As soon as he'd looked through the glass, Dornan wanted to die. Because there was a woman, maybe in her late twenties, and she was huddled on the floor, screaming. And she was pregnant. Very pregnant.

Dornan had slammed the viewing pane shut, but it was too late. He could still hear her screams, even though he knew that couldn't be possible. He finished up the other thirty-nine checks, most of them the same as cells two and three. Nobody else had screamed like her. Nobody else had made themselves heard like the woman about to become a mother, who vocalised her doom for nobody except Dornan to hear.

And then they were gone, loaded onto the truck, which rose on its bridge and disappeared into the sub-floor, ready to be driven out to make the scheduled deliveries.

His phone rang again, snapping Dornan out of the garish daydream he kept replaying in his mind. He looked at the screen. It was Viper again. Viper, along with a couple of other Brothers, was running the trucks tonight. It might be a situation. He took the cigarette from his mouth and hit answer. 'Yeah?'

The sound of heavy tyres on asphalt greeted him through the phone. It was loud running trucks back and forth across the zig-zagging roads of the United States.

'We got a situation, boss,' Viper yelled over the steady hum of the road noise. 'I need you to help with a clean-up. I'm pulling in to the rest stop.' He gave an address and Dornan memorised it. A clean-up. That was code. It meant one of the prisoners had died. *Fuck*.

Mariana walked into the loungeroom in a thin bathrobe that left nothing to the imagination, her hair wrapped up in a peach-coloured towel. Dornan fought the urge to tie her up and either interrogate her or fuck her senseless. His cock ruled him when it came to Mariana Rodriguez.

'Which one?' Dornan asked.

'Number four,' Viper replied immediately, and Dornan's suspicions were confirmed.

'Boss, it's fucking bad. Hurry.'

The line went dead.

Mariana hovered at the edge of his vision. 'Everything okay?' she asked.

Dornan raised his fist and slammed it into the counter hard enough that the whole thing shook. The immediate pain calmed him somewhat, but all that rage, all that fight, was still waging a war inside him.

'What happened?'

He raised his gaze to look at her. He drank her in for a good few moments, taking in the curve of her hips, her tiny waist, full breasts and slender neck before his almost-black eyes settled on her dark blue ones. Was she a liar? Had she betrayed him? If she hadn't yet, *would* she?

'Get dressed,' he ordered, thinking about the secret cellphone. He wouldn't let her out of his sight until he got an explanation.

'Why?'

He frowned. 'That's for me to know,' he said, his tone vicious. *Go on, resist me. Argue with me. Do something so I can fucking explode.*

But she didn't. Of course she didn't. Her ability for feeling out situations was just as good as his, if not better. She heard the danger in his voice and decided to obey. She nodded, pulling the robe tighter around her as if it would somehow protect her.

'What should I wear?' she asked softly.

'Something warm,' he said. 'Bring your coat. And your sneakers. We might be digging a hole.' He looked at her pointedly.

Her eyes went big and round, but she didn't protest. She backed away, not letting him out of her sight until she was at her bedroom door.

He hated scaring her. He loved her. But a small part of him, the vengeful, suspicious man inside, was secretly pleased.

CHAPTER TWENTY-SEVEN

DORNAN

FUCK.

It was the single thought that ran through his head.

Fuckfuckfuckfuckfuck.

Viper was opening the back of the large trailer, his face ashen. And there was the muffled, yet unmistakable sound of a woman screaming.

Dornan hadn't spoken a word to Mariana the entire way here. Almost an hour it had taken to arrive, and now she was sitting in the car, probably wondering why the hell she was suddenly privy to cartel activities. Well, until he found out where that fucking phone had come from, and what it was for, she'd be spending a lot of time with him. Fuck what anyone else thought. John might be the boss in name, but Dornan was the leader of this Gypsy pack.

'Why the fuck did you call me out here?' Dornan growled. 'You go in there and you shut them up!'

He was angry. He was angry and so fucking tired of having to deal with this shit day in and day out, so tired of the souls who begged him to let them go – and worse, the ones who didn't beg, the ones who sat in the deepest corners of their cages, defeated, having already given up on life. Yeah, he preferred the fighters. They still had a spark of something in their eyes. Hope.

Not that it ever did them any good.

'I've got a truck full of fucking deliveries,' Viper hissed, his normally tough demeanour dropped completely, replaced with horror. At first Dornan wanted to smash his fist into Viper's face, kick him in the ribs until he bled, and beat the sense back into him. He was a Gypsy Brother, for fuck's sake. What did he expect? Sometimes messed-up shit happened.

But now Dornan was here, and he could hear it too.

Screams that sounded like death cries.

He rushed to the back of the truck, holding his jacket up over his face to keep the rain off. The doors to the container had already been slightly propped open by Viper. The screams grew louder, more insistent, as Dornan walked down the narrow space in between stacks of containers that housed their flesh trades for the day.

He already knew which woman was screaming. Her eyes had been screaming at him inside his mind all goddamn day.

He got to the box, placed his hand on the lock and took a deep breath.

She'd been heavily pregnant. He had known that when he saw her earlier, but it didn't matter. It never mattered. They always took the pregnant ones at least a month before they were due, to make sure they made it to their new owner before they gave birth.

He opened the lock and pulled at the door. His gaze landed on a naked newborn baby, its face a purplish-blue, covered in blood and gunk. Its umbilical cord trailed away between the woman's legs. The woman's face was ashen; she'd lost a lot of blood, more than she should have, judging by the way she was practically bathing in the stuff. She was almost unconscious, her head drooped to one side. She was sipping in little breaths of air, sweat dripping from her forehead. This had never happened before. They'd had women die before, but they'd never had one give birth. This was *not* supposed to happen.

'Holy fuck,' Viper said, over Dornan's shoulder.

'Get outside and keep watch,' Dornan hissed, turning and shoving Viper. He scurried away, seemingly very happy to get away from the woman and her newborn.

'Please,' the woman whimpered. She was so pale, she looked like a corpse, but she was alive and she was still conscious. 'Please help my baby,' she said.

'She needs a doctor,' Mariana said behind him, taking off her coat. 'That baby needs warmth.'

Dornan turned on her, towering over her. 'What the fuck are you doing back here?' he roared. He looked past her to Viper. 'I said to fucking keep watch!'

Viper shrugged, clearly on the cusp of madness. Useless fuck. He'd deal with him later.

Mariana was dressed in just a thin striped tank top and black skirt, her cashmere coat bundled up in her outstretched hands as she glared at Dornan defiantly. 'Are you going to help them? Because if you're not, *move.*'

Speechless, Dornan moved aside so that Mariana could squeeze past him. The space between the containers was narrow, the air thick with horrors best left unseen, and Mariana was here in the middle of it. For so many years, he'd kept a wall up between the reality of what he did with these women and his Mariana, his secret, his dark lover. He'd drawn a line in the sand and made sure she never, ever knew of these things.

Except now she'd seen, and she knew, and would she ever forgive him? A hidden cellphone was nothing compared to this. Dornan knew this.

He watched wordlessly as she knelt down beside the woman and scooped the baby up. The baby wasn't moving. Wasn't crying. It was blue. She stuck her fingers in its mouth and made a scooping motion, then turned it over and hit it lightly on the back a couple of times. The baby started to pink up almost immediately, making a little mewling sound.

'Pocketknife,' Mariana said. 'Sterilise it first.'

Moving on a mixture of autopilot and awe, Dornan unclipped his knife from his belt and clicked it open, taking his lighter and heating the blade for a few seconds to kill any germs. Luckily, he was obsessive about keeping it clean. It had seen its fair share of death and destruction, and you could never be too careful with pesky things like DNA. The knife was clean enough to eat your steak dinner with.

He handed it over to Mariana, pocketing his lighter as he watched her work. She balanced the wrapped baby on her knees and grasped the long, coiled cord that attached baby to mother, cutting through it in one swift motion. Dropping the knife, she stood and turned, thrusting the baby into Dornan's arms. 'Hold him,' she said, and Dornan did. He was struggling to keep up with this. It was a *him*? This was already getting way too fucking personal.

Viper appeared with a large woollen blanket he'd retrieved from the cab of the truck. Mariana made a crude knot in the baby's umbilical cord with bloodied fingers.

'We need to get them to a hospital,' Mariana said, addressing Dornan and Viper.

Viper looked between Dornan and Mariana with a mixture of shock and brutality on his features. 'We ain't taking anyone to a fucking hospital,' he said. 'This is a one-way ticket.'

Mariana ignored him. 'Dornan,' she said, stepping closer to him and peering at the tiny baby, nestled safely in her cashmere coat. 'We have to help this woman. The baby needs to go get checked out, he's cold. He needs warming up.'

Dornan fixed his gaze down at her, frustrated and ready to fucking explode. 'How about I decide?'

Mariana's face twisted into a look of disgust as she reached for the baby and nestled him against her own chest protectively. Dornan was relieved to be free of the baby, who felt like a ticking time bomb in his arms, a burden that was going to be dire no matter which way he played this shitty set of cards he'd been dealt.

'Maybe decide before they both die,' she said pointedly, turning to look at the woman. The mother. The dying woman. Dornan made a mental note to chat to Mariana after he'd sorted this situation. She was getting far too mouthy for his liking. He thought of the hidden phone again and his gut twisted uncomfortably.

The bleeding woman, the product that was holding this entire gig up, was still slumped in the corner. She looked completely fucked. Dornan had to move her, couldn't deal with her in this tiny, confined space. And this truck needed to move, now, before the goddamn highway patrol drove past or something.

'Viper, help me move her into my car.' Mariana looked visibly relieved. Viper opened his mouth to protest and Dornan shook his head emphatically.

'Wait in my truck,' he said, offering his car keys to Mariana. She looked at them for a long moment before taking them. 'Put the heat on,' he added. She didn't answer, just made for the truck's cab and slid into the driver's seat, holding the baby close to her the entire time. A moment later he heard the engine of his truck turn over. Fuck. This was the worst situation he could have imagined.

'Dee, why the fuck are we putting this broad in your truck? She's made us both, and the accountant,' Viper said, pointing towards the truck where Mariana waited. 'And you know Daddy Dearest would never let a live one go, even if we could help the bitch.'

Dornan levelled his gaze at Viper. 'Shut the fuck-up,' he hissed. 'Do not question me. I will handle this. Now. Help me pick this woman up, and for fuck's sake wrap her up first so we don't get blood all over us.'

They got blood all over them anyway, despite the carefully wrapped blanket. Lucky they both wore black almost all the time. It came in handy when you didn't have time to change your clothes in between all the bloodshed and chaos.

A few minutes later Dornan was in the backseat, holding the woman who'd just birthed her baby and who was now dying in his lap in the back of his truck. She'd started to wail as soon as they moved her. It was obvious she was in a lot of pain and her noise was affecting the baby. He was bellowing as well, and it was enough to make Dornan want to eat his own gun just to get some fucking peace and quiet for five seconds.

'You want me to come back there so you can drive?' Mariana asked quietly, twisting in her seat to address him. 'Or I can drive them to the hospital.'

Dornan smiled at her, at his beautiful Mariana. This could be her in his arms, if things had played out differently. He'd saved her, but he'd learned a long time ago that you couldn't save them all. In fact, she was the one and only he'd ever managed to grip tight and raise out of the vicious fate she'd been careening towards, and there had been *thousands.*

He didn't speak. He didn't have to. He saw the recognition on her face as she clutched the baby tighter.

'Dornan,' she whispered. Pleaded. He felt his heart shatter and burst under the pressure of her horrified gaze.

Her horror would have to wait. The woman in his arms was bleeding to death, and she was dying in pain, and he just wanted to take some of her suffering away.

He put a hand to her neck and felt her pulse. It was erratic, all over the place. She cried out again and her back arched off his lap. Her eyes were full of anguish and the shock was starting to wear off. The woman was suffering.

'Will you help my baby?' she asked, looking up at Dornan with eyes that wouldn't be seeing this world for much longer. How did she even have the energy to form words? It was the strength of a mother's love, he reasoned. She wouldn't let go until she was sure her child would be safe.

Dornan nodded, feeling tears prick in his eyes. Goddamn, why did this have to happen now? Why had Viper called him? Why was it always his fucking problem when anything went wrong?

And why had he chosen this night, of all nights, to bring Mariana with him on a run, knowing she might be exposed to something like this, something that had the power to ruin everything between them. She'd never look at him the same way after this, and that realisation broke him inside. He'd done everything to protect her and she was probably going to end up hating him like every other woman he'd ever let in.

The woman's eyes fluttered shut and she relaxed a little. 'Promise me you'll take him some place safe,' she whispered.

Dornan wiped a tear from his cheek, and another. He shouldn't be upset. He didn't have the right to be upset and he certainly didn't deserve to get fucking emotional about this woman and her kid.

'I promise,' he said and he wasn't lying. In that moment he made a decision. He didn't know if it was wrong or right, but he did it because nobody deserved to suffer that much. He couldn't take her to a hospital, couldn't get her medical attention, because if she spoke – and they all spoke if they escaped, even the ones who promised they wouldn't – she'd be able to lead the police right to them. She'd seen Dornan's face, and Mariana's and Viper's. She's seen the interior of the truck, knew there were more like her.

No, he couldn't take her to hospital.

'Dornan!' Mariana protested, twisting in her seat.

'It hurts so bad,' the woman whimpered against his chest, opening her eyes again and peering up at him. 'Please, make it stop hurting.'

He nodded, stroking her hair with one hand and reaching for his gun with the other. It had the silencer attached, a small mercy. He pressed the barrel to her chin.

He hugged the woman to his chest one last time, tears forming in his eyes as he looked down into hers.

If she knew what was about to happen, she didn't show it. She didn't panic. She didn't struggle.

'Stop!' Mariana screamed.

A single, muffled shot rang out into the clear, soundless night. It was much too quiet, too controlled a noise to be the bang that ended a life, but it had ended it nonetheless.

She died instantly. Dornan made the sign of the cross above her face and let her sag onto the seat. He'd have to replace it. He'd have to replace the entire interior of the car, but it didn't matter. She was dead and nothing else mattered.

Mariana held the baby to her chest and stared at him with dead, loveless eyes.

'You fucking *monster*,' she said, turning away from him.

The baby began to cry.

CHAPTER TWENTY-EIGHT

MARIANA

'You could have taken her to the hospital.' I'd said the words at least three times, but it was too late.

His eyes glistened. 'She was going to die. Do you understand me? She was never going to make it to a hospital.'

We were parked in front of a 24-hour pharmacy. Dornan had just gone in and bought supplies at my insistence, despite him protesting that we really needed to get 'the kid' to a hospital. Diapers, bottles, a tin of formula and sterilised water were my list of demands and he didn't argue with me for once in our relationship. The baby was suckling on my little finger impatiently as his mother lay dead in the backseat.

Dornan shook a bottle full of powder and water to mix it together.

'How did you know to do all that?' Dornan asked.

I looked down into the baby's face, holding back tears. He'd just killed the baby's mother to save her a long and protracted death. A mercy killing, but why did she have to die at all? It wasn't fair.

Life wasn't fair.

'I watch a lot of television,' I replied wearily, cradling the baby closer as I looked up at the pharmacy sign. My breasts ached as I remembered holding my own little son, feeding him from my body just one time before they took him away. If I could have nursed that baby in the car, I would have without hesitation. He might not have been mine, but the sad fact was, he no longer belonged to anyone. I wondered who his father had been, if he'd even known. If he was a good man, or if the woman had already been a captive when she fell pregnant. Was this baby the result of something pure or something evil?

Not that it mattered. He was a baby and by definition that made him innocent. He was brand new and sacred and exquisite. And he'd been born into the pits of hell.

'You can't keep him,' Dornan said, almost reading my thoughts. 'Don't get too attached.'

I turned my head up to face him as he handed me a small plastic bottle of formula. 'Shut up,' I snapped at him, my mother bear out in full force as I snatched the bottle from his outstretched hand.

'Here, little baby,' I cooed, placing the teat near his mouth. God knows how long he'd been lying on the floor of that horrid little death cell before we'd arrived. It couldn't have been too long, because he hadn't been getting air until I scooped the gunk out of his throat so he could breathe, but it had been long enough that he'd turned cold and blue next to his dying mother.

'I mean it,' he said.

'I know,' I said forcefully. 'But what do you expect me to do? Leave him on the side of the road?'

Dornan scowled. 'We're dropping it off at the hospital.'

'He,' I clarified. 'The baby is a he.'

Dornan started the truck and it roared to life. We drove for a long time. As the trees began to thicken, I looked around outside, the baby now asleep, nestled against my chest. I'd managed to get a few drops of the formula in and to warm him up, at least.

The road we were on looked ... Familiar.

My stomach lurched as I saw where we were pulling into. The county morgue. The same place John and I had come to dispose of Murphy's body. Christ. The Gypsy Brothers and the Il Sangue Cartel were really keeping this place in illegal after-hours business.

I couldn't bear to watch as Dornan dragged the dead woman from the car and onto a waiting steel gurney. He paid the guy a wad of cash and then we were driving again. Pretty soon we were pulling into a dark corner of a run-down hospital parking lot. I could see why Dornan had chosen this place. It looked decrepit, and I doubted it had anything like surveillance cameras to record that we were ever there.

I hugged the baby tight. Was it terrible that I didn't want to let him go? Dornan came around to my side of the truck and opened my door, holding his arms out.

I looked down into the little boy's sweet face. He was still all squashed from having just been born, but his face would spring up soon, his nose would pop out, and he'd be cleaned up. He was going to be breathtaking.

'Ana,' Dornan urged.

With great reluctance, I handed the baby over. I didn't meet Dornan's gaze. I couldn't.

I couldn't bear to look at the man I loved, and see a monster instead.

CHAPTER TWENTY-NINE

MARIANA

An hour later, we were parked at an old warehouse by the wharf. It had started to rain again, gentle drops that pattered against the roof and windows with a soothing rhythm.

Me, I was exhausted. I'd been firing on adrenalin-fuelled cylinders for a couple of hours and I was ready to pass out and sleep for a year. I felt heavy. I felt so unbearably sad.

Plus, Dornan had just dropped a bomb in my lap the size of California. The drugs and guns weren't the only things the Gypsy Brothers and the cartel had been trafficking and selling. In fact, those were just two small parts of the sickening empire Emilio was running, and the third, very large, very lucrative part of his game was people. Women, mostly. Girls. No wonder he'd been so keen to sell me.

It was his fucking specialty, selling girls as slaves.

Not for the first time, I was weirdly appreciative of my unorthodox upbringing, the way I'd had to keep my father's finances afloat by money laundering and shady bookkeeping antics. It was those skills, self-taught and honed to a sharp edge, that had kept me alive all these years. It was those skills, dirty as they were, that had kept me out of the back of a truck on a one-way trip to hell itself.

I demanded answers as soon as we'd steered away from the hospital where he'd run in and deposited the baby on the reception desk. My heart still ached, knowing that little boy needed a mother, knowing he didn't have anyone. At least he was someplace safe. At least now he had some kind of a chance at survival.

'How could you do that?' I asked Dornan as we both stared straight ahead through the front window of the truck. The rain was swiftly growing heavier, and I couldn't help but remember the night I'd killed Murphy.

Dornan took off his shirt and offered it to me. 'Put some water on it. Clean yourself up.'

'Don't you think about them?' I continued, taking the balled-up shirt from his hand. 'Don't they *haunt* you?'

'Never thought about it,' he said quietly. 'Never let myself. Never made eye contact. God gave me sons and I was grateful. I never had to worry about them. I knew they'd be alright. I knew they'd never be a part of that world. At least, not the part that suffers.'

'You mean, the way you don't suffer? Because you're covered in the blood of a woman you just killed, and I'm pretty sure that look on your face is suffering.'

He smiled sadly. I took a section of his shirt and poured bottled water on it, offering it to him first. He had more blood on him than me. I'd only been dirtied by the blood that was on the baby from his birth. Dornan was soaked from head to toe in the blood of a woman he'd cradled in his arms as he shot her in the head. The gun might have been silenced, but a silencer didn't stop the blood spatter. Luckily, he was wearing dark clothes, and being soaked in blood didn't look too different from being soaked from the rain unless you looked closely.

'What made you realise what you were doing was wrong?' I asked.

Dornan flexed his blood-stained hands, took the wet shirt I was holding out and started to rub at his skin. I saw the twitch in his jaw, the way he ground down on his teeth. He was suffering. 'Always knew it was wrong,' he replied quietly, so quietly I almost couldn't hear him above the torrential downpour outside. 'Just never gave it much thought. Never really wanted to think about what happened to them. Where they ended up. If they survived.'

'So what changed?' I asked.

He cleared his throat, then examined one relatively blood-free hand before switching to the other. 'John went to prison. Caroline was pregnant when he was arrested and she just went completely fucking psychotic without him there to watch her every day. I had her committed twice. That bitch charmed the pants off those fucking doctors, convinced them she was on the straight and narrow. They let her out. They always did. By the time the baby was due, I was letting her shoot up on the couch in my office just so I knew she wasn't lying dead in a gutter somewhere with John's baby inside her.'

'Juliette,' I said.

He nodded.

'Caroline had that baby. And then she disappeared. Left the hospital, stole a car and drove away. And guess who was left holding a baby girl?'

My stomach twisted anxiously. 'You.'

He shrugged, dropping the shirt between us. 'Babies are all the same, boys or girls. They cry, they eat, they sleep. But she could've been *my* daughter. That's when shit got hard.'

Something about that made me angry. So, so angry.

'Then why do you do it?' I snapped. 'Because Emilio says you have to? Tell him you can't. Tell him you *won't*.'

'I've got too much to lose,' he replied, squeezing the steering wheel until his knuckles turned white. 'I have *responsibilities*. Much as I'd like to, I can't ever tell him no.'

He stared at me pointedly, maybe the first time he'd looked at me since he'd started recounting his story. His dark eyes glimmered as lightning lit up the car and I felt a lump rise in my throat.

'I do what I do and I get what I get,' he said, reaching across and taking my chin in his hand, brushing his thumb along my lower lip. Something about what he had said – *I get what I get* – stabbed at me painfully, demanding more answers. A creeping suspicion suddenly flooded me and I felt sick.

Me. He was talking about *me*.

I swallowed thickly, my voice momentarily frozen. I opened my mouth to speak and nothing came out. I felt his eyes drilling twin holes into mine.

'Don't tell me you're talking about me,' I said, tears forming in my eyes. 'Please.'

'I've never lied to you,' he said, taking my hand and squeezing it, almost to the point of pain. 'So if you don't want me to tell you ... *don't ask*.'

So it was me. I brought my hand up to my mouth, intending to muffle a sob, but Dornan took hold of it at the last moment. He held it up to the dim light in the truck. There were fine specks of blood. I watched, sobbing openly, as he took my hand and used a clean section of the shirt to gently wipe my skin.

I didn't stop crying. I was so damn emotional all of a sudden, and I didn't know why.

He loves me enough that he'll damn everyone else in the world just to keep me safe. And I hate him for it, but I love him for it more.

I thought of the kiss with John, and shame burned deep inside me. I was a horrible person. How could I be thinking about him while Dornan was shipping people off to their deaths in exchange for my life? I'd called him a monster, and he'd been doing all this for *me*? So that I was safe? So that Emilio didn't make good on his threats to sell me off as a slave, too?

'You should stop,' I whispered.

He took the shirt from my skin and placed it on the dash.

'No, I mean, you should stop ... whatever it is you're doing with these people – and if he gets rid of me, at least you'll be able to sleep at night. I'm not worth all this, Dornan. I'm not worth any of it.'

His head jerked to face me, and then his hands were coming at me, wrapping around my waist, pulling me to him. It was awkward, but the truck was spacious enough that he could drag me onto his lap without me getting jammed between him and the steering wheel. I ended up facing him, one knee on each side of his legs, our noses inches from each other.

I looked up at the roof of the truck. It was grey felt. I attached my gaze to a small tear in the fabric and held it there, trying to stop the tears from flowing down my face even as I felt my teeth chattering.

'Ana.'

I shook my head.

'*Mariana.*'

I tore my eyes from the roof and looked at him, because I knew if I didn't he'd wait all night for me to meet his gaze.

'You want to know what I wished for on my birthday?' I asked him. I couldn't even see anymore, everything warping and bending through the film of my tears.

I felt his warm hand cup my cheek, his thumb brushing away a steady stream of tears as he waited for me to speak.

'I wished that things were different,' I whispered. 'I wished that we could be free.'

He chuckled mirthlessly. 'You'd still love me if we were free?'

I nodded. 'So much,' I replied. 'More than you'll ever know.'

His face softened, almost as if my words had relieved some worry inside him. 'I can't imagine why,' he responded, his voice low and husky, cutting through the continual buzz outside as the rain continued to fall.

I tilted my head. 'You saved my life,' I whispered, shaken by the veracity of my words. 'You didn't even know me and you did that. You're still doing that. I'm sorry I called you a monster. You're not a monster. You're the reason I'm alive.' *And I don't deserve you.*

He moved his thumb along my lips, his gaze shifting between my eyes and my mouth. Something stirred within me and I had the sudden urge to kiss him.

So I did. I placed my hands on either side of his face, his stubble deliciously rough against my cold hands, and leaned down, covering his mouth with mine. He responded immediately, one of his hands fisting my loose hair, the other curling possessively around the back of my neck, pulling me even closer. His tongue met with mine, and a shiver ran down my spine. Our love was electric. Always had been. It was the rest of our lives that was the problem. But right here, right now, in the howling wind, with the metal and glass the only thing between us and the pouring rain, it was almost too easy to pretend that nothing else existed. I melted into him, wanting more, always wanting more. It was like we wanted to devour each other, and maybe one day one of us finally would. But until then, we were here, together, the windows fogging up under the pressure of our heavy breathing and the rain raging on outside. I felt wetness pool between my legs as my heart pounded faster, begging to get closer, to get rid of these annoying layers of fabric that separated us so that we could be together again.

I could feel him beneath me, hard already. Hard for me. And I wanted him. I needed him.

We didn't even need to speak to know what came next. Ours was a dance so finely tuned, we were in perfect sync. We needed each other like we needed air to breathe, and when time forced us apart, it made the world a dull place. Until we met again. And then sparks flew when we collided.

It had been like this for nine years, and I didn't ever want it to stop.

He placed both hands on my hips and lifted me off his lap. I braced myself against the steering wheel as he unzipped his jeans and reached into his boxers, gripping his cock with one hand as he brought his other hand up my thigh, underneath my skirt. I moaned softly as he pushed my panties to the side, his fingers pressing against my wetness. I moaned again, louder this time, when he pushed two fingers inside me.

My noise seemed to be enough to drive him over the edge. He slid his fingers from me, and I ached from the sudden loss. I needed him. I needed him inside of me, around me, possessing me in every way, and I needed it now. His mouth found mine again as he jerked me closer, my legs straddling him, the swollen head of his erection pressing impatiently against my entrance.

His hands went to my hips and his fingers dug into my flesh as he pulled me down onto him. His size made me gasp, all the air leaving my lungs as the noises coming from my throat were drowned by our kiss. With agonising slowness, Dornan pulled me down onto him until I was stretched and full with him, ready to explode.

'Fuck, you're so wet,' he groaned, his voice gravel and smoke, his hips continuing to rock, each thrust driving me wild. His hands moved from my hips, down to my thighs, and I flinched as he pressed against the fresh cuts I'd made just hours ago in the bath. He saw me flinch, connected the dots. His entire body stilled; though I could tell he was desperate to keep slamming up into me, his eyes demanded answers. He pulled the hem of my skirt up to my belly so I was completely exposed to him, scars and all.

'Mariana,' he said in a strangled voice. 'What did you do?'

I closed my eyes, fresh tears pricking at them, demanding release. 'Nothing,' I breathed.

I felt one of his hands wind around my long hair and tug, forcing my face to his.

'Open your eyes,' he murmured.

I did. I opened my eyes to see his own dark eyes staring back, the iris and pupil merging almost seamlessly in the dim light. His eyes looked black, but they were beautiful to me. They were everything.

'Why?' he asked. 'I thought we agreed no more.'

I didn't want to talk about it. I didn't want to think about it. I just wanted to come undone, to shatter apart with him inside me. I just wanted to forget how fleeting our time together always was. But I had made a promise to him not to cut myself years ago, and I had broken that promise.

I put my hands on his shoulders and started to move again, skin against skin, his hand tightening in my hair.

'Mariana,' he demanded. 'Stop.'

He pulled on my hair to the point of pain. I yelped, stilling.

'Look at me.'

I didn't want to look at him. He made me nervous when he spoke like this. I just wanted to fuck and forget. I squeezed my eyes shut.

'Fuck me,' I begged. 'It doesn't matter.'

'No.' He growled, shaking me. 'Tell me what this is. Tell me why. You know how many arteries are here? You could have fucking bled to death.'

You could have fucking bled to death. Yeah. I could. And the saddest thing was, he wouldn't even be the one to find me because he was always somewhere else.

'You're gone so long,' I croaked, opening my eyes again. 'It was my way of keeping track. You're always gone for so fucking long.'

His face fell as he studied the cuts on my thighs, his fingertips hovering over the barely healing flesh. 'That's what this is?' he said, his voice thick. 'You do this until I come back?' He looked closer. 'These are the days?'

My cheeks burned with shame as tears fell on them.

'Baby,' he said sadly. 'You know I want to be there every fucking minute with you. You know I can't live without you. I fucking love you. *Only* you.'

I nodded, still crying. My orgasm hovered inside me, almost there but not quite, and I wanted release. To not have it was painful. I lifted slightly on top of him and pushed down, and he resumed his almost violent lovemaking, leaning back and grabbing my hips again. He thrust deep inside me, and that was all I needed, that single stroke enough to make me cry out as I came around him. A few seconds later he tensed, his fingers digging into my flesh as he slammed home one more time and spilled himself inside me, hot and wet. We sat, unmoving for a few moments, before I disentangled myself from him and returned to the passenger seat, rearranging my clothes as I went.

It was completely fucked up, the way we went from arguing about human lives to screwing each other's brains out, but it seemed our primary method of connecting was physical. Our love demanded to be shown, to be shared. It wasn't good, and it wasn't right, but it was what we had.

Dornan leaned over and kissed me as he was zipping his jeans up. The kiss quickly grew frantic. Dornan grabbed a handful of my hair and tugged me closer to him, and I moaned into his mouth.

I came to my senses. Realised what we'd just done in here, in the same car where he'd shot and killed a woman. I planted a hand on his chest and pushed, breaking the kiss.

'I'd die without you,' he said, releasing his grip on my hair and grasping my chin between his thumb and forefinger.

No, I thought, *I'd* die without *you*. And it wasn't just about love. It was reality. Without him, I would have been dead a long time ago.

Just as I was opening my mouth to respond, the world exploded.

With a deafening bang, glass flew everywhere. I automatically put my hands to my face, feeling the shock of something devastating vibrating through Dornan's entire body. Cold rain that felt like tiny shards of ice poured into the car, the driver's side window no longer there. When the glass stopped falling and it was just the rain driving sideways into my face, I let my hands fall from my eyes, let them open.

I squinted through the icy sheets of rain that were pouring into the car.

Oh God. Dornan was bleeding. His chest was a mess of blood, the clean bullet hole cut neatly into his shirt bursting forth with dark red blood. Someone had just shot him through the fucking window, and he was literally bleeding out before my eyes.

Another shot rang out and I dove to the side as the front windscreen crashed down around us. Pain blossomed in my arm and I realised I'd been hit. *I'd been shot.* I fought the urge to throw up, gagging as the pain radiated through my shoulder and all the way down to my hand. I refused to look at it, though. If I looked at it I'd probably pass out, and if I passed out I'd probably die. We both would. So I swallowed back vomit and pretended it wasn't happening as I tried to get Dornan to respond. I felt glass cutting my arms and legs, everywhere I moved causing more lacerations.

'Baby,' I whispered, my voice barely audible over the rain.

Nothing. His face was ashen, and he'd slumped to the side a little. I felt sorrow rise inside me as I saw what someone had done to *my* Dornan. His belt was still unbuckled, for Christ's sake. They'd taken him at his most vulnerable moment and shot him from afar, like fucking cowards.

My blood was pumping hot, despite the cold. I could feel the white-hot anger searing a path through my circulatory system, my breath coming out in short, shallow pants.

'Dornan,' I said, a little louder this time.

Through the blistering rain, I heard the dim noise of a car door opening.

Close. Whoever it was, whoever had done this – they were close.

I didn't want to sit up and look, though, because I might get a bullet in the face for being nosey. No, I huddled in the footwell, pulling gently on Dornan's arm so he slid down onto his side, his arm and ribs pressing awkwardly over the glove compartment that separated our seats. It looked uncomfortable, the way he was twisted, but it was better than him being dead.

I snapped out of the haze I'd been in since the first bullet hit, reaching automatically for my purse and, within it, my gun.

Thank you for giving me a gun. Thank you for teaching me how to aim. Thank you for all of it.

Footsteps crunched over loose gravel, and my heart beat furiously.

Don't die, I silently urged Dornan. *Please, don't fucking die on me.*

I'd seen enough death to last me a lifetime.

And then the gravel stopped crunching.

CHAPTER THIRTY

MARIANA

There was a woman at the window and she was aiming a gun at Dornan. Her eyes were fucking wild. Her hair was long and dark, and her black T-shirt was stuck to her. She was soaked to the bone, but that didn't seem to be affecting her aim.

Allie.

Murphy's crooked cop girlfriend, the bitch he was planning to run off with. My stomach lurched painfully at the realisation that she had not, in fact, taken the money I'd transferred into her bank account and run like she should have. I would have run. What an idiot.

She was a cop. She'd just shot Dornan. And now, now she was here to finish the job. To finish me.

'Thanks for the money, cunt,' she spat, glancing at Dornan before shifting her aim to me. Bile crept up my throat and I swallowed forcefully – a side effect of having a gun pointed at your face.

'I'll ask you once,' she said, her teeth grinding each word out with measured rage. 'Where is Christopher?'

'Allie,' I protested. 'Come on. I know you're not that stupid.'

She screamed, frustration written all over her face. 'I don't believe you!' she said, wild with emotion.

'You were in love with him,' I realised all at once. I'd assumed she was just in with Murphy for the money. But the way she said his name – Where is *Christopher*? – the anguish in her words. She had loved him. And now she knew, beyond a shadow of a doubt, that he was dead.

'Allie, he was a bad man,' I said, trying to placate her. 'He killed innocent people. I did what I had to do, and I'm sorry.'

'Oh, you're sorry?' she repeated shrilly. 'You'll be sorry, bitch, when you watch your dirty biker bleed out in front of your eyes.'

My heart sank – she wasn't going to be talked around. She was here to get vengeance.

'Allie,' I said softly. 'Murphy wanted me to go with him when he left. He tried to rape me. He was naked in my bed when he died.'

She scoffed. 'You're a fucking *mexicunt* working at a strip club owned by bikers. You don't get *raped*. You open your mouth and suck and say thank you after you swallow.'

Well, I didn't know what to say to that. 'He asked me to go with him. He was never going to take you. It was all a set-up for you to take the fall.'

'Stop lying. Stop talking!' She shook the gun in front of her for effect.

I took a deep breath and tried to think. *Think!* It was hard to strategise with a gun aimed at you.

'Why Dornan?' I asked. 'He didn't do anything. He wasn't a part of this, Allie.'

'He's never without his fucking whore,' she spat, looking at me. 'Seems only fair that you get to watch him die before I kill you.'

I breathed heavily, my heart thundering in my chest – its low roar filling my ears. My gun, concealed by the darkness, itched in my hand. I had to shoot her. I had to *stop* her.

Allie sneered, letting her aim drop as she looked down into Dornan's lap.

I took my chance. It was the only one I was going to get. As the bitch laughed at Dornan's state of undress, I raised the gun in my hand and squeezed the trigger.

I recoiled as I felt her blood hit my cheek, the deafening roar of my gun something that was becoming far too familiar. Allie hit the dirt before I'd even blinked, the force of the bullet sending her straight onto her back. I rummaged around on the floor in front of my feet, looking for my coat, until I remembered I'd wrapped the baby in it. Desperate, I held a hand to Dornan's red-soaked chest as I tried furiously to slow the tide of his blood. With my other hand, I searched in his pockets for his cellphone. I scrolled through until I found John's number, called it, let it ring.

No answer.

I didn't know who else to call. I couldn't call his wife, could I? I wasn't supposed to exist. And Emilio? No way would I call that bastard.

Jesus Fucking Christ. Who else *could* I call? Not the police. I'd just killed a cop. Again.

John. Answer your fucking phone!

He didn't answer. Again. I looked at Dornan. The blood. There was so much blood.

Above the steady drum of the rain, I heard someone groaning outside. Allie? Jesus. Was she still alive? With a quick glance at Dornan, I opened the door as quietly as I could and slipped out, pressing it shut behind me. The rain was brutal, and I could barely see in front of me. I circled around the back of the pick-up, gun at the ready, my eyes searching for any movement as I rounded the corner of the truck and happened upon Allie. There was blood coming from her mouth, and she had one arm outstretched, reaching clumsily for her gun. In her dying moments, she didn't look like a bitch anymore. She looked like a sad, lost little girl, and I silently cursed Murphy for pulling her into this hellish existence. For the first time, I realised that she was younger than me, just a young woman who fell in love with the wrong man. Don't we all.

She saw me, and her hand reached for the gun more desperately. Before she could grab it and take a shot at me, I placed my foot on her wrist, pinning it to the ground.

She looked up at me, her eyes sad.

'I thought he loved me,' she choked.

I nodded, crouching beside her. 'That's the thing about men like Murphy,' I said softly. 'They're not capable of love, Allie. They only know how to destroy.'

She seemed to soften, her eyes closing momentarily. 'I don't want to die,' she whispered, blinking back tears. 'I didn't know.'

I nodded sympathetically, pushing her hair back from her face.

Before she could do anything, I placed my hand over her mouth and squeezed her nose shut between my thumb and index finger. Shock and realisation lit up in her eyes as she thrashed her head back and forth beneath my grip.

'That's the difference between you and me,' I said to her, as she clawed at my hand and sucked against my palm for air. 'I'm old enough to know better.'

She struggled some more, her face turning a dirty shade of grey as her eyes bulged with effort, then finally dulled and froze open, unseeing.

I took my hand away from her mouth, noticing her blood all over my palm. I wiped it against my side, reasoning that the rain would wash the rest away soon enough. Fuck. I'd just killed somebody with my bare hands. I was turning into someone I didn't even recognise. The terrifying part was the complete detachment I felt. Of course I killed her, I reasoned to myself. She was going to kill me. She shot Dornan.

And that was that. No guilt and long-winded self-searching. No beating myself up about taking another life. No, I took one look around to make sure I wasn't being watched, grabbed Allie's ankles, dragged her over to the side of the wharf and rolled her into the fast-flowing water below.

It sucked her down in a second.

And then she was gone.

***

I vomited beside the car, the act somehow cleansing me. That last vestige of doubt gone. Replaced by numb victory, by indifference. I was exhibiting all the classic symptoms of shock, but I didn't feel shocked. I felt like a fucking lion who'd just protected her cub. Allie had tried to fuck with someone I loved and I had put an end to that.

Dornan.

He was bleeding. He needed help, and quickly. I raced back to my side of the car and yanked the door open, sliding in and assessing how much worse he'd gotten since I'd been gone. He looked bad. His skin was so white he looked like he'd just fade away.

I remembered what he'd said to me. *I do what I do, and I get what I get.*

The knowledge of what he'd done – what he was still doing – slammed home that night. The fact that he was here because of me, that I had somehow caused this just by existing, just by being with him. He had wanted me back then, nine years ago, and he was still paying the price. I saw the souls of every life he'd trafficked in his grief-stricken gaze when he'd told me, and now I might have to live with the fact that we'd never get to say anything to each other again.

The only thing worse than finding out that the man you love has been dealing in innocent lives, buying and selling them and sending them to their deaths, is knowing that he did it for you.

On the floor at my feet, I saw the discarded baby bottle, the tin of infant formula, all covered in a thick sheen of his blood, and I began to shake.

CHAPTER THIRTY-ONE

MARIANA

I struggled to get Dornan out of his seat and into the passenger seat. He was two hundred pounds of solid muscle and rage.

Please don't be dead. You're not dead. You can't die.

You can't die.

I finally got him across the seat, first pulling his upper body across into my seat, and then hoisting his legs over one by one.

I started the ignition. 'Dornan,' I said. I could barely see, with the rain and my tears, but somehow I made it onto the road and towards the hospital where we had dropped the baby off. I prayed that they didn't have cameras. I prayed that they didn't know it was Dornan.

I prayed that this wasn't going to be the end for us.

Ten minutes later, I was back at the hospital, John opening my car door, worry plastered across his features. He'd finally answered his phone, and he must have broken several laws speeding to get to the hospital before me. On the other side of the car, two Gypsy Brothers – Jimmy and some other dude – were pulling Dornan out of the car and onto a gurney. The shock on Jimmy's face was evident as he saw his VP's blood all over the passenger seat. Wait until he got a look at the backseat.

Once Dornan was on the stretcher, some nurses raised the sides and whisked him away. Everything was moving too fast for me, and I felt like I was drowning.

'Get rid of the car,' John roared.

Jimmy moved into action, grabbing my waist and hauling me out of the way. He got into the truck, which was still running, and took off before he'd even closed the door.

I looked down at what was in my hand. My coat, the one that I'd wrapped the baby in. The one that I'd used to try and stem the flow of blood from Dornan's bullet wound.

Life begins, and life ends. So fast. So fleeting.

John grabbed my elbow. 'Hey,' he said gruffly, tugging me into the hospital. Dornan was gone, stretchered away somewhere into the labyrinth of hallways that faced us in the entrance, maybe gone forever.

There was somebody else with us. I couldn't remember his name. Which was bizarre, because I'd seen him enough times at the clubhouse that we were practically acquaintances. But my brain had frozen, stuck on a loop of horror – I heard the baby's pitiful little cry and saw Dornan stroking the mother's hair so tenderly, so softly, before he planted a bullet in her skull.

'Security footage,' John hissed at the guy, who nodded, making a beeline for the building.

'I need to see him,' I said, my tears suddenly stopping, my weeping replaced with an absolute conviction that if I didn't get to Dornan right now, he would die – and if he died, I wouldn't survive. I'd already lost everything else.

Este had been shot, and I didn't cry. I was still in shock. I didn't understand what was happening. But nine years of missing him, his lopsided smile and the way he squeezed my hand tightly to reassure me when I was afraid, the way he held our son and promised me we'd get him back one day? I knew, nine years later, the pain of watching somebody bleed to death in front of you, the regret of not saying goodbye. Because they're just *gone*, and nothing you will ever do for the rest of your existence can turn back time and make those moments appear again, those moments when you just want to say *I love you. I love you.*

John took my elbow again, pulling me along. He stopped short of the emergency doors and yanked me into a room with an empty bed, still messed up like someone had been sleeping there recently, an empty chair beside it. I wondered, briefly, if somebody had just died there. 'They won't let us in,' John said, blocking my attempt to leave the room. His blue eyes were wild, his dark blonde hair all mussed up from his helmet. He hadn't shaved recently, and I had to wonder what hell he had been toiling in. I mean, Dornan got the trafficking, what did John get?

Suddenly I needed to be sick. Very, very sick. I put my hand over my mouth, forcing my throat closed. I retched, but nothing came up.

I needed Dornan, and I needed him now.

'They won't let us in,' John said again. I ignored him, trying to push past him.

'Mariana!' he yelled, taking my shoulders and shaking me. 'Look at me! You can't see him!'

'Screw you!' I said, fighting off his grip. 'His wife will be here in ten minutes, John. His kids. Emilio. Do you think they'll let me see him then? Do you think I'll be allowed to go to his funeral if he fucking *dies*?' I was crying again, great shuddering sobs that hurt as they bubbled up in my chest and left my body. 'Do you think I'll be allowed to live if he fucking dies?'

'He's not going to die,' John said, with conviction. 'He's gonna live. I promise.'

I shook my head. 'Don't make promises you can't keep.'

I looked down at my hands. They were covered in blood, so much that I couldn't even remember who it belonged to anymore. In the space of three hours I'd seen two lives end, one begin, and the person who meant more to me than anything barely holding on.

'Fuck,' I remembered, my hands shaking as I held them up to John. 'I shot somebody. I killed somebody.'

John's eyes narrowed, his eyes searching my face. 'What?'

'It was Allie. She shot Dornan through the window.' I took in a ragged breath, reliving the moment all over again. The deafening blast. The way the light died in his eyes before they closed. So fast. It all happened so goddamn fast.

'Where did she go?' John asked, his tone dangerously calm. Too calm. I knew that tone. It was the eye of the storm.

It was hell about to be unleashed.

My skin hummed, where tiny pieces of glass were still stuck, and my feet were bleeding on the stark white of the hospital floor. My shoulder was pulsating where the bullet had nicked it. But it didn't hurt. I was flooded with adrenalin, with the sharp sense that I had to survive. I was like a deer, eyes wide open, looking for the threat as the bullet whizzes into its body and tears it apart.

'I shot her, but she wasn't dead,' I whispered, looking up at John with a mixture of dread and disbelief. 'I put my hand over her face until she suffocated, and then I rolled her body into the marina.'

John released his grip on me and took a step back, swiping his hand across his stubbled chin.

'You sure she was dead?'

I nodded, taking the gun from my waistband and holding it out to him. He looked around, seemingly shocked, before he shook his head and pressed my hand back to my side.

'Keep it,' he said. 'You might need it.'

I nodded, replacing the gun in the hollow of my back, the metal against my skin oddly comforting as I rearranged my tank top to cover it.

'I need to see him,' I repeated. 'Five minutes, John. I'll shoot *you* if I have to.'

John tipped his head to the side, my threat apparently lost on him as he looked down at me. 'No, you won't,' he said softly.

'Alright, I won't,' I mumbled. Across the hall, I spotted a laundry cart, stacked with fresh sheets and what looked like hospital-issue scrubs.

I raised my arm and pointed. 'Five minutes. That's all I need.'

John turned, saw the scrubs. He sighed, his resolve crumbling before my eyes. 'Wait here.'

He ventured cautiously into the hallway, looking around before darting over and grabbing a stack of folded green clothes. He brought them back into the room and tossed them on the bed.

'Hurry,' he urged, turning around to give me some privacy. I thought about our kiss. It was the wrong thing to be thinking about when my lover was fighting for his life in the ICU.

My heart in my mouth, I stripped my clothes off and wiped myself down as best I could with an extra shirt John had grabbed, before sliding the scrubs on and tucking the gun back into the waistband. I glanced in the small mirror that hung next to the bed. I still looked terrible, my skin caked with dried blood, but I was a damn sight better with fresh clothes.

'Okay,' I said, letting John know I was decent. He turned around and I gave him a tight smile. I was just about to pass him when he grabbed my arm again. I looked up, surprised, to see something else in his face.

Pity? *Affection*?

'Ana,' he said softly, pulling me to him. He wrapped his arms around me and squeezed me, and I melted into his embrace, comforted by the gesture. I felt his hand on my hair as he hugged me tight, as fresh tears started to flow.

'It'll be okay,' he murmured into my hair. 'He's gonna be okay.'

I gave a small nod, hovering there in the space his arms offered, part of me just wanting to stay here in the safe darkness of his embrace. But that was dangerous. Very, very dangerous. He smelled like pine needles and gasoline, and I probably held on to him too tightly. The realisation of what I was doing made me tense. *Dornan is dying in a hospital bed and I'm appreciating the way his best friend smells.*

'I would never let anything happen to you,' John said quietly, and my heart dropped into my stomach with a resounding thud.

Oh *fuck*.

As soon as he'd said that, he released me, but made no move to step back from me, my head barely reaching his chin. 'If he ...' John's face twisted momentarily. 'You'll be okay. Trust me.'

If he dies, you'll be okay.

I nodded again. We stepped out of the room, my bloody clothes discarded and forgotten, and made our way to the critical care ward.

To Dornan.

CHAPTER THIRTY-TWO

MARIANA

Did I ever say it?

I love you.

You saved my life.

Nine years, and I showed him, but did I ever say it?

You are my world.

You are my *everything.*

I didn't know. Standing in a hospital corridor that smelled like bleach, waiting for John to come back and tell me if Dornan was alive or dead, I didn't know if Dornan ever understood that I would have died for him in a heartbeat.

John came back to where I was standing in my green hospital scrubs, a surgical mask in his hand.

'Here,' he said gruffly, handing me the mask. His rough hand brushed against mine when he placed the mask in my outstretched palm, and he let it stay there for a beat too long. I stared at his hand, transfixed and probably in shock.

I wasn't there anymore, though. Maybe it was because I hadn't eaten, or because I was in shock, or because my shoulder had started to bleed through the hospital scrubs I was wearing. Whatever the reason, I was awake one minute, looking at John's mouth intently as he pointed to the blood on my shoulder, thinking *It's weird that I can't hear him all of a sudden.*

Then it was like somebody turned the light out. I didn't even feel it when I hit the floor.

Just ... nothing.

CHAPTER THIRTY-THREE

MARIANA

'You can go,' I said to John, even though I really wanted him to stay. But he had a wife and a daughter and an entire club that was no doubt reacting to the news that their VP had been shot.

He crossed his muscled arms across his chest, covering his Gypsy Brothers patch. His body language said he wasn't going anywhere.

I felt ... relieved. I'd fainted in the corridor on the way to see Dornan, which was both embarrassing and tragic – embarrassing because I wasn't the one who'd been shot in the goddamn chest, and tragic because now Dornan's wife was by his side and I'd missed my chance to see him. My shoulder had been bandaged, just a surface graze, and the bullet had taken a nice chunk of flesh with it. But I was okay.

A nurse bustled in, a clipboard in one hand and the jar I'd just peed in clasped in the other.

'Good news all round,' she said cheerily. 'Everything looks good from the baby's standpoint. Hormones are still high. You just need to eat something. Your blood sugar is low.'

I sat bolt upright in the bed, as John and I baulked in unison. '*What*?'

The nurse's face fell. 'The... pregnancy,' she said, all trace of cheer gone.

'I think there's been some mistake,' I said sharply. 'I'm not pregnant.'

She looked down at the chart in her hand. 'Yes, you are. Your hCG levels are through the roof.'

I laughed maniacally. 'You're crazy.' I looked at John. 'She's crazy!'

She looked at John, then back to me. 'Do you want me to call a psych down so you can talk to someone?' she asked quietly.

'What? No! I want to see my chart. There's been some mix-up. I'm on the pill. There's no way I can be pregnant.'

My stomach was sinking, sinking like quicksand. I tried to remember the last time I'd had a period. Nope. No idea. I thought back over the past several weeks, of how many times I'd puked or felt sick and assumed it was the stress of working for a drug kingpin or murdering a DEA agent that was making me constantly nauseous.

'This is a mistake,' I insisted, snatching my chart from the nurse. She looked affronted. 'Can you give us a minute?' I asked her, motioning to the door.

Before I'd had a chance to read the chart, it was snatched from my hands. John read through the notes as I fumed on the bed. 'Give me that,' I said. 'It's got to be a mistake.'

John's blue eyes looked at me over the clipboard in his hand. 'It's not a mistake. I just watched her test that jar in the next room.'

'Oh God,' I groaned, flopping back on the bed. This was turning into a fucking nightmare.

'Congratulations,' John said, and when I looked at his face, he seemed almost disappointed at the news.

I was pregnant. With Dornan's baby. And Dornan was in the ICU, being operated on, and he might not even live to hear the news.

CHAPTER THIRTY-FOUR

MARIANA

The doctors insisted on keeping me in for observation, which was ridiculous, but I wasn't about to argue with them. The hospital was where Dornan was, and if his wife ever left his bedside, I'd be able to go and see him.

At some point in the night, John woke me to let me know that Dornan had made it through surgery. He was going to be okay, Allie's bullet having narrowly missed his heart. The news made me cry. I suddenly realised why everything had been making me cry lately. Damn pregnancy hormones.

As morning broke, I was itching to see Dornan. John informed me, however, that Dornan's wife had spent the night at his bedside, once he was out of surgery. I was getting antsy in my own hospital room, so on impulse I rode the elevator to the third floor. The maternity floor. I hadn't been able to get the little baby boy from last night's horror show out of my head, and I'd even had nightmares that he was my baby, and I'd been the one who was shot by Dornan.

I tried to tell myself that I was just wandering the halls to keep my mind off Dornan, but it was more than that. I was gravitating towards the nursery, and soon I found myself right there, my hands pressed up against the glass window as I scanned the clear plastic bassinets all lined up inside.

He was there. The last bassinet, tucked into the corner. He was asleep, his little lips suckling away at the air as if he were dreaming of his mother's milk. The name tag on the end of his bassinet was blank.

My heart shattered.

That poor baby. Nobody would ever know who he was. His mother was gone and his future looked bleak.

I wanted to take him home and hold him and feed him and never let him go. I wanted to tell him how sorry I was that there were people like Emilio in the world.

People like Dornan.

Something brushed against the back of my neck and I jumped. I turned my face to see Emilio standing there, smiling indulgently at me. He was smiling like he knew a secret, and that made me fucking terrified.

'How are you feeling, Ana?' he asked, putting an arm around my shoulder. 'You were shot. You shouldn't be out of bed, dear.'

I looked at him for a moment before turning back to the babies. I kept my back rigid, refusing to make it comfortable for Emilio to drape himself around me.

'It was just a flesh wound,' I replied. 'I'm trying to stay out of your family's way until the hospital discharges me.' It was kind of the truth.

'How thoughtful of you,' Emilio said, pulling me closer to his side. 'Always so thoughtful. Tell me, did you decide to drop this little bastard off before his mother died or after?'

Oh God. Sweat started to gather around my temples, and

my skin was all itchy. I needed to get away from this man. I didn't say anything.

'I asked you a question, cholita.'

I yelped as bony fingers pressed into my bullet wound. I gagged, the pain so sharp that I almost puked right then and there.

'Ahhhhhhhh,' I cried, doubling over from the pain so my forehead was pressed against the cool glass window that separated us from the babies in the nursery.

Emilio didn't like that. He tugged on a handful of my hair, forcing my head back up, and pulled me along so we were standing directly in front of the *bastard* baby he was talking about.

Emilio grinned, his gold tooth reflecting the harsh fluorescent lights that hung overhead. Even after nine years, I'd never gotten used to that tooth, and it made me jump every goddamn time he opened his mouth.

'Mariana,' he said, his voice like chains being dragged through rocks. His eyes were so much like Dornan's that it scared me. How could you come from a man like Emilio Ross and not turn into him? That thought burrowed into my brain and sat there, dormant, waiting for the time when I'd have to rip it out and answer it.

Somehow, I knew we were heading towards destruction, even as we stood in the calm aftermath of Allie's failed attempt at vengeance.

It wasn't over. It would never be over. Emilio's cold hand squeezed the back of my neck as he directed my gaze towards the smallest baby in the line-up.

'I'm taking this boy home,' he promised, his words turning vicious. 'I'll raise him as my own. And if you ever try and leave your post ...'

I sobbed from the pain of his fingers inside my wound. 'I've given you almost ten years,' I whispered. 'You told me you'd let me go once I repaid the debt.'

He chuckled. 'That was before. This is now. Do you have any idea how fucking marvellous you are at what you do? I was going to shoot you that night but you insisted on coming with me. You've only got yourself to blame, dear.'

I couldn't stop crying. The pain! I just wanted him to get his hands away from me.

'You try and leave, and I'll find you, Ana,' he continued. 'I'll find you and I'll make you watch while I kill that boy in front of you.' He returned his black eyes to me and grinned. 'It's a shame your family is dead. Your sister would be much more fun to kill while you watch than a fucking child.'

My blood ran cold. Even though I knew he was talking about this baby who'd been born in the back of a trafficking truck, all I saw was Luis. And it wasn't just Luis any more. There was another baby, a secret that lived inside me.

I had to get out. I had to find a way to get out of this hell, for both of my children.

CHAPTER THIRTY-FIVE

MARIANA

Dornan woke up.

But nothing was ever the same between us.

Because when I looked into his eyes, I no longer saw the man who had saved me all those years ago.

I saw the man who'd morphed into a monster before my very eyes.

Part of me thought it would have been better if Allie's bullet had killed him, so I wouldn't have to keep living this lie. The bullet didn't kill him, though. It didn't kill him, and he got better, and I still couldn't bring myself to tell him that I was pregnant with his child.

CHAPTER THIRTY-SIX

MARIANA

I still hadn't told him.

This great weight inside me, this thing, this child I carried like a sinful secret. It burdened me and lightened me at the same time. I wanted to tell him, and I didn't. Thirteen weeks now, it had been growing inside me. After I'd found out, I'd dithered and ummed and ahhed and ached. Because I wanted it. And I didn't. I wanted it because it was mine, loved it like I loved the first baby I'd birthed so long ago. Hated it because it was forcing me to choose. Life or death. No matter which one I chose, I was going to regret it. Kill my child, the child Dornan and I had unwittingly created? Or keep it, bring it into this world, only to have it taken from me just like Luis.

I hated myself because I was so selfish. Because if things had been different, if I had been free, I would have been ecstatic to have a baby growing in my womb, even if it was Dornan's.

Especially if it was Dornan's.

I loved him. I loved him even in my darkest moments. Even in his.

But I still couldn't reconcile the man I loved, the father of my child, with the man who had shot that woman in front of me while I held her baby in my arms, begging him to stop.

I still couldn't fathom that the man I loved had been doing this – taking women and selling them as slaves and handing me the money afterwards – and I'd been blissfully unaware.

I knew they were bad people. I knew that. But I'd never known how complicit I was in it all.

And as much as I tried to convince Dornan to stand up to his father, he insisted that he couldn't. That there was a bigger picture to think of. That it wasn't just me he had to worry about.

'You're the kingpin of this operation,' I protested. 'You're the one in charge of all of this.'

'It's not like that.' Dornan replied, stonewalling me.

'It's exactly like that. You let me see something like this and then you pretend that you're doing it for me? Well, don't do it for me. I'd rather die than be the reason for all of this.'

'Shut up,' he growled. 'You don't know what you're talking about, and if he ever hears you—'

'Let him hear me, Dornan,' I cut him off. 'Let him hear everything I say. Because if he thinks he can make you do this for him and use me as a threat? I won't have it. I'll let him sell me as a fucking sex slave before I let you traffic one more soul in my name.'

'Don't you get it?' he yelled. 'This isn't just about you. You're one form of currency, Ana, but I have kids. I have friends. I have a club. How many people do you think had to die before I agreed to do this for my father? I'm no kingpin,' he said bitterly. 'Emilio's the kingpin. I'm the pawn, and so are you.'

'He's your father,' I protested.

'Exactly.'

'Who did he kill, Dornan? Who did he kill to make you go along with this?'

He was silent for a beat.

'That woman I told you about, the first woman I really loved. Her name was Stephanie.'

He'd never told me her name before.

'My father was putting the pressure on for me to join his trafficking operation. Said he needed someone he could trust to run it, and who can you trust more than your own flesh and blood? And I refused. I said no. I said fuck you, do your own dirty work.'

'What happened?'

'She disappeared. I said no, and she fucking vanished into thin air. I already had kids at that point. I didn't love their mother, but I sure as hell didn't hate her enough to risk her. To risk my boys. No. I showed up. I did what I was told to do. I kept my family safe.'

'Your sons – they're his family. That's Emilio's grandsons you're talking about.'

He raised his eyebrows. 'When I say my father's a snake, I'm not fucking kidding around, alright? He'd slit his own mother's throat if it got him where he wanted to go. He'd sell my boys just as soon as he'd sell you.'

'Dornan,' I whispered. 'I don't know if I can live like this anymore.'

I cried. I always cried.

'Really?' he said, and his face twisted with rage. 'And what can you live with? Huh? What's the alternative? You want to leave?'

'I don't want to leave you,' I muttered. 'I want to leave this craziness. This is no place for a—' I'd almost said baby, the word on the tip of my tongue.

'For a what?' he pressed.

'For a life!' I answered.

He just chuckled. 'That's funny,' he said cruelly. 'I thought you understood after all this time. There's only one way out of here, baby, and it's not pretty.'

There has to be a way, I thought to myself. *There has to be something.*

CHAPTER THIRTY-SEVEN

DORNAN

Dornan moved the food around on his plate.

'You don't have to eat it,' Celia said quietly. She took the plate from in front of him and held a cool palm to his throbbing forehead. 'You feeling okay?'

Dornan grunted in response and leaned back so his wife wasn't touching him anymore. Her touch made his skin crawl, made him want to lash out and strike her. But tonight he couldn't even be bothered making a shitty remark about her cooking, so he said nothing. For some reason, ever since he'd been shot, he couldn't stomach eating. The thick steaks Celia had cooked were still bloody in the middle, and that was probably the issue. He'd seen too much blood lately.

Celia – cold, beautiful Celia – shook her head, and then left the kitchen. Dornan didn't care. After this many years of marriage, he was completely disillusioned with the concept. He had thought about divorcing her, but he needed to be close to his kids. He'd been able to get sole custody of his three older sons when he divorced his first wife, Lucia, but her family was nobody special. Celia, on the other hand, had powerful mafia connections on the east coast, their grandfathers very distant relatives somewhere along the line, and she'd probably be able to wrangle shared custody.

Dornan wouldn't have that, and he'd told her exactly that on more than one occasion when she demanded a divorce. The only way she'd be getting away from him was through death. Over the years, their marriage had turned into something of a business alliance. Celia was smart, she was feisty, and she was crucial to getting their east coast relatives to play fair. Their current arrangement worked well enough.

But it wasn't a marriage, and he didn't love her, and he knew every time she looked at him she was probably counting down in her head the minutes until he'd leave again.

He didn't even care anymore. Having Celia – who, he knew for a fact, was fucking somebody else – gave him a measure of protection, a cover story, something to distract people from asking what he was really doing. Sometimes he fantasised about somebody kidnapping Celia, holding her for ransom, and then going to collect her and to pay the kidnappers off, and shooting her in the face instead. Because even though she was his wife, she was also a rather heavy piece of baggage he had to drag around. The thought of getting rid of her tantalised him. Because if she was gone, he'd be able to spend every goddamn night buried balls-deep inside Mariana, fucking her into oblivion and then laying tender kisses on her afterwards.

Dornan wasn't a tender man — in fact, he was the opposite — but Mariana made him want to be a better person. At least she had, until he'd found the fucking cellphone buried in the back of her kitchen cupboard. The question had been on his lips in the truck, just before the deafening bullet had torn apart his chest and his sanity.

Who's the phone for, Ana? He'd convinced himself that there was a perfectly legitimate answer for the secret phone. It could be Guillermo's. It could be he'd forgotten about it. Because if it was anything else – if she had betrayed his trust – he couldn't bear to think what would come next. What he'd have to do to her. How he'd have to punish her.

His chest was aching, that phantom bullet still metaphorically jammed up against his heart, its shards spreading through his ribcage, tiny specks of poisoned lead. And it ached for her. He couldn't bear that she might have already betrayed him. He couldn't deal with that shit. It was easier to pretend like he'd never seen the phone, or at least keep the knowledge of its existence in his back pocket, ready to pull out when she was least expecting it. He imagined her eyes widening in fright, because he knew he frightened her. Would she try to lie about it? Or would she confess? Had she been calling somebody without him knowing? The thoughts were like a cancerous rage, swirling inside him. He had to fucking stop thinking about it before it consumed him.

His stomach twisted uneasily again. Maybe he'd caught something. He never got sick, though. Ever. It was something else.

Yeah, come to think of it, he wasn't any better than his father and the rest of the Il Sangue Cartel. He thought of Mariana's face when she'd realised what exactly it was keeping her alive, Dornan's end of the grisly bargain he'd struck with Emilio all those years ago. One life in exchange for many. He tried to forget the horror in her eyes when she'd learned the truth, just before he'd been shot, but it was impossible.

He was snapped back to the present moment by the urge for a cigarette. He could light up, inhale and try to burn the memory of her sad eyes from his brain, one puff at a time. His cigarettes were in the bedroom. He pushed back from the table and made his way to the master bedroom, finding his pack of smokes and lighter in the pocket of his leather jacket.

The light was dim in the cool and quiet bedroom. The kids were always loud, and sometimes this was the only place he could find any peace in this fucking house. As he lit up, he continued to think of Mariana, always alone in her apartment, always lonely. Always begging him to stay.

He thought of the way she'd cried out as he fucked her perfect round ass, the way her light brown skin shimmered as he pulled those tight globes of her ass onto his cock again and again, and the thought made his dick grow hard almost instantly.

He shifted slightly to relieve some of the unbearable pressure of denim on his growing erection, and saw movement out of the corner of his eye.

'Dear husband,' Celia said, leaning against the doorway. 'Care to spare a smoke for your lovely wife?'

Dornan raised an eyebrow and stuck his cigarette between his teeth. 'Knock yourself out,' he said around the stick of tobacco, gesturing to the packet on the bed beside him.

She ignored the packet, instead slinking towards him. Kneeling on the floor in front of his legs, she burrowed her lithe body into the V between his open knees. Her mouth curled up into a smile as she looked towards his lap.

'Happy to see me?' she asked, reaching for his zipper and boldly tugging it down. Dornan watched his wife like one would watch a snake, keeping his eye on her so she didn't suddenly strike. He didn't respond, just watched with detached indifference as she pulled his straining cock out of his jeans and wrapped her lips around the head. It felt good, but knowing it was her made his blood run cold. Didn't make his dick any less stiff, though. He was a man, and what man didn't enjoy a surprise blow job?

She must have wanted something. That was the only explanation for her sudden interest in his dick, after so many years.

He rested back on his hands, cigarette still between his teeth, as he watched his beautiful, cruel wife suck him. She was really getting into it, using both hands. Taking one of his hands off the comforter, he threaded it into her hair and pulled her head back. 'What do you want?' he muttered around the cigarette.

She pouted, her hands still around his erection. 'Nothing. Can't a woman give her husband a blow job anymore?'

He let go of her hair and gestured as if to say, *Don't stop on my account.*

She resumed her sucking, making a small gagging noise as he hit the back of her throat. That amused him more than it should, and he found himself holding back a snicker. His cell vibrated in his pocket and he pulled it out. It was Viper. Christ, what now? Last time Viper had called him, he'd ended the night with a bullet to the chest.

'Yeah?'

It was quiet. Eerily quiet. The only noise on the other end of the phone was steady breathing.

'What?' Dornan asked.

'Boss,' Viper spoke, an urgency in his tone. 'I found her.'

Dornan transferred the phone to his other hand; he could barely hear Viper, he was speaking so quietly. 'Everything all right?'

'Dee,' Viper said.

'What is it?' Dornan asked, impatience growing in his gut.

'Don't freak the fuck out. I found Stephanie.'

Stephanie? *Fuck*. It had been what – sixteen, seventeen years? An anxiousness began to build inside his chest, an annoying, gnawing buzz that ate away at him.

His heart squeezed painfully.

Dead. That's what Viper was going to say, he knew it. Knew it in his bones. The first woman he'd ever truly loved, one he could have imagined leaving this life for. Hell, once he'd even proposed the idea. He would kill everyone in the cartel, and they could leave, go someplace where nobody would ever find them.

She'd laughed.

He'd pretended he was kidding, and they had never mentioned it again. And not long after, she had vanished from the face of the earth, swallowed up no doubt by the same people who had killed Dornan's brother back when they were still weedy teenagers on the verge of becoming men. Gunned down, left in their front yard as a message, and he just knew Stephy had ended up the same way. That knowledge had almost killed him. He'd been a zombie, then become cruel, sadistic, letting her disappearance ruin any good that had existed within him. So he embraced the dark, and he was very, very bad. He killed. He coerced. He traded in lives.

And then he met her.

Mariana.

And she blew his goddamn world to pieces.

She was different from Stephy in every way possible. Mariana was Colombian; Stephy was born-and-bred

Texan. Mariana had dark hair and bronze skin; Stephy had strawberry blonde locks, the consistency of fairy floss, and pale skin thanks to her Irish-American ancestry.

Mariana was alive, and Stephy was not.

At least, that's what Dornan had believed for the past sixteen-odd years.

He held the phone so tight, it was a wonder it didn't shatter in his hand.

Viper seemed hesitant. Dornan could've reached through the phone and ripped him a new asshole for not hurrying the fuck-up and spilling what he'd discovered.

'She dead?' Dornan grunted, feigning indifference, but inside, he was ready to explode.

'Dee,' Viper said. 'Where are you right now? I should be telling you this man to man, not on the fucking phone. Where the hell have you been, man?'

'Keep talking,' Dornan said. He struggled to keep his voice steady as he pushed Celia away, and she fell on her pert ass with a thud. 'Tell me.' He tucked his cock back into his pants and started working on the zipper – not easy with one hand.

Celia was on her feet now, staring right at him with dead eyes. She looked positively pissed and like she might want to cut his balls off and shove them down his throat.

Stephy had to be dead. After all this time, it was the only explanation. He knew someone had taken her, probably used her for their own sick pleasure and then murdered her. His chest grew uncomfortably tight as he remembered her hair, those bright eyes, that smile. The one woman he'd truly loved. The woman who'd accepted him with open arms and a laugh, even though he was married, even though he had kids, even though he was a Gypsy Brother with so much baggage it could spell death for them both. She'd started out working in the bar at the clubhouse, but she wasn't a club whore. She was just a university student trying to supplement her income, and when Dornan had found out about Celia's cheating, how she was pregnant and it might be with some other motherfucker's kid, Stephy had been the one who had listened to him. He'd confided everything in her – things about Emilio, about the trafficking, about the government connections. He'd been so smitten with her, and then she'd just ... *vanished.*

She'd gone and fucking disappeared on him, so abruptly it was almost as if she'd never existed. He'd gone to her apartment and everything seemed normal. Her purse was still there, all her ID, some cash, her cellphone. It was all normal – too normal. He'd called a crime-scene tech he knew and asked him to check out Stephy's apartment with luminol, and that place had lit up like a fucking Christmas tree in Times Square. There was blood all over the apartment, invisible to the naked eye since someone had painstakingly mopped it all up, but it had been there, and nobody could lose that much blood and still be alive. He hadn't loved another woman for many, many years. Not until Mariana.

They never found Stephanie's body. Dornan had grown older and more bitter, refusing his wife's half-hearted attempts at reconciling, burying himself in his work, waking up at night covered in sweat as he imagined Stephy being brutally murdered.

Imagining it was Emilio who'd been holding the knife. Because she had known too much. Dornan had been too naive, entrusting this girl with cartel information, and so he was certain his father had had a hand in her death. He pictured a bag of bones in a shallow grave, some piece of clothing or a deathbed confession the only way to truly know they were Stephy's remains. It had been so long ago that it would be impossible to identify her. Her flesh would have rotted into the earth a long, long time ago, eaten by greedy worms and insects.

Viper cleared his throat. And he said something that would change the very fabric of Dornan Ross's soul, extinguish the love he felt for the girl he'd long given up for dead, and replace that feeling with a rage so brutal it demanded blood. Simple words was all it took.

'Dee, listen to me. I found her. I found Stephanie. She's alive.'

'Come again?' If the fucker was having a joke at his expense, it would be the last joke he ever made, because Dornan would drive over to his house and kill Viper with his bare hands.

'That's not all,' Viper said.

There was something else? Dornan could hear the reluctance in Viper's tone. *There was something else.*

'Go on,' Dornan ground out.

'She's got a kid, man. A son. He's fifteen. I'm pretty sure he's yours.'

Fifteen.

FIFTEEN.

The kid was fifteen.

He had a son out there, somewhere, and *he hadn't even known.*

It all fit together now, all made total, devastating sense. She hadn't been taken – hadn't been killed.

She had run away. With his baby inside her.

She had stolen something that belonged to him.

Dornan's grip on the phone became even tighter, the plastic starting to buckle under the pressure.

'Boss?' Viper said nervously.

Few things were capable of shocking Dornan Ross these days, jaded and weary as he was, but this was like someone had just dropped an atomic bomb in his lap and asked him to please sit still.

'Where is she?' Dornan asked, feeling almost two decades worth of sadness and guilt collect into a vortex of what could only be described as a black, festering rage.

'Dee—'

'*Where*?' He was so enraged by her apparent betrayal, he couldn't even bear the weight of her name on his lips.

'Colorado,' Viper conceded. 'I'm texting you the address right now.' A brief pause. 'What are you going to do?'

Dornan started to pace, completely ignoring Celia, who was watching his every move. He wondered if she could hear Viper's side of the conversation. Doubtful. Dornan could barely hear him.

'I'm going to go on a little road trip,' Dornan said, ending the call.

He needed to smash something. Now. Celia was in front of him. No. She didn't deserve his wrath, not over this. He tamped down his rage momentarily, as his phone buzzed again with a text message. He glanced at the screen and saw a Colorado address flash up. Took a deep breath.

'Who was that? Everything okay?' Celia asked in a small voice.

No, everything was most certainly not okay. It was the furthest place from okay that was humanly possible.

'Work,' he lied, though he didn't need to explain anything to her. The way she was staring at him was making him itch. The bitch would do well to remember who was in charge in this relationship.

'Dornan,' she said quietly.

He expected her to launch into a tirade – it was her go-to – but instead her eyes filled with tears.

'Fuck,' Dornan muttered. Perhaps a better man would have felt regret over his callousness, over his rough rejection. Not Dornan. All he felt was annoyance. '*Celia*.'

She dissolved into sobs. Dornan hastily did his belt buckle up and glared at his wife. He looked at the screen on his cellphone and back to Celia. Her hands were covering her face now, her shoulders moving up and down as she cried silently.

'Celia, just tell me what you want,' he said gruffly.

'Why don't you touch me anymore?' Celia said, her voice small and lonely. 'Why don't you love me anymore?'

Dornan raised his eyebrows. 'I never loved you,' he spat. 'Not sure where that idea came from.'

Dornan shrugged his leather jacket on, swiped his cigarettes from the bed and shoved them in his pocket. He thought of the deal breaker, the night he'd found her fucking some other guy. *While* she was pregnant with Dornan's fucking kid. With that memory implanted firmly in his brain, any trace of guilt he felt for pushing her away evaporated. He'd punish her until she either left, or died. *Fuck* her.

'I want a divorce!' she screamed.

He laughed. 'You sucked my dick so I'd grant you a divorce? You're crazier than I thought, Celia.'

Mascara streaking down her cheeks, Celia looked like one of the strippers at the club.

'Why won't you just let me go?!'

His chest tightened. He thought of her leaving, their sons in tow. No.

'You know why,' he said.

'They're mine!' she cried. 'They came from me! They grew inside me, and now you want to take them from me? I tried to make you love me, and you just push me away.'

Dornan spread his hands. 'I let you stay here. I let you spend whatever you want. I didn't try and take our sons from you. But I will not forgive what you did, Celia. And I will never let you take my sons from me. Ever. You want to go? There's the goddamn door.'

She pouted, crossing her hands across her chest. 'I fucking hate my life.'

Dornan shrugged as he left. 'Survival of the fittest, baby,' he called over his shoulder. 'We might not like it, but it's better than the alternative.'

'Good luck out there,' Celia snapped sarcastically. 'Don't get shot.'

He had to clench his fists to stop from laying one into her pretty face. He concentrated on the image of Stephanie and what he would do to her when he got to Colorado.

It wouldn't be pretty.

***

He drove all night and into the next day, only stopping when his gas tank ran low. He had just crossed from Utah into Colorado, and to have to stop now was excruciating.

As he was filling the tank of his newly fitted-out truck at a gas station, somewhere near Grand Junction, Dornan's phone rang. It was his lawyer. Jesus, what now? He answered.

Celia had filed for divorce. She'd signed over full custody of their sons.

She'd give up her own children, the things she loved most in this world, just to be rid of him.

Dornan didn't know whether to laugh or smash his fists into the hood of his truck and cry.

CHAPTER THIRTY-EIGHT

DORNAN

The house was a modest affair: a single-storey stucco building that sat, squat and neat, between other houses that were exactly the same. Inside it was tidy enough. Chequered tea towels. Kitschy shit that cluttered the mantlepiece above the open fireplace, the coffee table, the windowsill above the sink in the kitchen. Useless possessions irritated him. What was the point of them? They took up space and gathered dust, and then you died and littered the world you left behind with your crap.

There were photographs hanging on the white panelled walls. A baby boy, with Dornan's eyes, his colouring, his DNA. Everything about the kid screamed Dornan. He looked more like him than any of his other sons, for fuck's sake. How was that for irony? He hadn't even known the kid existed, and here he was, his carbon copy, smiling Stephy's lopsided smile, her dimples passed down to *his* son.

His son. Those two words wrapped around him like a vice, pulling tight until he could barely breathe with the injustice of what this bitch had taken from him. He wasn't a good man, had never pretended to be anything remotely in the realm of good, but he loved his children with a ferocity that knew no bounds. He was the father lion, possessive, pride of the pack, poised to strike at and rip the throat from anyone who dared to shatter his carefully constructed world.

Viper had been useful. Giving him the time the bitch was due home, the kid, too. He still didn't know what he was going to say to them, but he was pretty sure it was going to take everything inside him not to smash her face into the kitchen table until she passed out. Sixteen years. And all the time, she'd let him believe she was dead in a shallow fucking grave somewhere.

And *he had a seventh son.*

He found her gun in the second drawer he opened. He knew she'd have one stashed in easy reach, and ironically it was the same one he'd given her. Fucking bitch. He flicked open the chamber, was mildly impressed at the recent cleaning and oiling of the weapon. He emptied the bullets into his pocket and replaced the gun in its spot.

He sat at the kitchen table. It was cheap pine and it looked like someone had traced their initials into it. JP.

His son's name was Jason. He didn't even have Dornan's last name. But he would.

Dornan's hand went into his pocket and he squeezed his fist tight around the bullets he'd just reclaimed.

And then he heard her car in the driveway.

He didn't bother hiding. You couldn't see the kitchen from the front door, so he helped himself to a glass of milk, sat back down at the kitchen table, and he waited.

She took a while. He heard several doors opening and closing, the screech of metal that needed to be greased, the jangle of keys in the door.

And then she was in front of him, her mouth hanging open, the paper shopping bags in her arms falling and crashing to the floor.

Dornan eyed the contents momentarily before returning his gaze to her. He felt beads of milk clinging to the stubble above his lip. He wiped it with the back of his hand and smiled at the bitch who was having conniptions in front of him.

Goddamn, she was still beautiful.

'Hello, Stephy,' he said. 'You got a real nice house here.'

She was frozen. She couldn't form words. Dornan laughed, taking another gulp of milk. He would have preferred beer, but she didn't have any in the refrigerator.

She was so fucking obvious. He saw her eyes dart over to the kitchen drawer where her now-empty revolver was hidden. She rushed over, the shock still sharp on her face, opening the drawer and taking the gun out.

It was stupid, the way his heart hurt when she pointed the gun at him.

'That's not very nice, baby,' he said, his voice low and rough. 'I come all the way here to visit you, and you pull a gun on me?'

She cocked the revolver in trembling hands. She still hadn't said a word to him. Was he really that frightening? She'd loved him, once. She'd let him hold her life in his hands, and now she wanted to end his?

'How's my son?' Dornan asked, his tone shifting rapidly, acerbic and bitter.

She huffed. 'He is not your son.'

So she did speak.

Something broke inside him, something he'd been trying to push down and keep locked away for fifteen years. Longer. Sixteen.

He had loved her, goddamn it! He. Had. Loved. Her.

And she was staring at him like she'd never laid eyes on him in her life. No, it was worse than that. She was staring at him like he was a fucking monster.

'That's funny,' Dornan replied looking at the framed photograph on the wall of a small boy, maybe seven, his dark brown eyes and hair a dead ringer for Dornan's. 'Because I'm pretty fucking sure he is.'

'Get out,' she whispered, her eyes full of tears, her aim steady. 'Get out or I'll shoot you, Dornan, I swear to God.'

Dornan nodded, reaching for his own gun. Terrified, Stephy aimed at his chest and pulled the trigger. And pulled it again. And again.

'It needs bullets to work,' Dornan said calmly. 'Here, have one of mine.'

He aimed at her shin and pulled the trigger on his own Glock, smiling with satisfaction as she went down hard, her lower leg exploding in a mess of blood and bone fragments as she landed between a bunch of bananas and a loaf of bread.

Dornan took a deep breath, the victory of vengeance singing in his veins as he stood up and drank the rest of his milk. He let the empty glass fall to the ground at his feet, where it shattered.

'Stephy,' Dornan teased, stepping between the fallen groceries to get to her.

She cowered in the corner, her hands covering her face, which was turning swiftly pale. She had hurt him, and he was going to hurt her back. He was going to hurt her very, very badly. And the thought filled him with relief.

He holstered his gun. He didn't want this to go too quickly; no, he wanted to draw out her suffering, the way she had drawn out his suffering. His endless fucking pursuit of a shallow grave, of a confession from her killer, of something. And all the time, she had been here, living and smiling and bearing his fucking child.

He knelt beside her, his boots crunching on the broken glass. 'Let's get you cleaned up,' he said, smiling. 'Where's your bathroom?'

She whimpered. She didn't answer. Sighing, he balled his fist up and slammed it into the side of her face. Not too hard, because he didn't want her to pass out. Just hard enough to hurt like a motherfucker.

'Let's try that again. Where's your bathroom?'

She pointed down the hallway. Smiling, Dornan grabbed a fistful of her long blonde hair and started dragging her. She half-crawled, half-limped alongside him, crying out in pain the whole time.

She had a bathtub. Excellent. Dornan rolled his eyes as she started to beg, scooping her up and throwing her hard into the bottom of the tub. She struggled to sit up and he hit her again. His fist throbbed in pain. It felt good. He'd never hit a woman before, not like this.

But she deserved it for what she'd done.

'Here's the deal,' Dornan said, crouching beside the tub and brushing her fringe from her face. 'You tell me when my son is due home, and I promise I won't kill either of you.'

She swallowed thickly. 'School finished at three-thirty,' she said shakily. 'He's usually home by four.'

Dornan nodded, taking a syringe from his pocket, and a vial of morphine he'd made damn sure to bring with him on his long journey. Stephanie stared in horror as he stabbed the syringe into the vial and drew up a colourless liquid.

He filled the syringe, and her eyes grew wide as she realised what it was.

'Please,' she begged.

'You remember this, don't you? Just like smack, only better. You liked it the first time. Remember how you used to come underneath me? How I'd give you a hit of the sweet stuff at just the right time? Do you remember that, Stephy?' He wrapped a rubber tourniquet around her arm.

'Dornan!' she cried. 'Please don't do this. My boy needs me, I'm all he has ...'

My boy. That made Dornan angry. He pulled the tourniquet tighter and a juicy blue vein popped up against her pale arm.

'You promised,' she said, blood spilling out of her mouth from the spot where he'd punched her. 'You promised!'

Dornan smiled, pushing the plunger down and delivering enough morphine to stop her heart five times over. 'I did promise,' he replied cheerily. He felt crazed. He felt high. He'd loved her, and he'd mourned her, and now he would end her.

'Remember how you promised you'd love me forever? How you'd never leave me? You lied, baby.'

Her eyes started to flutter shut. 'You promised,' she whispered.

He grinned wickedly. 'I know. I lied, too. How does it feel?'

She couldn't answer him, though, because she was dead.

***

A few hours later, the boy came home. *Jason.* His son's name was Jason.

He was exquisite. Dornan could think that without feeling stupid, because he was laying his eyes on his son for the first time, as if he'd just been born, only fifteen years too late.

The boy found the kitchen a mess, and soon after his mother. Dornan confronted him, told him who he was. The boy put up a solid fight, made Dornan proud at the way he punched and kicked, but he had twenty-five years and change on the kid. He knocked him out, injected him with some tranquilliser to keep him subdued, and placed a call to John.

He answered on the second ring.

'Hey, Dee,' John said.

Things had been tense between them of late. Dornan knew the shooting had been stressful for John, and the mystery surrounding Murphy's disappearance hadn't helped matters. He'd also heard through the grapevine that Caroline was up to her usual, so it was no wonder he hardly saw his best friend outside of official club business these days.

'Hey, buddy,' Dornan said, a strange calm descending upon him as he surveyed the damage he'd done to his first love and their son. 'Something's come up. I need you in Colorado, now. Bring Ana.'

While John asked questions, Dornan picked through Stephy's groceries, finding things to fix himself a sandwich. He poured himself a fresh glass of milk and sat at the table, which was covered in Stephanie's blood, and proceeded to eat his first meal of the day as he waited for John and Mariana to arrive.

CHAPTER THIRTY-NINE

JOHN

Dornan had found her.

He'd fucking *found* her. And along with her, his kid.

John hung up the phone and looked around his kitchen, rage and guilt rising inside him. The conversation hadn't gone down well. Dornan had demanded his presence in Colorado, and insisted that he bring Mariana.

Did he know about Murphy? About the kiss? Did he know about the way John had put his hands all over Dornan's woman, about how he wanted to do more and no matter what he tried to do to take his mind off it, he couldn't get her out of his fucking head?

'That's a fifteen-hour drive,' John had protested, as soon as Dornan had made the request. 'I'll grab a flight. Or ride it. I can ride faster than I can drive a car.'

'You're not riding with Mariana on the back of your bike,' Dornan had growled. 'Where are you?'

John glanced at his daughter, lying on the couch as she watched TV. Caroline was in bed, where she'd been for the past three days, only getting up to take more pills. Sometimes she liked uppers, but this week she was systematically knocking herself out for six hours at a stretch. He'd been sleeping on the couch to stay away from her. Their bedroom smelled like unwashed bodies and stale beer, and he wasn't about to go in there and clean it up. At least when she was on a downer, he could keep tabs on where she was.

'I'm at home,' he said. 'Tell me what's going on.'

Dornan cleared his throat. 'I've found Stephanie.'

So it was true. Fuck. Did he know the rest, too? Did he know that John had already known where she was all along?

'Alive?' John asked finally.

'No. Well, yeah. She was alive when I got here.'

Jesus.

John wondered about Jason, Stephanie's son. Dornan's son. He couldn't very well ask about him, though. He wasn't supposed to know Jason existed.

'Okay, you wanna tell me what happened?'

'Not particularly. You'll see soon enough.'

'Give me an address,' John said reluctantly. He didn't write it down. He didn't need to.

He knew exactly where he was going.

CHAPTER FORTY

MARIANA

Somehow knowing that I was pregnant made the nausea worse. It had ramped up significantly since the shooting, and it was taking everything I had to keep it concealed.

Guillermo's mother had improved, and so he'd come back to the apartment. I had hardly seen Dornan in the past few weeks and I'd mostly kept my head down. I'd called Miguel and checked on Luis, desperate for information. My family had been buried in a plot without a funeral. There had been no investigation.

The corrupt fucking police force that was supposed to protect my country was probably being paid by the cartel to do their dirty work. I mean, it made sense. Emilio had Colombia by the balls, and he paid the police commissioner handsomely. I would know. I was the one who organised the cash transfers into his bank account.

It was around eight at night and I was cleaning up the dinner plates after Guillermo had cooked tacos. It was the only thing he knew how to make, and he'd already started before I could protest that my ass was going to get fat from the food he kept bringing home. There was a knock on the door. Guillermo looked at me from his seat at the breakfast bar.

'You expecting company?' he asked, one hand going to the gun at his hip.

I shook my head. 'Nope. You?'

He shook his head, sliding off the stool and approaching the front door. He moved like a freaking cat, he was so stealthy, his feet gliding along the tiles as if they weren't even touching them.

He keyed in the code and the door clicked, whoever was on the other side opening it immediately.

Guillermo aimed at whoever it was, until the person smacked the gun out of his hand and grabbed his arm, twisting it behind his back and slamming him face-first into the wall.

'John?' I asked, watching the gun slide across the tiles.

Guillermo stopped struggling when I said his name.

'Prez?' He frowned, apparently confused.

John let him go with a shove, stepping back and removing the hoodie from his head. 'What the hell was that?' John asked, his face red and his breathing fast. He looked pretty fucking stressed out, and that made my stomach do all sorts of weird things.

'I didn't know it was you,' Guillermo muttered, looking embarrassed.

'What happened?' I asked John.

Guillermo walked back towards the kitchen, massaging his elbow, as John slammed the door shut.

'Pack an overnight bag,' John said tersely. 'Now.'

He never spoke to me like that, and in light of everything that had happened with Murphy, I didn't see the need to ask questions.

'What's going on?' Guillermo asked, looking between John and me.

'Dornan happened,' John said impatiently, looking at me and pointing to my bedroom. I nodded, passing him and entering my room, where I grabbed a duffel bag and started gathering jeans, underwear and make-up. I dumped it all into the bag and zipped it, coming back into the hallway a few moments later.

'You need me to come?' Guillermo asked, an off look on his face. Surely he couldn't tell anything had happened between us just by looking at us, but he had suspicion written all over his face.

'Stay here,' John replied, opening the door and motioning me outside. 'And, call Dornan. He's got about fifteen hours to fill you in while we drive to Colorado.'

Colorado? Where did I know Colorado from? Those post-it notes that John was always giving me, amounts each month to send to a bank account in Colorado. The wire transfer. I wondered if it was related. Probably not, but I made sure to file that mental note away for later.

Once we were on the freeway, I rounded on John. 'What happened?' I asked. 'Guillermo's not here now. You have to tell me. What's in Colorado?'

He stared straight ahead, seemingly in deep thought. Just as I was about to press him again, he started to speak.

'Has Dornan ever mentioned a woman called Stephanie?' he asked, glancing at me before looking back at the road.

My stomach dropped. 'Yeah. His girlfriend? From before we met. Did something happen to her?'

'She disappeared,' John said. 'Sixteen or seventeen years ago, I can't remember exactly when.'

He didn't offer any more.

'Sometimes I'd like to disappear,' I said after a few moments silence.

John's hand shot out. He grabbed hold of my wrist and squeezed tight.

'Ow,' I said, glaring at him. 'You're hurting me.'

'Do you have any idea what we're going to walk into tomorrow?' John hissed. He didn't ease up on the squeezing. I pressed my teeth together in frustration.

'No, I don't know where we're going,' I snapped, finally managing to tug my wrist out of his grip. 'That's what I'm asking you. What happened to this Stephanie woman?'

John's lips pressed together to form a thin line. 'Dornan happened to her,' he said finally.

I thought of the woman from the trafficking operation, the mother who Dornan had shot in the head. I thought of our baby.

'What did he do,' I asked, a lump rising in my throat.

'I'm not entirely sure,' John said. 'Dornan's always thought she was dead, that her body might turn up one day.'

Realisation settled into my bones like an old friend. 'You helped her get away,' I whispered.

John raked a hand through his hair, agitated. 'She was pregnant,' he said. 'She was pregnant and freaking out, and I did the only thing I could think of. I gave her some money and got her out of town.'

I looked back to the road, slumping down in my seat. Shit, it seemed like history was repeating itself.

'Did you – Were you with her?' I asked, jealousy stabbing me in the chest for some unknown reason. I'd kissed him exactly one time, and now I was suddenly jealous of some woman he may or may not have been involved with sixteen years ago? I was losing it. I was really, really losing my fucking mind.

'No,' he said sharply. 'Not at all. Caroline and I, we were good back then. Things were good.'

'Does Dornan know you helped her?' I asked quietly.

John shrugged. 'I don't think so. I don't know.'

Impulsively, I reached for his hand in the dark. He looked down as I laced my fingers in his, as if I'd just given him an electric shock. He didn't pull away, though. He looked at the road, squeezing my hand in his, and I felt tears well up in my eyes. How had things gotten to this? How had we ended up with the terrible burden of Murphy's demise hanging between us like a fatal secret? How had I ended up pregnant with Dornan's baby? How had we ended up in this car, barrelling down the freeway, on our way to Dornan and the woman he had probably killed?

'The baby,' I said suddenly. 'The one she was pregnant with when she left. What happened?'

John looked like the weight of the world was pressing down on his shoulders as he drove.

'He's fifteen years old,' he said wearily, 'and I'm pretty sure his father just murdered his mother.'

I took my hand away, crossing my arms over my stomach, convinced that if I tried to leave I'd be next on my lover's hit list.

Fuck.

We stayed on the road all night and into the morning, checking into a seedy motel that charged by the hour after about ten hours of driving. I'd offered to take the wheel so we could keep going, but John could see how exhausted I was, how nauseous, and he'd insisted we sleep for a couple of hours before we drove the final stretch to Colorado.

The room was like a matchbox, small and threadbare, and when I sat on one of the beds it sagged dramatically. Great. All the trimmings of a five-star establishment. John disappeared for a while, returning with burgers and fries. I inhaled mine, then curled up on the bed furthest from the front door and passed out into a dreamless slumber.

Well, it was dreamless at first, but then I started to have a nightmare. Dornan had his hands around my neck, and he wouldn't let go. He squeezed and squeezed until my neck broke and I died in his hands. I woke up with my own hands at my throat, as I sat bolt upright and gasped for air.

John must have been a light sleeper. As soon as I sat up, he turned on the bedside lamp and jumped out of bed, reaching out for me.

'Are you okay?' he asked, not looking even slightly sleepy. He still looked as wide awake as when we'd arrived, and I guessed that he hadn't slept at all.

'Yeah,' I said, tears streaming down my cheeks. Fucking hormones. John saw my tears, a concerned look on his face as he sat on the edge of my bed and rubbed my bare shoulders. His palms were large and warm, and I wanted to melt into his touch.

Stop! I had to stop reacting to him.

'Bad dream?' he asked, smiling sympathetically.

I nodded.

'You're okay,' he said, reaching up and brushing hair from my face. I leaned into his touch, the move almost an unconscious act, and I saw something shift in his gaze.

I reached for him in the dark like my life depended on it. Without giving myself even a moment to stop and think about what I was doing, I pressed my lips to his, opening my mouth, seeking his tongue. He didn't hesitate, his hands in my hair, at my waist, palming my breasts through the thin material of my tank top. I moaned when he did that, my nipples hardening to stiff peaks when his hand came into contact with them. He pressed into me and I laid back against the pillows, John shifting so his top half was over me. Just as I was losing all sense of reason and reaching for his belt buckle, he pulled back.

'I can't,' he said, pushing me away.

I put a hand over my mouth, scooting up the bed so I was sitting with my back against the headboard. I didn't want to look at him, but I couldn't look away.

'I'm sorry,' I said weakly.

He jumped up and began to pace beside the bed. 'I'm sorry,' he said, his hands balling into fists that looked like they really wanted to smash something. 'You're having his baby. We can't do that ever again, you understand?'

I just watched him pace.

'If I wasn't having his baby, then what?' I asked quietly.

John shook his head, agitated. 'No,' he said, 'no. You're not mine to touch. You're his.'

'Oh, I'm a fucking possession now?' Suddenly I was livid. 'What, I'm Dornan's toy, so you have to find another one?'

He glared at me. 'I don't want another one,' he said. 'But this one's taken. By a man I call my best friend.'

'Huh,' I said. 'Some best friend. You've got a lot of secrets for a best friend, John.'

He scoffed. 'Most of them are yours,' he said angrily. 'Let's not forget that.'

It was like he'd punched me in the face.

'You're right,' I said. 'I shouldn't have called you that night.'

'You should have called Dornan,' John said flatly.

'I did call Dornan,' I snapped. 'He was busy with his wife.'

John eyed me from the end of the bed. 'Do you love him?'

I sighed, frustrated. 'I don't know,' I said, throwing my hands in the air. 'Yes, I do. But he's not the person I met nine years ago. He's scaring me. I don't know how to help him out of this darkness he's sinking into. It's like poison, and I'm scared he's going to pull me in with him.'

'You gonna tell him about the baby?' John asked, gesturing to my stomach.

I took a deep breath and let it out in a long whoosh. 'I don't know,' I said again. 'I don't want to. I'm afraid of what he'll do.' I started to weep. 'I just want my boy back. I just want to leave and never come back. I want to have this baby where no one will ever find her, or me, or Luis, and we can just stop being afraid.'

Oh God, how it felt to finally externalise that awful, aching longing I'd been carrying around for my Luis.

'Her?' John asked.

I nodded. They'd scanned me before I left the hospital after the shooting, and I was already far enough along for them to tell the sex of the baby.

'It's a girl,' I said. 'I can't bring a little girl into this world, John. The things Emilio would do to her.' I shook my head. 'No. I get out or I have a termination. I can't do this if I'm still here. But I don't know if I have it in me to try and run. I don't want to live every day of my life worrying about when a bullet's going to hit me.'

John nodded, coming back to sit beside me and pulling me into his arms.

'I'm glad you called me that night,' he said.

CHAPTER FORTY-ONE

JOHN

Complete and utter carnage.

That was the only way John could describe what he was looking at. Dornan leaned against the basin in the small bathroom, irritation and fatigue competing for real estate on his face.

'You stop in Canada on the way?' Dornan asked.

John ignored the question. Dornan looked wild, still covered in the blood of the dead woman in the bathtub beside them.

'You didn't have time for a shower?' John asked, looking his best friend up and down. Jesus, the smell of old blood in the room was overwhelming, crawling up his nostrils and burrowing in. He wanted to get the fuck out.

'The shower was taken,' Dornan snapped.

Mariana, who'd been explicitly told to stay in the kitchen, appeared in the doorway. Dornan stared at her, and she did the same to him. They didn't speak.

'We need to get her out of here,' John said, positioning his body so that he was blocking Mariana's line of sight to the bathtub.

At his words, Mariana stiffened. 'I'm not going anywhere,' she said, and Dornan chuckled.

'Not you,' he said, studying his knuckle. 'Her.'

Mariana pushed past John and laid eyes on the woman in the bathtub. John scrubbed his hand across his chin, glaring at Dornan.

'What did you do?' Mariana whispered.

'Let me handle this,' John barked, and Mariana's eyes went wide. 'Go and take care of the boy,' he said, gentler this time.

She nodded, disappearing from view.

'You didn't have to do that,' John said.

'Do what?' Dornan asked, grinning.

The bastard was smug. He'd killed the woman he'd been willing to leave the cartel for, and he was fucking smug?

'Let her see ... this,' he said, gesturing to the carnage. 'Was that really necessary?'

Dornan didn't answer. He pushed off the vanity, where he'd been resting one foot, and brushed past John.

CHAPTER FORTY-TWO

MARIANA

I'd never seen Dornan so indifferent in the face of death.

When he'd killed the woman in the backseat of his truck, he had cried. Wept as he pulled the trigger and delivered the bullet that ended her life. I'd seen the anguish in his eyes, seen the devastation that engulfed him.

Now he seemed almost bored with the fact that he'd just killed someone. And not just anyone.

He'd loved her, once. That was the part I found the hardest to accept. He'd loved her, and she'd left, and this was what happened when you left a man like Dornan Ross and never came back. Eventually, he found you, and brutally murdered you.

All of these things raced through my head as I stood in a small bedroom and watched the rise and fall of a young boy's chest.

He might have been fifteen, but in deep sleep he looked younger. He was gorgeous, with olive skin and dark, long eyelashes that covered his closed eyes.

He looked exactly like Dornan. Like a miniature version, though he was almost as tall as him. I held a hand over my mouth as I took him in silently, not wanting to make a noise and risk waking him up. But it seemed like he was knocked out, and that he'd sleep through anything.

I wondered if he'd found his mother. As I was thinking all of this, Dornan entered the room and stood beside me, his hands in his pockets.

'You can stop looking at me like that,' he said, his voice like gravel. He pulled out a cigarette and lit it, sending smoke wafting across the room.

'You shouldn't be smoking in the house,' I said warily, and that made him chuckle. 'Why not?' he replied, tapping ash on the carpet. 'The house is about to burn down.'

I thought of my family. How Emilio had burned them.

How the apple never falls far from the tree.

I looked from Dornan to his unconscious son, a coldness settling into my being. I felt shards of ice travel along my veins and arteries, turning everything frozen and black inside. Everything.

'How could you do this?' I asked him.

Dornan looked at the ground and then back at me, the fury in his eyes unmistakable.

'What would you have done,' he asked darkly, 'if someone had stolen your child away from you?'

I thought of Murphy, the way he had been so heavy in death. Of Allie, her threats against Luis, and how much lighter she had been as I had stolen her breath away and then rolled her body into the water.

I decided that I wasn't one to judge, after all.

CHAPTER FORTY-THREE

DORNAN

They'd cleaned the scene as best they could, and after a lot of convincing on John's part Dornan had agreed not to burn the house down. It was unlikely anyone would trace Stephanie back to Dornan after sixteen years, and he might decide to come back for the boy's things. He was still having trouble referring to Jason as his son. He was like a stranger, this kid who he had to keep sedated to manage, even with his shocking resemblance to Dornan.

They'd buried Stephanie in the woods nearby instead, Dornan insistent on being the one who shovelled dirt onto her bloodied face. He couldn't separate the hate from the love, and the rage, the rage was the worst part of all. At one point, when half her face was still visible, Dornan had started smashing the shovel down onto her head, until John managed to get the shovel away from him.

He wanted to scream and gnash his teeth and bash her fucking head in, but it wouldn't matter because she was already dead. He didn't regret killing her, though. The only thing he regretted was not drawing out her death.

They travelled to a motel, Mariana in the backseat

of John's truck, cradling the boy protectively. *At least he'd have her to take care of him*, Dornan mused silently. She'd be a good mother. He'd told her that once, and now she'd have someone to mother. All these thoughts swirling in his brain made perfect sense. He didn't once stop to consider what would happen when the boy woke up. It was a problem that he'd deal with later, and the boy would eventually come around. He'd be mad at first, but he'd understand why his mother was a lying bitch who deserved to die.

They got two rooms at the motel. Dornan dragged the boy in and dumped him on one of two beds in the first room, John and Mariana following on his heels.

'You want to take first shift?' he said, addressing John. 'I know he's tied up, but the little bastard is strong. Like his dad.' Dornan smiled proudly, but neither John nor Mariana smiled back. He was starting to get annoyed by their reactions. Didn't they understand that he'd done this out of love for his son? He was the victim here. He'd just had fifteen years of his child stolen from him, and he intended to make up for lost time just as soon as the boy was awake and calm.

Not now, though. There was no calm space inside Dornan Ross. He was crazed. Drunk on death, on killing. He needed Mariana's softness, needed her around him. Stephanie's blood was on his hands, soaked into the fibres of his clothes. He just wanted to forget.

'I want to talk to you,' he said, tugging Mariana from the room. She looked back at John hesitantly, who seemed to want to say something.

'I'm not gonna kill her,' Dornan said, looking between the pair. Something was off, and he wondered if it was just him, in the aftermath of what had happened, or if there was something he was missing.

John closed his mouth, and Mariana followed Dornan slowly out of the motel room and into the adjoining room. He closed the door behind her. The room was identical to the other one. Two beds. A minibar. A bathroom.

Perfect.

He turned to Mariana, who was hovering at the door, looking everywhere but at him.

'Get on the bed,' he growled, lunging for her. Mariana backed away from him, only stopping when the backs of her knees hit one of the narrow double beds.

'Baby, you're scaring me,' she said, her eyes glassy.

'Why would you be scared of me?' he asked, pressing himself against her so she was forced backwards onto the bed. Her eyes lit up and she pushed her palms against his chest, trying to push him off of her. He didn't like that. It made him mad. Didn't she want to make him feel better? Didn't she want to help him forget?

He grabbed her wrists and forced them over her head, using his weight to press her into the bed. Her eyes grew wide as she struggled against his stronghold.

'Dornan!' she hissed. 'What are you doing?'

He laughed. 'What do you think I'm doing?' he asked, letting go of her wrists and taking hold of the waistband on her pants, tugging hard until the material slid over her hips and down to her knees. She continued to thrash, but he held onto her hips so hard his fingernails drew blood from her flesh.

'You're hurting me!' she cried, pushing at his chest.

He didn't stop. Couldn't stop. All he saw was red.

'Dornan!' More forceful this time.

'Shut up!' he snarled, taking hold of her hips and flipping her onto her stomach. He unzipped his jeans, letting out a breath as he pressed his cock between her ass cheeks.

'It's not too late,' Mariana whispered, her voice shaky. 'You can stop. I don't want to do this. You're not giving me a choice.'

He thought about that *choice* as he spat on his hand and rubbed between her legs. 'No,' he said finally, 'I'm not.'

He thrust into her, and she yelled, her sounds muffled by Dornan pushing her face into the pillow.

He pressed his other hand into the small of her back, needing release, needing calm before he snapped again and hurt her. He'd stop soon enough. Just a few minutes, and then he'd stop. She was upset because of Stephanie, but she'd understand. She loved him. She'd want to take his pain away.

She started to really struggle against his hands, turning her head to the side to look at him, and that made him fucking angry. Couldn't she see, after everything, that he needed her? After everything he'd done for her, after he'd changed his entire existence for her, couldn't she just shut her mouth and let him give her some of his rage, some of the ache inside him?

He laid over her, his large body enveloping her small one. She softened immediately, as if she were relieved. That made his gut twist, made his veins sizzle. Was she a liar, too? Was she just waiting for the moment when she could stab him in the back and run? He collected her small wrists in one hand and pressed them above her head until she whimpered and pressed her eyes tightly shut.

He barely even heard her gasps. There was only need, thick and present and requiring satiety.

He dragged a hand through her thick, silky hair, stopping at the ends and tugging hard. Mariana didn't resist his insolent tug, following the movement like a good little kitty so her neck was outstretched, exposed. He imagined biting into her throat like some kind of lovesick pseudo-vampire, but instead he wrapped his hand around her pretty throat and squeezed.

Her dark blue eyes came alive once more, still wet, but this time tears started to streak across her skin, mixing in with clumped mascara so it looked like she was weeping blackness. It didn't make sense. Their fucking was like fighting most of the time, animals in heat, pain and blood and submission the things that got both of them off. A small part of him knew this was different – that this wasn't good for her, that she had said no, that she was crying as if he were *raping* her – but he pushed that aside, because it didn't matter what she needed in that moment. It only mattered that he get rid of this feeling inside, that he get rid of the image of Stephanie lying in the tub begging for her fucking life, and replace it with something else.

Mariana struggled underneath him, her nails digging into his hand that was clasped at her throat. She took in tiny sips of air, her eyes streaming with tears, the fear inside them both comforting and nauseating at the same time. The only sound was skin slapping against skin, the small choking sounds coming from her throat, and the bed banging against the thin stucco wall with every brutal thrust into her pliant flesh.

CHAPTER FORTY-FOUR

MARIANA

It felt like my wrists were about to snap in two. My throat, though, was where most of the pain blossomed from. I could take in shallow breaths, but Dornan's weight crushed me into the lumpy motel mattress, and my lungs burned, begging to be filled with oxygen. The room started to spin. There were tears in my eyes. *He's supposed to love me.* And I guess the most fucked-up part of all was that he did love me. Even as he held me down, he loved me in the only way he knew how. With violence. With anger. With pain.

I'd become hardened over the years but I'd never, ever felt this torn beneath him. I'd wanted to tell him about the baby for a split second there, but after what I'd seen – how he'd butchered his ex-girlfriend – everything inside me said to shut my mouth, to give nothing away.

And my heart. My heart was hurting, because it was breaking in two. I still loved him, deep down in the dark places inside me. But I was afraid of him. I hated him. I was terrified of this man.

And John. I wanted John. He was safe. He was gentle. He didn't look at me like a possession. He didn't lock me up and have me followed and hurt me. He didn't murder women – not that I knew of anyway. He was tender. He was loving.

Love. I choked tears back, clinging onto consciousness by a tattered thread, as Dornan finished with one final thrust and collapsed on top of me.

I sucked in a breath the moment his hold on me loosened, coughing and choking as fresh air burned my lungs.

In the shock that came after, I imagined stepping onto a plane with Dornan's baby nestled inside my belly, safe and hidden. I imagined the utter relief as the plane took off. And then he would be there, dragging me from my seat, shoving me inside a toilet stall and killing me with his bare hands while his dark eyes burned with *Why?*

I lay on the edge of the bed, not daring to move, until the last of the sticky liquid had seeped from inside me and turned cold beneath my thighs. I waited until Dornan was sleeping, his breath coming in slow increments, his form still. Rolling my legs off the side of the bed, I moved slowly and silently, heading for the bathroom. Once I was in there, I locked the door and stepped into the shower, turning on the hot water.

I'd never been raped before. Is that what it was like? It had been less traumatic letting Murphy fuck me than it had been begging Dornan not to. I was shaking and I couldn't stop.

I held my wrists up to the weak light the bare bulb was throwing off overhead. I saw fresh bruises blossoming across my skin, and marvelled at how close love and death could become. Dirty, messy, inexplicably intertwined. I didn't cry. I was numb. My heart beat in a steady rhythm, and I imagined the second tiny heart within me. Pressing a hand against my flat stomach, I said a silent prayer for the life inside me.

I remembered the piece of paper the ultrasound technician had handed to me, the one I'd been supposed to give my doctor.

The baby inside me was a girl.

She was a girl, and I wanted her more than anything, but at the same time my heart told me it was utterly selfish to bring a little girl into this world I was imprisoned in. Would she be corrupted? Would she be sold? Would her father end up destroying her?

Weary but warm under the generous hot water, I said a silent *sorry* to my daughter, whatever her fate might be. I pleaded for her forgiveness – for my carelessness, for my selfishness, that I wasn't even sure if I had the strength to be her mother. Because she might be inside me, but I'd never stared into her eyes, never held her in my arms and begged to keep her as she was ripped away from me. No, at the moment she was nothing more than a blurry picture and a plus sign on a pregnancy test.

It wasn't too late for an abortion. I still had time. But that time was fast running out, and if I decided to terminate I'd have to make plans. Get help. *John*. It would always come back to John.

I could terminate the pregnancy, but I'd heard her strong little heartbeat thundering along in my ears. I'd seen her move. She had arms, and legs, and a heart. She'd already survived Murphy, and Allie shooting me. She was a fighter. She deserved a chance.

On the other hand, she had a father who was a murderer. A grandfather who was a monster. A family wrapped up in lies and death and torturous pain. She'd either become one of them or be imprisoned by them, and I didn't know which one was worse.

Whatever happened, if she even survived long enough to be born, her life wasn't going to be easy.

The merciful path would be to make the choice for her, to lie down on a hard hospital bed, spread my legs and let a stranger vacuum her from me. To let her fade away before anyone ever knew of her existence.

But I knew I couldn't do that.

I couldn't bear to destroy the one good thing Dornan and I had left.

CHAPTER FORTY-FIVE

MARIANA

Dornan rolled over and kissed me on the mouth, tasting like stale whiskey and lies, before closing himself in the bathroom. The motel would have to burn the sheets, streaked with blood from where he'd slept.

While he was showering I dressed and headed outside, making sure to wrap a scarf around my neck to hide the bruises Dornan had left. I couldn't bear to spend another moment with him, but I was ashamed that I'd been so fucking weak. I could have yelled for John. But I hadn't, because being forced was preferable to watching John and Dornan kill each other if I'd cried out for help.

I just wanted to be alone for five minutes, so of course as soon as I opened the front door I ran smack bang into John.

He looked shattered, and I realised he hadn't slept for days. I gave him a sympathetic look, affronted when he returned it with a tight-lipped stare.

'Bad night?' I guessed.

He sneered, looking past me. 'Not as good as yours,' he said cruelly, flicking his gaze up and down me. 'You get off on Dornan killing people?'

Furious, I yanked my scarf down and tipped my head back so he could see the bruising across my neck. 'Go fuck yourself,' I said, swallowing back tears as his face fell.

'Are you alright?' he asked, reaching out a hand to touch my neck. I pulled away sharply, narrowing my eyes at him.

'I'm fine,' I snapped. 'Don't you worry about me, John. I'm just fine.'

CHAPTER FORTY-SIX

MARIANA

It was a tense drive home. I sat in the back of the truck with Jason, who Dornan had drugged yet again. I was starting to seriously worry about him killing his new son, who I'd still not actually seen awake in almost twenty-four hours, with an overdose. The kid had wet himself in his comatose state, and we drove home with the smell of piss filling the car.

When we finally arrived back in Los Angeles, John drove to my apartment. When we pulled up, I didn't move. After a few moments, Dornan turned around, looking at me expectantly. 'You can get out,' he said.

I didn't budge. 'Where are you taking him?' I asked, pushing the boy's fringe off his face.

'To the clubhouse,' Dornan replied. 'Don't worry, I'll take good care of him. I'll let him wake up and give him something to eat, introduce him to his brothers. He'll be fine.'

I felt my mouth open in shock. 'You just fucking murdered his mother,' I hissed. 'You can't just feed him and expect him to be okay.'

Dornan's mouth twisted into a grimace. He got out of the car, yanking my door open and gesturing for me to get out. I hesitated for a moment, and he took hold of my arm, pulling me to my feet.

I looked down at John, who was watching with a detached expression on his face. I knew there was nothing he could reasonably do, but it still pissed me off that he was just going along with everything without questioning Dornan's sanity.

'I'll be back in a sec,' Dornan said to John, placing his hand in the small of my back and taking my duffel bag from me. I cringed against his touch as he escorted me up the stairs, remembering how he had forced himself into me, while I'd been begging him to stop. As soon as we were at the front door to my apartment, I took the bag from him, unlocking the door and letting myself in.

The apartment was empty, Guillermo nowhere in sight. As soon as we stepped into the kitchen I turned on Dornan.

'You need to bring Jason up here,' I said. 'I'll take care of him. He doesn't belong at the club.'

Dornan raised his eyebrows. 'And what are you gonna do with him, huh? You're not his family. You're not anybody. What makes you think he'd be better off here with a stranger?'

I laughed in disbelief. 'A stranger?' I echoed. 'You're a stranger! He doesn't even know you. The only thing he knows is that you murdered his mother!'

Dornan stepped forward and slapped me across the face, so hard I tasted blood. I brought my hand up to my cheek, shocked by his sudden outburst, but not surprised.

'You're losing it,' I said coldly. 'You're really fucking losing your mind.'

'I thought you, of all people, would understand,' he said, and for a moment he sounded like a lost little boy, completely at odds with the way he'd been acting.

'I don't understand,' I said. 'What happened to you? So she left you. Why would she stay here and bring a baby into this fucking mess?'

'Shut up,' he said through gritted teeth.

'No,' I replied. 'No, I won't. You tell me, Dornan. Tell me why she should have stayed with you – while you were married, by the way – and had a baby in this fucking life? She deserved better. Your son deserved better than this.'

'Shut up!' he roared, pushing me hard against the wall. He charged at me, and before I could get out of his way, I felt a hand around my throat and a fist in my stomach. I doubled over in pain, gasping silently for air that wasn't there, but he didn't release his grip. I saw stars, then brilliant bursts of white that spread across my vision and merged into one, and still he wouldn't let go.

CHAPTER FORTY-SEVEN

MARIANA

The bleeding didn't start right away.

I was out for a while. How long, I'm not sure. All I remember is that the sun, bright and unrelenting, started to bother my eyes and finally I had to open them.

The ache was dull, low in my abdomen. It wasn't so bad at first, just like I was having a period.

For a while, I forgot I was pregnant. Must've been from when I knocked my head against the tiles.

Then I started to notice a dampness between my legs, like I'd just peed my pants.

And then the pain, sharp knives stabbing into my womb, one after another. I gasped at the intensity as I struggled to sit up, wetness flooding between my thighs. I winced, one hand to my stomach as I came to a sitting position, and it was only then that I saw the blood streaking my thighs and pooling onto the floor beneath me. And I knew.

I expected to feel sadness, grief at losing the baby that had gone undetected by anyone else so long inside me. I knew immediately that there was no hope for the tiny creature who'd been a part of me for three short months. I watched, nauseated, as she bled from me and onto the stark white tiles.

He did this, I thought to myself. *He killed his own child. For nothing.*

Dornan would be back at the clubhouse by now, now that he'd kidnapped his secret son and dragged him back to Los Angeles, a son who would no doubt hate his father for ripping him from the only life he'd ever known. And in doing so, inadvertently, Dornan had killed something that hadn't even lived.

There was a knocking at the door. Three sharp raps at first, then a yell.

Was he back already? God, no. Not now. Not like this. Another yell.

Relief flooded through me.

John.

I heard the lock hiss and the front door open.

'Jesus,' John said, falling to his knees beside me. He pulled my head into his lap, taking out his phone. His voice calling for an ambulance sounded so far away, it was like I was listening to someone in another universe.

'Mariana!' I heard him yelling. The sound was so faint. I opened my mouth and tried to respond, but the pain was too much, and the sound came out as a whimper.

I blacked out again.

CHAPTER FORTY-EIGHT

MARIANA

I was awake for bits and pieces of the ambulance trip. The emergency line operator had tried to convince John to drive me to the hospital, telling him that a miscarriage wasn't life-threatening, but he'd been insistent. And with good reason. I wasn't just having a miscarriage, I was haemorrhaging, and the bleeding wouldn't stop. I came to in an operating theatre, my legs in stirrups and a kind-faced nurse stroking my cheek as I closed my eyes again.

Later, when I woke up, I was in a regular hospital bed. I tried to sit up, but the pain was excruciating. Even though no one had told me, even though I had no real way of telling, I knew the baby was gone.

John was dozing in the seat beside my bed, and when I tried to move he woke up, his bloodshot eyes finding mine. He reached for my hand, and I let him because I couldn't bear not to touch him any longer.

'Don't sit up,' he whispered. 'You've just come out of surgery. You lost a lot of blood. Here, I'll move the bed.'

He took a remote in his other hand and pressed a button, slowly inclining my head. The change in pressure made me dizzy, and I closed my eyes to stop the room from spinning.

'Where's Dornan?' I asked immediately, and John's face fell.

'Not here,' he said, his mouth twisting. 'Not yet, anyway.'

I nodded, squeezing his hand.

'What did he do before I found you?' John asked. 'He says he hit you, but not hard enough to hurt you.'

I laughed mirthlessly. 'It was hard enough,' I said.

'You lost the baby,' John blurted out.

I nodded again. I looked at the ceiling for a moment. When I looked back to John, I saw angry tears in his eyes.

'I'm okay,' I said, 'really.'

He shook his head, standing and pressing his lips to my forehead. It felt good. It felt wonderful.

'What do you want to do?' he asked me.

I looked at the door, making sure we were still alone. 'I want to take these kids. I want us to get Juliette, and Jason, and I want us to leave, before it gets any worse.'

John swallowed thickly, nodding. 'I have to get Juliette from school,' he said, placing my hand back on the bed and stepping back. 'I'll come back to check on you. You want me to call Guillermo to come sit with you?'

I shook my head. I wasn't afraid of Dornan showing up. I had nothing left to lose.

John just stood there, his leather jacket over one arm. He didn't want to go. I could see that it was killing him to leave me.

'Go,' I said. 'I'll be here when you get back.'

Eventually he left, trudging down the hallway until I couldn't hear his boots any more.

It was strange that I wasn't bawling my eyes out. But I was eerily calm. Maybe even grateful, in some small way. My love for Dornan had been the thing that was keeping me stuck, stopping me from taking any real action in my life. I had a son waiting for me in Colombia and access to millions of dollars in cartel money, and yet I'd been sitting on my hands waiting for something I could react to.

But now I could see my future, and it was as stark as it was brutal. If I stayed, I was going to end up like Stephanie and Murphy and Allie and everyone else who had ever been touched by the cartel – dead or, worse, like Dornan. I'd already killed two people. How long would it take for me to kill five? Ten? How long would it be before I started to accept what they did to those girls, before I grew totally complacent?

I was thinking about all of this when Dornan arrived. His helmet in one hand, tears on his cheeks as he stared at me with those midnight eyes. He looked positively grief-stricken, and his indulgence in such a display of emotion at something he had caused made me turn cold and dead inside.

He made a beeline towards me, dropping his helmet on the floor and gathering me in his arms. I didn't return the embrace, freezing until he finally pulled away.

'Did you know?' he whispered, his low voice vibrating in my chest.

I nodded. 'I was going to tell you, but then Colorado happened.'

'Fuck,' he said, falling into the chair by my side, covering his face with his hands. 'I'm sorry,' he said, taking my hand and pressing his lips against my fingers. His kiss was cold. He must have ridden with his visor open, the wind chilling his skin.

I didn't reply.

He leaned over and pressed his cheek against my stomach. 'I'm so fucking sorry,' he said, his deep voice breaking.

I should have felt something. Pity. Anger. Hatred. But I didn't. I felt nothing for the man who had once been my entire universe.

'You didn't mean it,' I said blankly, threading my fingers through his hair. In my head, I was already planning how to get away from him because he'd destroyed our love so swiftly, so brutally, I barely remembered what it was that had tethered us together for so many years.

CHAPTER FORTY-NINE

JOHN

'Daddy?' Juliette said, her big green eyes welling up with tears as she craned her neck to look at him. 'Daddy, what happened?'

She darted a hand towards his cheek, touching the bloody skin before he could catch her wrist. As his hand grasped her small arm, her eyes went wider, her skin paled and she flinched, as though he was going to hurt her.

'Shhh,' he ground out, trying to sound comforting as he released her wrist. 'It's okay. Everything is okay.'

He clamped his teeth down on the inside of his lip, hard, so he wouldn't argue with her.

'Who did this to you?' she whispered, drawing her hand back to her side.

John couldn't help but stare at her hand, transfixed, as though she might become infected now that she'd seen and touched the horror that he was trying to keep away from her.

'It's not my blood. It's Mariana's. She ... She fell. She was hurt, badly. It's her blood.'

That was the moment something broke inside him; first strung tight, like a bowstring, a delicate cord that snapped under the weight of her words.

Who did this to you?

He was ashamed that he didn't have a good answer, that nobody had done anything to him, that he had done nothing to stop this from happening, and that Mariana had almost died because he'd let Dornan walk her inside without following.

Part of him wished that Dornan had just knocked him out when he'd had the chance.

But another part of him, a part that sounded extremely familiar, like a beautiful young seductress, had the loudest voice of them all. *We have to take these kids, and we have to leave.*

CHAPTER FIFTY

MARIANA

Six weeks later

Nine years is a long time, and it isn't.

Nine summers.

Nine falls.

Nine winters.

Nine springs.

Nine anniversaries that marked the night Este bled to death, a bullet in his chest, his only crime the fact that he was with me.

I thought I knew how my life would end. In fact, I'd fantasised about it enough times to know the details intimately. I'd drive my car off a bridge and let myself drown. Or I'd cut into the soft flesh at my wrists until I hit an artery, letting my life force pour from me until I was a bloodless husk, floating in water that would grow cold. Or, more realistically, I wouldn't have to end my own life at all: it'd be snuffed out by Emilio, or Murphy, or even by Dornan himself. I imagined a smooth silver bullet, puncturing my skull at point-blank range, tearing through bone as it bedded into my brain and exploded.

I'd resigned myself for so long to the fact my life was in somebody else's control, that I assumed my death would be as well.

But that was before, when I was selfish, when I only thought about myself. That was back when I was in love with the man who'd saved me, instead of just afraid of him. And I was afraid of Dornan. Afraid of what he was. Afraid of what he was becoming. There was a darkness within him – there always had been – but it was growing, threatening to swallow up everything else in its wake.

I was terrified.

***

I held John's hand in the dark. Nobody knew he was here with me. He'd come in like a ghost and he'd leave the same way. We were lying on the floor in my bedroom, the door locked in case Guillermo got back to the apartment and came knocking. We were on our backs, side by side, and we'd just done something very, very wrong.

But it had felt so good.

I rolled onto him again, feeling his bare skin underneath mine. I straddled him, splaying my palms over his warm chest as he grew hard underneath me once more.

We didn't speak. Didn't make any noise. I lowered myself onto him, stretching around him until I felt like I could barely breathe. Slowly, gently, I rocked against him as we tried to devour each other with our mouths.

He was everything Dornan was not. He wasn't a fucker. He was a lovemaker. I didn't even know what I felt for John, but when he moved inside me it felt like he was loving me, even if only for a fleeting moment.

But it wasn't just some kind of love that drew us together, at least not in the typical way.

It was desperation.

He kissed me, his lips soft, his stubble deliciously rough, lifting my hips up and pressing me into his lap as he thrust into me. We came at almost the same time, so, so quietly, and that made it feel even more illicit, more exciting. Even when Guillermo wasn't around, after I'd relayed news of Agent Lindsay Price bailing me up in the gym showers, we'd convinced ourselves that we were being watched. And who knows? Maybe we were, even then.

John supported himself on his hands, covering my body with his as he withdrew from me and went in search of his clothes.

I heard the shower start, decided I might as well join him. We didn't turn any lights on. I'd already lit candles everywhere, and they illuminated the bathroom enough that we could see.

Somehow, it felt safer in the dark. Part of me couldn't believe how brazen we were being – carrying on while Guillermo could come back to the apartment at any moment.

I slipped into the shower and found John, pulling him towards me. He held me tight, pressing his lips to the top of my head. I didn't even know how this had happened, but it had.

'What's going on in that head of yours?' John asked, cupping my chin and bringing it up to meet his eyes. They shone bright blue, even in the dim flicker of candlelight.

'Hawaii,' I said, smiling tiredly.

He grinned. 'Hawaii?'

'Yeah,' I said, leaning my head against his chest as he held me tightly. 'We could do it. Take these kids and get the hell out of here.'

'If they found us, they would kill us,' John said soberly. 'Remember Colorado?'

'Of course,' I said, pulling away so I could see his eyes. 'Of course I remember. That's why, if we did leave, we'd have to kill them first.'

To be continued in
Empire ...

The

CARTEL

series continues ...

EMPIRE

The irresistible conclusion to the Cartel trilogy

As dark secrets come to light, and with the blood of innocents on her lover's hands, Mariana is forced to choose between the man she loves and the man who threatens to destroy her carefully built web of deceit.